LOVE, JULIE

LOVE, JULIE
•
Christine Bush

AVALON BOOKS
NEW YORK

Published by Thomas Bouregy & Co., Inc.
160 Madison Avenue, New York, NY 10016

Library of Congress Cataloging-in-Publication Data

Bush, Christine.
    Love, Julie / Christine Bush.
        p. cm.
    ISBN 0-8034-9786-5 (acid-free paper)
    I. Title.

    PS3552.U816255L68 2006
    813'.54—dc22
                                2006003149
PRINTED IN THE UNITED STATES OF AMERICA
ON ACID-FREE PAPER
BY HADDON CRAFTSMEN, BLOOMSBURG, PENNSYLVANIA

This book is dedicated to
HARDY BUSH (1954–2003),
my brother, my hero, my friend.

Chapter One

Julietta Brightingham stuck her head out the window of the stagecoach, taking in deep breaths of fresh Montana air and squinting in the spring sunshine. It even smelled like freedom out here.

The coach bounced along the bumpy path, the white-haired driver adroitly dodging the uneven ruts and occasional rock that loomed on the way.

Almost all the rocks, Julietta amended, as the stagecoach gave a sudden lurch and she smacked her head on the side of the window.

She rubbed the spot and laughed out loud, tucking in the stray piece of nondescript brown hair that had escaped from her bun, and straightening the reading spectacles that had threatened to slide down her nose.

A new person, a new life. The past would never catch up to her.

Excitement and anticipation bubbled in her twenty-four-year-old heart, overriding the other emotions that

1

had been plaguing her. The sadness, the anger, and the fear had all been dwarfed by the Montana sky. She drew in breath after breath, taking in the crisp, fresh air. After three weeks of traveling, she was almost there.

Good-bye New York! Hello Grey Eagle, Montana! Her life as Julietta Brightingham, unwilling heiress, was but a memory as distant as the harsh New York skyline. Her new life was beginning. She was Julie Bright, the newest resident of Grey Eagle, Montana, already in love with a town that she had never even seen.

Her hand felt for the crinkled piece of paper she carried in her skirt pocket, her letter of introduction to the town sheriff. She knew it by heart, but she opened it to read it one last time for assurance before arriving in Grey Eagle.

April, 1890.
To Sheriff Jack White, Grey Eagle, Montana:

Please allow me to introduce Miss Julie Bright, your new schoolteacher, who is traveling to Grey Eagle to accept the post as teacher in my stead. Circumstances in my life have made it impossible for me to fulfill my obligation to travel to Grey Eagle as your new teacher.

As your need for a schoolteacher is immediate. I have located a replacement and have used the funds provided to pay for her passage instead.

Although I know your preference was for a schoolteacher who was more mature in years than Miss Bright, I assure you that her levelheadedness, experi-

ence and maturity make her a most acceptable can-
didate for the post. I offer the highest recommenda-
tion.

　I wish you the best.

Sincerely, Mrs. Mabel Mayberry,

New York City

Deftly, she refolded the familiar letter and repocketed it, once again thanking the aging teacher who had assisted with her escape. Memories threatened. Sighing, she sat back in the leather seat, suddenly glad that she was traveling alone on this last lap of her journey.

She was lost in her thoughts when the trouble began. The thundering rhythm of the horses hooves increased, and the stagecoach lurched forward.

"Haw, haw, giddy-yap!" she heard the driver cry, as the whip snapped in the air above the already tired horses. They had been driving since dawn.

A new sound became audible. Another horse was approaching from the rear, its hooves pounding the rocky ground ferociously. Julie peeked out the rear window of the coach and saw the masked rider bearing down on them. The tired stage horses were no match for the angry black stallion he rode and it was only seconds before he was upon them.

There was a loud thump, and Julie realized the attacker had leaped onto the coach, struggling with the driver above her. The stagecoach veered and slowed to a stop.

She wasn't going to bet that the white-haired stagecoach driver would be the victor in a fight with the masked marauder who had ridden the magnificent black horse. The odds were certainly stacked in favor of the bandit.

And when he won, he could come after her next. It was one thing to worry about what could personally happen to her, but if he stole her bags, he would be stealing her dreams as well. She had come too far to let that happen.

It was up to her to change the odds, and once decided in a flash, she didn't hesitate for a moment. Silently, she slipped open the catch on the stagecoach door, and put her booted foot to the ground without making a sound. Bending quickly, she scoured the ground for the loose rocks she had been seeing along the path all day.

Her small fingers bent around them, one in each hand, the exact size of a baseball.

Baseball, her teacher's mind recited. *The form used today originated in 1839.*

She crept around the coach, where grunts and groans and occasional thumpings of fist hitting flesh could be heard. The stagecoach driver was doing better than she'd expected.

She saw the two man grappling on the front bench of the coach, her driver's eyes growing large as he saw her emerge from the shadows of the coach. The bandit mercifully had his back to her.

Baseball originated in Cooperstown, New York.

She wound up, swung her arm, and pitched the first rock with all her might. It hit the bandit square in the back, and he yelped out loud. But he didn't go down.

Baseball, she said to herself again. *Invented by Abner Doubleday.*

She wound up, and let her second pitch sail with gusto.

Crack!

It hit the bandit right in the back of the head, and he dropped like a stone.

An amazing man, that Abner Doubleday!

"Geez, Miss," gasped the white-haired driver, his chambray blue shirt now caked with dirt, blood dribbling from a split lip. "You knocked him out cold. Where'd you learn to throw like that?"

"In the borough of Manhattan, sir. Central Park West. I can throw a player out at home base from center field without turning a hair. Now, can we tie him up and get on our way? I'm in quite a hurry to reach Grey Eagle."

The driver looked stunned as he plopped his hat back on his head.

"Sure thing."

The bandit was tied and draped over the top of the coach, still out cold. "I'll take him to Sheriff White. He'll know what to do with him."

The big black horse had come up beside them, and was angrily pawing the dusty ground.

"And bring the horse, of course. That's one beautiful animal."

"Looks a mean one, if you ask me," the man grumbled, tying the horse to the back of the coach as the beast bared its teeth.

Julie looked back at the glistening animal as she stepped back into the stagecoach, noting the vicious scarring along his flanks, where spur and reigns had been cruelly applied.

The horse pulled angrily on his lead, then raised his gallant head. She looked into his eyes sadly, nodding.

"Perhaps he just wants to be free."

The stage continued its bouncy path until the late afternoon sun cast rays of orange across the plains, and the first glimpse of Grey Eagle, Montana, came into view.

Julie's heart was hammering as the stagecoach rolled down the main street of Grey Eagle, her eyes darting back and forth as she took in the sights of the town. In the late afternoon sunlight, there was a rosy glow to the colorful wooden store fronts that lined the street. Grey Eagle was a small town, but a thriving one, she knew. It had originally sprung up because of the mining industry, and the LaPierre Copper Mine still employed a large number of its citizens. But the start of the Davis Grain Mill, which they had passed on the way into town had added to its prosperity.

She had learned all she could about Grey Eagle from Mrs. Mayberry, who had been not only one of Julie's early governesses and favorite teacher, but her stalwart supporter when she had admitted her dreams.

The stage came to a halt in front of the town hotel, a large clapboard building that had been freshly whitewashed. From the stage window, she could see the sign for the sheriff's office across the street. Excitedly, she gathered up her two well-stuffed carpetbags and neatly tied her bonnet on her head. She smoothed the skirt of her servicable brown traveling dress, and took a deep breath. She stepped out of the stagecoach door as it opened, and put her feet for the first time on Grey Eagle soil.

Someone large stepped in front of her. The setting sun blazed over the corner of the town hall, silhouetting the

huge figure that blocked her way. He was at least 6'6"
tall. She registered massive shoulders, thick arms, and a
hat that seemed like it could keep the rain off a square
city block.

She squinted out of her spectacles, trying to see the
features of the man who stood before her, but his face was
shadowed by the contrast of the setting sun behind him.

She tried to step to the side.

He stepped to the side.

She stepped to the other side.

He followed.

"Excuse me," she mumbled, slightly exasperated, as
she spun to avoid him. He deftly moved in front of her
again, but this time, the sun wasn't behind him, and his
face was clearly visible.

"Welcome to Grey Eagle," the deep, resonant voice
said in an authoritative tone. "And who might you be?"

She looked up and saw blue eyes the color of the
Montana sky. They were a most beautiful shade of blue,
but at the moment, they didn't look particularly friendly.
They looked arrogant and decidedly bossy.

His eyes narrowed as he saw the man tied up on the
top of the stagecoach, and the disheveled appearance of
the driver.

"I might be offended," she said jauntily, straightening
her bonnet and pulling herself up to her full 5'2" height,
"if you don't get out of my way. It's been a bit of a harrowing trip. I'm expected. I'm the new schoolteacher."

The giant man narrowed his sky blue eyes and stared
at her.

"No, you're not. I don't know who you are, young
lady, but you are not the new schoolteacher. We're not

too fond of impostors in this town. We don't need any troublemakers here."

Troublemakers?

She took a deep breath to answer him back, but was interrupted by the stagecoach driver, who had come up beside them, motioning to the bandit, who was beginning to stir.

"Caught us a real bad one, Sheriff, about two hours south of here. Gotta fill out a report for the stage company. I figure your men can take care of him."

Sheriff? The giant was the sheriff? She had been in town only minutes and already she was having a confrontation with the man who ran the town? There was a sinking feeling in the pit of her stomach.

Several men lifted the bandit from the top of the stage and carried him toward the jail. The big black horse was led off to the livery at the end of the long street.

"Good job," the sheriff said over his shoulder, addressing the driver, but not taking his eyes off Julie.

He was really making her nervous. She had to fight the urge to wiggle like a bug on a pin under his gaze.

But there would be no wiggling for Julie Bright, she suddenly affirmed. She had come this far, and she would not go back. She would introduce herself to this overgrown mountain of a man in his ridiculously big hat, despite his breathtaking blue eyes. She would prove that she was just what she stated, a simple, refined schoolteacher who had travelled to educate the children of Grey Eagle.

"I *am* the expected schoolteacher, Mr. Sheriff," she said with an obedient smile. "I can explain . . ."

"You should have seen her," the stagecoach driver began in a tirade. "The bandit was whackin' me but good, and all of a sudden, this mild lookin' little lady—"

"Was ready to faint," she interrupted quickly, darting a warning look at the befuddled driver.

It would do no good to have this already suspicious sheriff learn that she clobbered people with rocks. Unsuitable, that's what he would call her.

"But this brave driver was a true hero. Knocked out the attacker and saved my life." She fanned herself meekly. "I shall always be thankful for his heroism."

The dusty driver sucked in his stomach in surprise and stood tall.

A small crowd had gathered around the stage, and someone yelled, "Hip hip hooray!"

The driver beamed uncertainly, as he was led off to the hotel across the street for a celebratory drink. He looked over his shoulder at Julie as he left, and she gave him a quick wink, and he squared his shoulders and gave her an answering nod. Let him enjoy being the hero. He deserved it.

The sheriff shook his head. "Well, I'm glad you aren't any worse for wear after your trip, young lady, but we still have a problem. We *are* expecting a schoolteacher here in Grey Eagle, that much is true. But you don't fit the bill. After what happened before, I was down right specific about our needs . . ."

Julie took a deep breath and pulled out the letter from her pocket, handing it to the sheriff.

"This will explain, Sheriff," she said confidently.

He opened the letter and looked down at it for a moment. Then, he folded it again and stuck it in his shirt pocket. His chin was firmly set and his eyes glared at her.

"This explains nothing." He said darkly. "I'll get you settled in the hotel for the night, and you can take the stage heading back east in the morning." He bent and lifted her two bags, a look of surprise on his face.

"Geez, Lady, what do you have in these bags? Solid gold ingots? They weigh a ton."

"Books, Sheriff," she said haughtily. "And they're worth their weight in gold. They are the basis of education. Books hold the key to the universe. If they are too heavy for you, I'll be glad to carry them myself."

He had the grace to blush. "You'll do no such fool thing. I didn't say I couldn't carry them. They just caught me by surprise."

He stomped off across the street, and she could tell he was intent on getting her out of his hair and safely deposited at the hotel.

"She may not look much like a proper schoolteacher," she heard his frustrated mumble as he mounted the hotel steps, "But she sure has the sharp mouth of one. The sooner she's on her way the better."

We'll see, Mr. Sheriff, she thought determinedly as she signed her name in the hotel register. "Julie Bright, Schoolteacher." *We'll see.*

Chapter Two

Sheriff Jack White bounded down the steps of the hotel and crossed the broad main street of town, heading toward the sheriff's office. He punched open the door, startling Marcus, the young deputy who sat at the desk.

In a rush, he locked the office door, and pulled down the shade.

"Whar you comin' from with yer pants on fire?" the young man asked, pushing his hat back on his head, grinning broadly at the big man who was his boss.

"Don't try to be cute, Marcus. It's lost on me. Get over here and help me with this darn thing."

Sheriff White yanked out a chair and sat on it backwards, arms leaning on the high ladder back, as he pulled Julie's letter from his pocket and opened it hastily.

The deputy came and stood behind him, looking over his broad shoulder.

"It's a letter," he said.

"Brilliant deduction. So what does it say?" Sheriff White scowled at the pen stroked words.

"I still can't believe you can't read a word, Sheriff. Makes a feller want to hoot."

"You'll be hootin' for a new job if you don't start reading me this correspondence, and keep your insulting comments to yourself, Marcus Reilly. I'll learn to read when I'm good and ready, and if word leaks out in this town about me, I'll know who to blame!"

"Yer secret is safe with me, boss!" Marcus grinned, and then scrunched up his face to read the letter.

"To the sheriff of Grey Eagle . . ." Dennis began in a flat voice, punching each word as he figured it out. It took an hour, but he read Jack the letter, every word.

So now what was he going to do? It was just like life, he decided. Just when you thought you had things all figured out, a snake jumps out of the dang brush and spooks your horse. Or lightning strikes the barn. Or the cow falls sick. Or. . . .

No sense grumbling, he reckoned to himself. It was just going to take longer to reach his goal than he had wanted. But he'd get there. Somehow.

At thirty-two, Jack White had been roaming around Montana almost all his adult life, since losing his folks and the family ranch after a bad fire at the age of fourteen. He had done it all since those early days on his own. He'd been a cowpoke, a builder, a horse trainer, a mill worker, a miner, and had even done a stint as a short order cook, more or less wandering through life until he found his true calling.

Which he had. Being Sheriff of Grey Eagle, Montana,

was like a dream come true. It fit like a glove. And he'd gotten this dream by accident, or a stroke a fate, whichever you'd prefer to call it.

He'd been given the job by the town council's unanimous vote over five years before, as a reward for his "heroic" acts during a bank robbery attempt. To this day, his actions seemed only common sense to him, and not heroic at all. But the story had gone down in local lore as a bigger-than-life tale, told around bar tables and ranch bunkhouses for miles around. It had brought him fame and respect, which he enjoyed, as well as his job as Sheriff of Grey Eagle, which was his life.

He had been helping Mr. Baker of the Mercantile on the day in question, who had just received a large delivery wagon of supplies for his store. The new barrels and boxes had been neatly stacked in the storage shed behind the store, and Jack had been rolling an enormous empty sugar barrel back to the wagon to be shipped for refilling.

It was a peaceful summer day, with many local folks in town for shopping and visiting. When the noise broke out, with the sounds of yelling and gunshots, Jack had reacted immediately. The bank was right next to the mercantile.

Looking up from his stead by the wagon, he saw a single bank robber backing his way out of the bank, a large muslin money bag thrown over his shoulder, a gun still trained into the doorway of the bank. He was a wiry little man, with a stance that said he had nothing to lose.

"Don't move, or I'll shoot another one," the low voice had growled with menace, and he sounded like he meant it.

Someone was crying from inside the bank.

Most bystanders had immediately disappeared, either ducking into nearby stores, or running down the dusty street. The bank robber's horse stood waiting only yards away.

In a split second, Jack had realized that if anyone was going to stop the gun-brandishing stranger, it was going to have to be him. And he was going to have to be quick. He had no gun. But he had a plan.

Without hesitation, he had lifted the empty sugar barrel from the edge of the wagon, holding it upside down. He had silently stepped the few steps to the bank doorway. As the bank robber stepped backwards out the door, still intent on holding the people inside the bank at bay with his gun, he had simply lifted the big brown barrel up into the air with his 6'6" frame and well-developed muscles, and had plopped it down over the startled little man's head. Heck, he'd trapped muskrats even harder than that.

Startled and stuck in the thick, dark barrel, the man had been easily apprehended and jailed, and the money had been restored.

But sadly, the old sheriff had been a casualty inside the bank that day. It took only hours, in the midst of the panic and confusion, for the town council to name Jack as his replacement. The first tales of Sheriff Jack White had hit the circuits.

He'd taken his job as sheriff to heart since that very first moment, and cherished his town and all the folks in it. He took pride in its growth and stability, and had high hopes that Grey Eagle would be known as a gem in the new west.

They had a well-run hotel, thriving shops, and recently, a barber had settled from back east and set up shop. They had erected a church right outside town, and had a small office outfitted with medical supplies for the doctor who came monthly as he made his rounds in this region in Montana. And the schoolhouse . . .

A frown settled on his wide brow.

They had all joined together to build the school house over a year ago. Its neat, white clapboards sat gleaming in the Grey Eagle sunshine, bell firmly attached in a steeple that rose from its slate roof. But the bell hadn't rung.

Education was the key to a better world, Jack White firmly believed. It was the key to success. It was also a major thorn in his side. Living on a destitute dirt ranch as a kid, his parents struggling for existence, and then losing the battle at an early age, Jack White had never learned to read. His parents hadn't known how to read. His grandparents before them hadn't known how to read. He didn't blame them for what they didn't know.

But he was deep down ashamed.

When the schoolhouse had gone up, his hopes had, too. He would bring in a school marm to teach the children of Grey Eagle, to make sure that the citizens in his care had the best that life had to offer. And somehow, someway, he would get that schoolmarm to teach him the secret of words, too.

So he had begun his quest, with the help of Marcus Reilly, his reading deputy, and the only witness to his lack of reading ability. He would hire a teacher to live in Grey Eagle, an older, experienced, proper lady who wouldn't marry and run off to have babies and leave the schoolhouse empty. He'd hire a staid, no-nonsense woman who would fill the bill, and then he'd somehow get the courage to approach her and admit his secret desire to learn to read. No one else need ever know. He, Jack White, Sheriff of Grey Eagle, would finally learn to read.

But suddenly, the vision of those round brown eyes came to mind. Those funny little spectacles had done nothing to hide them. He'd seen those trim little booted ankles stepping from the coach, that petite little body who had threatened to carry her own bags containing at least seventy pounds of books, if he were any judge. He'd seen the way she'd confidently thrust her letter at him, seeing him as the authority of the town . . . Respect. . . . and the assumption that he could read her letter. His face burned with shame.

Could he ask that spritely little lady, who had to be even years younger than himself, to teach him to read? Never. Never.

And having heard the letter was from Mrs. Mayberry, the teacher who had fit his criteria, but who was obviously not coming to Grey Eagle, he was now without a teacher for this town who needed one so badly.

Miss Bright had come. Miss Bright would stay. According to the letter from the trusted Mrs. Mayberry, she was a most suitable replacement, and he would take her word. He owed the young woman an apology for his rude welcome. She would fit the criteria for Grey Eagle, which was most important. The town would rejoice. If it meant that his own personal dreams would just go up in smoke, it wasn't the end of the world. He'd keep his secret a while longer, that's all.

With a heavy but resigned heart, he plopped his hat back on his head, and nodded to Marcus, who wisely kept quiet. He pulled up the shade, unlocked the office door, and marched his 6'6" frame back across the street to welcome the new schoolteacher.

Chapter Three

W hen the door had shut behind the hotel porter, and Julie finally found herself alone in her room, she collapsed on the bed, spread eagle, lying on her back in a most unladylike position. She stared up at the high white ceiling.

"Well, I'm here," she said to no one in particular.

It had been a long and grueling trip, leaving New York in secret, traveling on the first of the amazing but deafening big black trains that now crossed the wide expanse of the United States. No matter how much she had read, no matter how many maps she had studied, the actual size of this great country had seemed astounding when she had actually traipsed each mile of it. And it was growing every day. Montana, with its growing population of 142,000, had become a state in 1889, and rumor had it that there were more territories on the brink.

She had seen the bustle of St. Louis, Missouri, then action packed Chicago in the state of Illinois. She had seen thriving farm land, spring fields freshly planted. She had seen the breathtaking mountains change their colors as the sun crawled westward each day, changing shadows and reflections like an inspired painter. It was a beautiful country they lived in.

When she had left the train in Helena and had embarked on the last lap of her trip by stagecoach, she had fallen in love with Montana most of all. The plains, the distant mountains rising from the land to touch the sky, the biting fresh spring air . . . all had affected her greedy senses.

Freedom, and a new life. That's what Montana meant to her.

Julietta Brightingham had been born the only daughter of James and Mary Brightingham of Park Avenue, New York. Rich and important in a city that was exploding with power and influence, James Brightingham had been a man born to be in charge.

And in charge he had been.

In his international shipping company, where his business genius and his economic daring had made him a millionaire many times over, employees quaked at the sound of his forceful footsteps approaching in the hallway. Following his commands and being a success were the adamant rules. Those who failed to comply were gone without a second's dismay. Those who simply failed despite their most valiant attempts were treated no better. Only winners could stay at Brightingham's.

One of Julietta's worst memories about her father concerned an unfortunate employee. Even though it had occurred when she was only ten, the thought of it still made her eyes burn with tears.

It had been Christmas eve, only moments before dinner. Her father had been home when a messenger had appeared on the gracious marble doorstep of their elegant house.

"It's about Petey," the white-faced man had stammered to his boss. Petey had been an office clerk at Brightingham's, fired earlier in the day due to a mail delivery mix up. "He couldn't face his family after losing his job at Christmastime, Mr. Brightingham. He just up and threw himself out the seventh story window, dead the instant he hit the pavement." The man's voice had been shaking with emotion.

"Pity," her father had responded. "Must have made a mess on the pavement. Make sure it's cleaned up right. We can't have something like that on Christmas day."

He had sent the man away, and Julietta was sure he had never given the unknown man named Petey another thought. But Julietta had. She had never forgotten her father's coldness.

Mary Brightingham, Julietta's mother, had died a year later, and she still missed the sweet gentle woman who had been so kind and good. She had been an obedient, proper wife to James, always at his beck and call, willingly molded into the society lady that he desired in his home. She hadn't admired that meekness in her mother, but she had understood it.

Her mother had enthralled her with her laughing eyes, her fondness for books and storytelling, and her soft blond looks. Julietta knew she looked like her.

She had removed the bonnet from her head when she had entered the room, and now put her hand to head, feeling the stiffness of the faded brown hair that was pulled into a tight bun. What a color!

The bottle of hair color rinse was hidden in the bottom of one of her bags, its sickly smell always threatening to gag her when she washed her hair and reapplied it.

It had been a brainstorm and a gift from Cloris, the mansion cook. The color was boring and hideous, and it made her usually soft hair stiff. It may not have been pleasant, but it was effective. It had hidden her blond curls when she escaped from the city, and made her seem more serious and mature, more scholarly, as she began her life as a schoolteacher here in Grey Eagle. Which she would do, despite the extremely large and unwelcoming sheriff.

She didn't bother fully unpacking her bags, as she had no intention of staying in the hotel for more than one night. She lit the lantern that stood on the dresser. The sun was setting and the room was darkening. Tomorrow she would visit the schoolhouse that Mrs. Mayberry had described. The thought made excited chills travel down her spine.

A knock at the door revealed a chambermaid, who had brought her warm water in a basin and some fresh towels. Gratefully she accepted it and proceeded to wash some of the stagecoach grime from her face and hands. Traveling was such dirty work!

Dinner would be served soon, she knew from checking in, and also from the wonderful smells that were wafting through the building, making her stomach rumble. Eating had always been one of her favorite past times, much to her father's chagrin.

"You eat like a horse, not like a lady, Julietta Marie," he would boom as she filled her fork. "I will teach you to be a lady if it's the death of me!" he would routinely threaten.

Well, he was dead. And she still ate like a horse. She grimaced at the face that stared back at her in the looking glass. Both were facts that couldn't be changed.

Her stomach grumbled again. She replaced the spectacles on her nose, and the room came into focus. Crossing to one of the overstuffed bags, she rummaged deep into its depths and pulled out an elegantly embroidered pouch, clutching it fondly to her chest for a minute. Her mother's jewels.

She looked quickly around the room, trying to decide on a suitable hiding spot. The room, while neat and clean and comfortable, didn't hold many surprises. With a shrug, she lifted up the mattress on the bed, and stuffed the pouch underneath, smoothing the bedding again when she was done.

Glancing out the window to the clear view she had of the main street below, she suddenly spotted the sheriff emerging from his office, his long legs carrying him quickly toward the hotel.

Was he coming to see her? Did he have more reasons why she should leave Grey Eagle? He was going to find out that she was not so easily corralled. She may look like her mother, but she was simply not the obedient, acquiescent sort.

She was, to quote her Uncle Edward, "and uncontrollable brazen young upstart." She was staying in Grey Eagle. And she was going to teach.

Quietly, she left her room, closing the door soundly

behind her, and started down the steps, to meet him head on.

Julie's mind was racing with all the clever, resourceful and assertive things that she was going to spring on the sheriff to convince him to give her a chance to prove her suitability as Grey Eagle's first schoolmarm. She wanted to teach. She desperately needed to teach. Somehow, she would make him understand that.

She heard the bell above the broad door of the hotel jangle when the sheriff pushed it open and stepped inside the spacious lobby.

My, he seemed to fill a room. He was so large, so alive.

She was half way down the wooden staircase, and heading right toward him, when he looked up. Their eyes met across the distance, and instantly, the strangest thing happened to Julie Bright. Her breath caught in her chest, surprising her. She faltered in her step, and automatically extended an arm to grab the dark wood of the bannister before she tumbled down the remaining steps. What was the matter with her?

Many years before, she had felt the same stunning feeling, breath rushing from her lungs and leaving her speechless. Of course, at the time, she had been attempting to shimmy down the copper drain pipe in the back of the Brightinghams' stately mansion on an early Saturday morning. She had been determined to escape to Central Park to join a lively group of street urchins who were willing to teach her to play baseball. Getting wind of her unladylike plans, her father had ordered her to the confines of her bedroom to spend the afternoon in a more demure pursuit, perfecting her needlework skills.

It was far from the first time (or the last) that she had shimmied down the drain pipe, but she had been in too much of a hurry. She had lost her grip, and landed in the bushes below with a resounding thump, air rushing from her lungs, and making her world spin. Like today, except without the drain pipe.

Fingers tightly gripping the bannister, the fleeting feeling passed. She sucked in a large breath of welcome air. On that long ago day she had recovered and had gone to play baseball. Today she would recover and prove her mettle to teach. A person could do *anything* they set their mind to, she always said. Julie Bright, formerly Julietta Brightingham, was not the type to swoon over a man, no matter what his attractive attributes. Or how big he was.

But she was going to stay on her toes and watch out for those startling blue eyes that were still staring at her intently and affecting her in such a strange way.

She continued her descent, stopping on the step that was second from the bottom. The sheriff had moved across the lobby toward her, and now stood at the bottom of the stairway. From her elevated location, she was face-to-face with the tall man.

She dared to tackle the blue eyes again.

"Sheriff," she bravely began, relieved to hear her voice sounded normal. "I'm happy to see you again. It's important to discuss the teaching position . . ."

"No discussion needed." He had removed his hat and was tapping it against his thigh. She did not want to look at his thigh. She schooled her eyes to ignore the motion.

"Certainly there is discussion needed, Sheriff White."

Was he going to simply refuse to speak to her? To reject her without even a chance?

She was horrified to find her eyes burning with tears at the thought. He couldn't. He wouldn't. Perhaps it had been wrong to come without warning, to take Mrs. Mayberry's place when it had been offered to her without getting prior approval, but given the circumstances she had no choice.

"I may be younger than you expected, but I'm clever. I'm a hard worker."

"If I may repeat myself . . . no discussion needed."

Her hands closed into tight fists at her sides. She couldn't let this big lawman stomp on her dreams. Not when she was this close. Was this how her life was to be forever? Would people be forever determined to negate her needs, to decide that she was unsuitable when she had a goal? Desperation was welling up inside of her and frustration had her temper mounting.

"I'm an excellent teacher," she sputtered, head held high. "And if you weren't such a stubborn mule . . ."

"And so humble . . . and mannerly."

She had the grace to blush, as he continued.

"There is no discussion needed, Miss Bright." He held up his hand to silence the retort that was promising to come out of her mouth. "And that's on account of your letter from Mrs. Mayberry. We do need a teacher in Grey Eagle. You are not what I expected, for sure. But I will take the recommendation from the Widow Mayberry and I will give you your chance. One month."

The breathless feeling was back again. She was getting her chance.

"Thank you, Sheriff," she said softly, feeling the joy well up inside of her. "You won't regret this."

He gave a short grunt, as he stuck his hat back on his blond head. "I regret it already. Stubborn mule, so you say." His voice sounded stern but there was a definite twinkle in his eyes, gone as soon as it had come.

But she had seen it. The big, mean lawman had been trying not to laugh!

"I'm sorry I was so rude," she said softly, confusing emotions swirling.

"I'll bet. Just be ready after breakfast tomorrow morning. I'll have a wagon to take you and your overloaded luggage out to the schoolhouse so you can get started. Tomorrow you'll get settled in your living quarters, and get the classroom ready, and the next morning the children will come."

It was all she could do to refrain from jumping up and down and clapping her hands. She nodded demurely instead.

"One month, Miss Bright," he said under his breath as he turned to stride out the door leaving an exuberant Julie behind.

What was the matter with him? What was he getting himself into, allowing this schoolteacher to stay? She was little more than a child herself, and she had this way of tying him up in knots . . . one minute making him want to shout, and the next minute making him want to . . . well, comfort and assure her. And laugh.

At that instant when she really thought he was going to send her away he had seen those big eyes threaten to fill with tears, and he had just about lost it. It wasn't the crying that got to him. He wasn't one of those men who went to pieces when a woman decided to cry. In his opinion, most of the ones he'd seen could bring on those crocodile tears in a lightning flash if they thought it would get them their way.

No, this was different. Julie Bright was determined *not* to cry, that's what he found so touching. It was those little clenched fists, that daring defiance and those un-shed tears that had touched his heart.

His heart? What was he thinking? The outspoken miss had actually compared him to a mule. A stubborn mule.

He was shaking his head as he reached the sheriff's office. It was going to be one heck of a long month. At least once he had her out at the schoolhouse and settled, she'd be out of his hair, quietly doing her job and edu-cating the children. He had a strong feeling that the less time he spent in the company of Miss Julie Bright, the troublemaker with the green eyes, the better.

Chapter Four

It was all Julie could do to stay in bed that night. She was so full of excited anticipation, sleep was out of the question. She tossed and turned, making plans, and counting the minutes until dawn. By the time the sun crept over the windowsill in the cozy little hotel room, Julie was already up and dressed and sitting on the edge of her narrow bed, bags planted at her feet, ready to go.

It was nearly 8 A.M. before the knock sounded on her door signaling the sheriff's arrival. She was wearing a simple but neat dress of navy blue, its high collar trimmed with white piping, spectacles perched on her nose, mousy brown hair sternly under control in her orderly bun. She glanced in the looking glass before opening the door. She looked like a teacher. She *was* a teacher.

The young chambermaid stood there, about her same age, smiling broadly.

"We're so glad you have come to be our teacher, Miss

Bright," she said cheerfully. "I'm Jane Adams. My little brother and sister will be coming for school tomorrow. We are quite proud."

Julie beamed at the young woman.

"I wish we could have had a teacher earlier here, when I was still of school age," she said wistfully.

"You are never too old to learn, Jane. Don't forget that."

As she reached out and patted the girl's arm, there was a gruff cough from the steps behind Jane.

6'6" of sheriff had mounted the steps behind her. He had a most strange expression on his face as Julie looked at him.

"I'm ready, Sheriff White. I was coming right down."

"I thought I'd help with those bags of bricks you are carrying."

He crossed in front of her and picked up the over-loaded bags.

"Bricks?" Jane asked quizzically.

"Books. Bags of books." Julie laughed. "The sheriff finds my luggage to be a challenge."

You got, that right, Miss Bright, he thought sadly. *Your bags of books are a challenge. Because I can't read them.*

Within seconds they were down the wide staircase, through the sunlit lobby, and bouncing down the rutted street in Sheriff White's open wagon.

Julie reveled in the beauty of the morning, taking in the expanse of blue sky, smelling the springtime smells of damp earth and enjoying the bite of the morning air on her cheeks as they traveled through the town toward the schoolhouse that sat on its northern edge.

She was aware of the bigness of the man beside her, his presence simply not to be ignored. But she wasn't going to let him get under her skin, to rattle her in any way. It was much too important a day for that.

The white schoolhouse came into view, and she felt a definite thumping in her heart. Julie Bright, Schoolteacher.

She had made the long journey, emotionally much longer than the hard traveled miles over land from New York to Montana.

Julie had, she now knew, been born a teacher. There are those who are born to sing. There are those who are born to lead. From the first day that a governess had placed a book in her eager little hands, in the nursery of the Brightingham mansion, high above the sidewalks of New York City, she had been in love.

She had fallen in love with the written word. She had become enamored with the whole idea of learning about the world; its history, its geography, its possibilities.

And from the time that she had begun to explore the world that bustled outside the safety of that cloistered nursery, she had wanted to share that excitement with others. She had wanted to teach.

But teaching wasn't on Mr. Brightingham's agenda for his heiress daughter. There was no need for her to associate with the riffraff of New York City. The world, he strongly believed, was divided into two categories: the socially acceptable and the socially unacceptable. And it was unacceptable for the daughter of James Brightingham to teach.

Learning was wasted on the lower classes. Learning was provided for the upper classes, mostly from the grateful hands of young impoverished gentile relatives or well recommended widows. It was an occupation suited to those whose circumstances had left them little option.

According to her father, Julietta Brightingham was simply not a candidate for such a slide from grace. She was the only daughter of a millionaire, an heiress in her own right. She was a woman who should learn, instead, the intricacies of supervising a large household of efficient servants, the social skills for entertaining the well-polished dignitaries who had traveled to the very places that she dreamed about. She should take pride in her embroidery and needlework skills. She should revel in the latest fashions and be a pillar of polite society. While she may pity the poor, she certainly was not expected to mingle with them!

As James Brightingham's daughter, she had fallen a little short of the mark.

And as the determined man that he was, he had criticized her, admonished her, and punished her, bound to break her spirit and bend her will. She would stick out her chin, and refuse to back down, even when she saw the fury in his eyes.

"Troublemaker!" She could remember him ranting and raving at her. "Disobedient and insubordinate!" He would yell.

"Mary, if you can't convince her to follow my instructions, kindly send her to her room."

She had spent a lot of time in her room.

She had also spent a lot of time going up and down the drain pipe. One could say it had been her favorite mode of transportation.

Her series of governesses had been both frustrated and amazed. She had been an avid learner. She had been a voracious reader. She had welcomed any chance to explore the world, whether it meant visits to local museums, or the astounding New York Public Library. But she had also welcomed any opportunity to escape to explore on her own, a habit that had resulted in the replacement of many a governess through her adolescence.

A troublemaker. That's what she had been called.

Adventurous. That's what she called herself.

Incorrigible. Her father had said.

Inventive and determined. That was her description of herself.

Mrs. Mayberry had understood her from the very start. She had been Julie's last governess, arriving when she had just turned fourteen. She had recognized the excited look in her young pupil's eyes, the thirst for knowledge, the curiosity about the world. And she had nurtured it, rather than be intimidated by it, as so many before her had been.

And she had understood Julie's love of teaching.

From the time that Julie had been about ten, she had realized that people were treated differently in the world, and that some children had not been taught to read. Finding so much joy in books herself, she had taken it upon herself to right that wrong. She had begun to teach.

First it had been the cook's children, their excited little faces upturned in the kitchen lamplight as she had shared her story books with them, teaching them the alphabet and the wonder of words. Her mother had recently died, and the excitement of teaching the children had given her some happy moments of relief from her grief.

"Take yourself right back upstairs, young lady," her father had bellowed when he had caught her on one of her kitchen sojourns. "It is not your responsibility to teach the masses."

But she had decided that it was.

She would often stop and chat with grubby street children, teaching them to play hopscotch, and therefore learn their numbers on her "fresh air walks" in Central Park. Her early governesses had practically had apoplectic attacks.

But once Mrs. Mayberry had arrived, things had changed. Mrs. Mayberry had understood, taking her stocky little body to the nearest bench to "sit a spell" and feed the pigeons in the park, while watching Julie from afar.

By the time they were ready to return home, the sidewalk had been decorated with the letters of the alphabet, right alongside the hopscotch grid. Over several weeks time, she had taught the growing group of children to write their names, to say the alphabet, and to do basic sums.

But when her father had gotten wind of their afternoon "classes," the walks in the park had ceased.

"Can't you understand that what you are doing is unsuitable for a young woman of your stature?" he had bellowed. "You are my daughter, and you *will* act accordingly."

Julie had feared that his anger might lead to Mrs. Mayberry's dismissal, but that hadn't happened. He had been at a loss about his daughter since the death of his dear wife, and he had come to depend on the solid lady who seemed to actually enjoy working with his head-strong daughter.

She had stayed until Julie was seventeen and ready for her "coming out", the societal signal that childhood was past. Julie felt a warmth in her heart for the little lady who had been such a positive force in her life, including giving her this opportunity to fulfill her dreams.

The wagon slowed in front of the schoolhouse, with Julie leaping down before the vehicle rattled to a complete stop.

"It's beautiful, it's wonderful," she exclaimed, throwing her hands in the air and actually jumping up and down.

Jack White felt his heart jump in his chest at the sight of her exuberance. Did she know the effect she had on a man, that quiet, soul searching way she had about herself one minute, and full of energy like being shot from a cannon the next?

But he didn't have time to think, if he wanted to be the one to introduce her to the schoolhouse and her lodgings, which consisted of two cozy little rooms built onto the back of the building. She was already running up the schoolhouse steps, peering into windows, and rattling the door handle, which, of course, was still locked.

"Hurry, hurry," she admonished him, watching impatiently as he unfurled his 6'6" self from the wagon bench.

"What's the dang rush, that's what I want to know," he muttered to himself, as he fumbled in his pants' pocket to locate the big brass key. He stomped up the wooden steps to stand beside her at the door, ready to complain about her impatience.

But then he saw her eyes.

She was crying.

He was baffled.

The schoolhouse was absolutely fine, he knew. It had been built with the love and pride and hard work that was the very core of Grey Eagle. There was nothing she could object to about the schoolhouse, was there? Frantically. He looked around.

He looked at her again.

Tears were streaming down her face.

Uh oh, he thought. *What am I going to do now?*

"Miss Bright?" he said hesitantly.

"Are you going to just stand there gabbing, or are you going to unlock this door? Because if you aren't going to get this door opened quickly, I'm going to break it right down with my foot. And don't think that I can't."

She raised a booted foot up in the air.

"But you're crying, Miss Bright. I'm just trying to figure out what's made you so upset."

"Upset?" she giggled through a mist of tears. "I'm not upset. I'm happy. Delirious. And impatient." She reached down and started rattling the door knob. "Now open this door!"

He shook his head and reached out with the key. If I live to be a hundred, I will never understand the mixed up mind of a woman, he complained, wisely to himself.

One turn of the key and the door opened. Julie leaped into the room. "I'm a teacher. I'm a teacher!" she exclaimed, darting across the room, laying a hand on each desk, each shelf, each bench. There were eight long benches in all, four in a row, two rows. Long desk tables stood in front of each. There was a large square teacher's desk with a ladder back chair.

The room smelled like fresh hewn lumber, clean and new. Tall plate glass windows lined each side wall, letting in the morning light. In the corner, a round bellied black stove sat ready to heat the room.

"It's wonderful. It's, it's perfect," she said quietly as she turned to face him.

He felt a swell of pride. He had done a fine job with the design of the schoolhouse. Her praise made him feel like he was ten feet tall.

He deposited her heavy bags in her living quarters, while she roamed around, sighing and exclaiming about each new thing that she saw.

"We didn't get books yet," he said in a way of apology. "Didn't know what you'd need. So it's good you brought that ton of books with you to get you started."

There were stars in her eyes. Their happy twinkle went right to his heart.

"Yes indeed," she said. "I can't wait to meet the children tomorrow. Thank you, Sheriff. I'm most impressed."

He felt like he had been given the moon.

"It's nothing," he said.

"It's everything. And most of all, it shows how much your education has meant to you, to want to share it like this with the children."

He felt like he had fallen off the moon, plummeting to earth like a stone. He had to leave. He needed to get out of there.

"Well, if there's nothing else you need, Miss Bright," he said formally, "I've got a passle of things to do so I'll be on my way."

He tried not to notice the hurt look on her face at his abrupt dismissal, the way the light dimmed in her eyes. He tipped his hat, and turned on his heel, boots clunking down the wooden schoolhouse steps and across the spring grass schoolyard to the wagon.

How much his education had meant to him? He could feel the blood rising in his face, the rush of feelings. It was the biggest mark of a man, his ability to read the words that other people had written down, his ability to write down his own ideas. He had never had the chance. He longed for the chance. He was the sheriff. He was supposed to be a leader in this town. And he wouldn't feel that he deserved the job until he could do those things. He longed for the chance to learn. But to admit it would expose his greatest fault.

He climbed into the wagon, took the reins, and headed back to the sheriff's office in Grey Eagle, where his secret illiteracy would be safe from prying eyes.

Chapter Five

Julie sighed a deep breath as she watched Sheriff Jack White disappear from sight down the road. What was the matter with the man?

He went from cheerful to ornery faster than a spitting cat. Was it her? Had he seen her inside his much loved schoolhouse, and decided that she didn't belong there? Had he decided she was unsuitable? Was he sorry he had hired her?

She willed away the fear that was building in her stomach. He would get over his reservations. She would simply make him get over them. She turned and glanced again around the wonderful schoolhouse. It was all she could dream of.

Busily she unpacked her bags, placing her much loved and much used books neatly on the waiting shelves. She had brought twelve small square slates, at Mrs. Mayberry's suggestion, and an abundant supply of chalk for the children's writing. In no time at all, her simple classroom was set.

She tackled her own room in the back of the schoolhouse next. Her clothing took only minutes to organize. There wasn't much of it. Given the choice of filling her bags with books and supplies or clothing and shoes, the books had won.

She thought, momentarily, of the closet full of party dresses and elegant clothing still at home. She had given many things away, trading with the staff in her own house, as well as in houses on the block, who had been in cahoots with her plans to leave New York City. Her expensive satins had been exchanged for simple muslin dresses. A fur jacket for a calico day dress. Jewel tipped dancing slippers were traded for servicable boots. Beads and bangles for bonnets and her sturdy grey travel coat.

The recipients had been ecstatic. And she had been . . . freed.

Abraham Lincoln had freed the slaves almost thirty years before, but Julie had learned that there was more than one kind of bondage in the world, and that it didn't necessarily have to do with color or poverty.

For some, her life of possessions and privilege might seem like a desirable one. But for her, the limits and prejudices of that high society had been intolerable. She had run away from it all to be her own person.

She wondered if anyone missed her. She didn't wonder at all if her disappearance had caused a ruckus. She had known that it would. But once her decision had been made, she had gone full force ahead. No one was going to control her life ever again.

Her disguise had been simple and effective. The darkened hair, the plain and proper appearance, the switch to simpler clothing had done the trick. She had anonymously crossed the great expanse of country without raising a single eyebrow.

Not that she hadn't had a few moments of doubt and fear. In Chicago, she had seen a copy of a newspaper at a newstand in the train station. An almost lifesize sketch stared back at her from the front page, like looking in a black and white mirror. "SEARCH CONTINUES FOR MISSING HEIRESS," the headline above her face had read.

In St. Louis she had seen a reward poster plastered to the station wall. A $5,000 award had been offered for any information that lead to the location of Miss Julietta Brightingham, the missing heiress of the Brightingham shipping fortune.

A crowd had gathered to read the message. She had stood, frozen in fear, waiting to be recognized by the excited people around her.

"I'd like to get my hands on a reward like that," one man had exclaimed, turning to look right at her. But he hadn't even blinked. It didn't cross his mind that the mousy little woman who stood surrounded by her heavy bags could be a missing heiress.

And so gradually, she had gotten more secure in her new anonymous look, so different from the debutante pose in the paper. And she had looked ahead, instead of back.

But sometimes the past crept up on her, bringing a deep wave of sadness. Who would truly miss her? Who would miss her for herself? Only the household staff, who would soon be dispersed to new positions, since her father's death. And Mrs. Mayberry, who was now living with a married daughter.

Would her father have missed her if he had still been alive? Perhaps. He had been a complex man, born to control, and dictate to others. He had attempted to rule over Julietta every day of her life. But he had loved her in his own way, she knew. He truly thought that he knew what was best for her, as wrong as he had been. As angry as he had made her, she missed him. She was sorry for the heart attack that had taken his life during a pressure-filled business meeting with his board of directors, but she wasn't totally surprised. He had lived life with an intensity she knew was unhealthy.

She could even find it in her heart to forgive him for the things he had done to her in his life, his criticisms, his complaints. But it was going to take a month of Sundays for her to forgive him for what he had done to her in his death. It had only been his intention, she knew, to make her live the way he thought was necessary. He had had no idea of the devious plan his selfish brother would hatch.

Julie suddenly wanted to escape the dark thoughts of the past, so she slipped out the door of the schoolroom and slowly began to walk around the property, letting the warmth of the midday sun caress her shoulders and dry the unwanted tears that had crept down her cheeks. It felt good. She turned her face to the sun, remembering her mother's early remonstrances about "ladies" and their "pale ivory skin." She could hardly remember her mother without both hat and parasol.

This is another world, Mother, she said gently to her memories. *I can enjoy the sun.*

She traipsed around the schoolhouse, noting the large oak tree that would be perfect for a swing, and its shady umbrella of leafy branches that would be cool and enticing when classes were held on a very hot day.

A small barn sat on the far corner of the property, a neat little wagon parked inside. Transportation for the schoolmarm? But the barn itself was new and unused, no horse apparent, though several bales of hay were neatly stacked. She'd tackle that dilemma later.

The warming breezes of spring were flowing gently over central Montana, the tufts of prairie grass poking through the earth, and giving a greenish tinge out over the prairie as far as she could see. Far in the distance to the west, the Rockies rose straight to the sky. Majestic.

A splash of color caught her eye, and she bent to pick a few wild posies that had blossomed in the sunlight. She'd find something to hold them, and put them on her desk.

It was a beautiful day. From the front porch of the schoolhouse, she could just barely see the end of the main street in town. Giving in to the urge to explore, she wandered farther and farther from the back of the schoolhouse, away from town. The land became rougher, rockier, and she sometimes heard the scuttering of little prairie animals she disturbed in her route. When she lost sight of the schoolhouse, she arranged rocks in little arrow formations to be assured she knew the way home. Getting lost on her first day on the prairie would be a calamity she would avoid at all costs.

Several miles from the schoolhouse, the terrain rose to a higher elevation, large boulders squatting amid the rocky landscape.

She was surprised to see the sun begin to dip in the sky, the sign that the afternoon had evaporated, and the day was waning quickly, and so she made an about-face and retraced her steps. She'd explore further on another day.

As she left the boulder-strewn area behind her, she thought she caught sight of movement in the rocky shadows. She strained her eyes, but couldn't define what she had seen.

She found each arrow of rocks, attempting to retrace her path. She had placed the stones in a straight line. At least she thought she had. About a mile into her return trip, with the sun rapidly threatening to retire for the night, she realized that her path was not straight. She was zigzagging back and forth over the prairie, following the arrows.

She was still basically heading in the right direction, she knew, keeping the location of the setting sun in sight. But it was taking her much longer than she expected. Had she really wandered in such a meandering route?

She quickened her pace, almost running, and calling herself all kinds of names for her stupidity as she hurried to beat the lengthening shadows. As the sun dropped, so did the temperature. She could feel the evening chill going straight to her bones.

How could she have been so mistaken? She started to think of an explanation that she would have to give to the giant blue-eyed sheriff, if she got lost. He was already convinced that she was unsuitable for her beloved job.

The schoolhouse finally came into view, with the last of the daylight, and she was flooded with relief. Looking back over her shoulder, where the prairie was almost totally dark, she tried to gage the distance she had come, and figure out how she had travelled so uneven a path. A flash of movement caught her eye, gone in an instant.

Was someone following her? The schoolhouse loomed ahead, and she charged toward it full speed, grateful. But as she left the prairie, she thought she heard a sound, lightly carried by the spring evening breeze. It sounded distinctly like a giggle.

Julie had no time to ponder strange sounds, though. Ahead she saw the schoolhouse, and noticed with a start that it did not sit dark and deserted as she had expected it to be. The windows were blazing with light. Three wagons were parked in front.

She gulped and bounded up the wooden steps.

The new schoolmarm had unexpected company.

There was an excited buzz of voices when Julie exploded into the door of the schoolhouse.

"Surprise!" the small crowd hollered in unison. "Welcome to Grey Eagle!"

Eyes enormous in shock, Julie looked over the group that filled the schoolroom, seeing smiling faces of every shape and size. Old and young, rancher and shopkeeper, the citizens of Grey Eagle had come together to show her that they were glad she had come.

Julie's eyes felt misty.

"Oh, my!" she exclaimed, taking in the table that had been erected along the wall of the room, overladen with food, and the bowl of punch that was being ladled out by the stagecoach driver. His eye had blackened, and his lip still looked awful, but he winked and smiled.

Jane Adams, the young woman from the hotel, was by her side.

"Oh, I'm so glad to see a familiar face!" she said to Jane.

"They'll all be familiar faces, soon, Miss Bright."

"Please, Jane, call me Julie, won't you? And let's be friends. I feel a bit overwhelmed by all this."

Jane smiled happily and took hold of her arm, guiding her through the crowd, introducing her along the way.

"This is Mr. Henry Baker, from the mercantile, and his wife, Bonnie. She makes the best cookies in town."

"This is Harvey Mills, who runs the livery and does the blacksmithing." The swarthy, chubby man blushed, and extended his work-worn hand.

"Most welcome, Miss Bright. While I ain't got no younguns' yet, I sure do reckon the ones we got in this town can do with some serious learnin'."

Julie smiled as she was led away and Jane whispered, "Why that's the longest speech I believe Harvey's ever made, Julie. And you sure did make him blush!"

"It's a pleasure to have you, my dear Miss Bright," interrupted a tall, spare woman wearing a lacy high necked dress with a matching bonnet who positioned herself directly in their path.

"May I introduce Miriam Davis, the wife of John Davis, who owns the Davis Grain Mill outside of town." Jane said softly, bowing deferentially to the self-assured matron.

"And on behalf of the Ladies League of Grey Eagle, we'd like to invite you to our monthly tea at the hotel next week. Four o'clock on the last Tuesday of the month. The league will be honored to assist you in getting settled here."

"Well, thanks," exclaimed Julie, slightly overcome with all of the attention she was receiving. But when Mrs. Davis had moved on, she noticed Jane's somber expression.

"All of a sudden you look like your shoes are too tight, Jane. What's the problem?"

Jane shrugged sadly. "Just jealous, I guess. Those Ladies League ladies don't even give me the time of day. Every month I wait on them at their tea at the hotel, and they treat me like I'm invisible." She pursed her lips. "Like I'm not good enough."

Julie grabbed her hand and squeezed it. "You're plenty good enough, Jane, and don't you forget it."

"Well, maybe you don't know, Julie, what rich folks can be like. They just don't care about everybody, you know, only their own."

Julie felt a sting of shame. She *did* know what rich folk were like. First hand. She didn't speak.

Jane sighed. "And I guess they've decided that you are 'one of them,' being the new teacher and all." She sounded wistful. "I sure wish I could read and be a teacher, too."

Julie smiled. "Then you will be. I will teach you."

Jane looked at the new schoolteacher as strangely as if she had sprouted horns. "If only that were possible."

More townsfolk were approaching them with introductions, and the conversation changed. She met the banker and his wife, Peter and Olive Newby, several local ranchers, and Marcus, the sheriff's deputy.

Her eyes kept scanning the crowd for the taller-than-life blond head that belonged to the sheriff. He was nowhere in sight. Evidently, he hadn't thought it necessary or desirable to celebrate the arrival of the new schoolteacher in Grey Eagle.

She already knew his opinion. So why did his absence cause such dismay?

The guests were happily dishing up the food that had been contributed, and there was a cheerful buzz of talk in the room. Suddenly feeling like the room was closing in, Julie slipped out the door to the porch of the schoolhouse for a breath of air.

She found him then. He was hatless for once, sitting on the porch steps with his long legs bent so that he could rest his elbows on his knees. She stood soundlessly behind him, noticing the curl of the shaggy blond curls at the back of his hair, the breadth of the shoulders that strained against the chambray shirt.

"Evenin' Miss Bright," he drawled without turning around.

She was startled. How had he known she was there?

It was as if he heard her unasked question.

"Had to be you," he said, still not turning his head. "It's that smell. Like violets."

"I didn't see you inside."

"I'm not exactly the party type. Seems too much work to walk and eat and talk civil to folks at the same time."

"It was sure nice of them to do this."

He stood up then, and turned around, standing at the bottom of the steps and looking directly into her eyes.

"It means a lot to them, having a schoolteacher in Grey Eagle."

"It means a lot to me, too. I won't let you all down."

"Didn't really think you would. I just wonder why you're here, though, pretty young thing like you."

"I'm here to teach, Sheriff White."

"We'll see. Schoolteaching's not an easy job, so I hear. These western towns are interestin', you know. Nothing but prairie here even twenty years back. Then people start arriving from points unknown, all aiming to start a new life. They all come from somewhere, leaving another life behind. Like you. What life did you leave behind, Miss Julie Bright?"

His blue eyes were piercing her, creating havoc inside. Her past. Why was he talking about her past? Could he know who she was? What did he know? Her hands were shaking. This would not do. She had faced down the intimidation of many a tough pitcher at bat. She would not falter.

She found her voice, and said in a much more casual tone than she felt, "And what life did you leave behind, Sheriff White?"

He froze and stared at her.

She felt like the air around them was crackling with electricity, and had the most idiotic urge to touch him. Why did this man do this to her?

He stared at her long and hard, then looked away to some unknown focus point in the distance. "Might as well call me Jack, Miss Bright."

A truce?

"Jack, then. And you may call me Julie."

He held out his hand to her, and she looked at the large, masculine palm and swallowed hard. She raised her hand to shake his offered one. Would he feel how her hands were shaking?

The large fingers enveloped hers, and the warmth from his hand spread through her like a flush. Friend or enemy?

She didn't know. She just knew that she felt a great sense of loss when he took his hand away.

Chapter Six

The morning sun crept over the eastern horizon bright and clear. Julie's heart was hammering in her chest as she stood at the doorway of the schoolhouse. It was the first day of school in Grey Eagle.

The children would soon be arriving.

She hadn't been able to sleep after the welcoming party last night, with thoughts spinning in her head.

She had met so many people, the ranchers, the farmers, the mill workers, the banker, the mercantile owners. The townsfolk of Grey Eagle had made her feel welcome and a part of their growing community.

And now the children would be coming to begin school. There was a cloud of dust in the distance, the first sign of a wagon making it's way toward the schoolhouse. She turned and surveyed the room behind her, ready for its first students. With two shaking hands, she grabbed the long rope that was attached to the school bell, high atop the building and pulled with all her might.

The school bell clanged resoundedly. Within minutes, the first wagon had arrived, followed soon by children on horseback, and on foot. They came from town, and from the outlying ranches and farms.

The new era of Grey Eagle had begun, she thought, as she welcomed each freshly scrubbed face. She faced her first official class with excited enthusiasm. An hour later, she was giving serious consideration to passing out.

They ranged in age from six to fourteen, including a family of seven. There were thirty-two children in all, filling every available seat and bench. The noise level was deafening. The older ones shouted to each other across the room, and the younger ones scurried around, chasing each other in and around the benches.

The Perkins twins spilled a bottle of ink on the new schoolroom floor. Julie darted around, bravely trying to ignore the chaos that she had no hope of containing.

She tried to speak to each child to ascertain any educational skills they may have. Several children knew how to write their names. A few could actually read. But the majority had only the vaguest concept of reading or writing. And they had no understanding of classroom deportment and behavior. The morning flew by in a haze of havoc, and Julie felt frustrated and sick.

How had she ever considered herself capable of being a teacher? At most, in New York, she had taught a handful at a time. She had taught the Brightingham staff's children in the shiny bright kitchen. She had taught small groups of children in the open spaciousness of Central Park. What did she know of managing a class of western hooligans who were used to open ranges and constant freedom?

Only the Adams children, the youngest siblings of her friend Jane from the hotel, were quiet and obedient. Their solemn dark eyes followed her around the room as she made notes.

At midmorning, she glanced up as a shadow filled the doorway, and found Sheriff Jack White blocking the sunlight. He looked around at the chaos around her, and watched her with expressionless eyes. He was gone as quietly as he had arrived, shaking his head and leaving her with an even deeper feeling of dread and shame that he had witnessed her failure. With burning eyes, she returned to her pupils.

Then the pendulum clock on the wall announced noon's arrival, and the end of the horrible morning.

Julie moved to the front of the room and stood before the class. Hungry, they gave her their attention. Finally they were all in their chairs.

They're probably exhausted and hungry from all the jumping around they did, she thought ironically.

"I guess it's time for dinner, class," she said softly to the group. Her confidence was gone, and her hopes were smashed. She would somehow get through the afternoon, finish this day, and admit her defeat. She obviously was a failure as a teacher.

A lone hand went up in the back of the room. It was one of the famous, ink-stained Perkins twins, a twelve-year-old boy with bright red hair.

"Can I ask ya a question, Miss Bright?" he said in his high-pitched voice. "Did ya really come all the way to Montana from New York on that thar big black train we heared about?"

Instantly, thirty-two sets of curious eyes were upon her.

"Well, yes," she said hesitantly, watching the children watching her with interest.

"Only it wasn't just one train. I rode on several trains. In some cities you have to get off one train and get onto another. But yes, the track continues all the way from New York to Montana now. And even further. It goes all the way to California. All the way across the country."

"Was it a long trip?" another young boy asked.

"Was it horrible loud?" asked a tall dark girl. "I heard it roars like a lion."

"Did you see any train robbers?"

"What makes it go?"

A tiny flicker of hope began to flutter in Julie's heart as she watched their eager faces. They were asking questions. They wanted to learn. She drew in a deep breath.

"I'll tell you what. It's time to take a break for the dinner you've brought to eat. We'll go outside in the fresh air and do that, and when I ring the bell, we'll come back in. If you are much more quiet than this morning, and stay right in your seats, we'll start the afternoon learning about the Pacific Northwest Railroad. No yelling. You'll sit still. And I will tell you all about the trip. How does that sound?"

Their delighted shouts filled the air and they sprung from their seats and bolted out the door.

We'll tackle deportment later, she thought. *First I have to get them in their chairs.*

She followed the active children out the door.

Recess was not exactly uneventful. There were two fist fights between the older boys, one a dispute between ranching and farming; one over who was the favorite of MaryBeth Newby, the banker's daughter. From all Julie could surmise, MaryBeth didn't much care for either one of them. The second fight had resulted in a bloody nose.

After playing referee, she organized the younger children in a game of hopscotch that she had learned in Central Park. They were quick to learn how to draw the boxes and corresponding numbers in the dusty ground. They laughed as she demonstrated standing on one foot and picking up her tossing rock, and eagerly tried it themselves.

She was hot and a bit mussed by the time recess was over, but ready to tackle the afternoon. Her stubborness had returned, and with it, her good humor. She was going to teach these children if it killed her. Or unless the sometimes surly sheriff killed her, which was, she knew, a distinct possibility!

She was hotter and even more mussed by dismissal time. Her throat was sore from constant talking. Her head ached from thinking. But they had been taught. They had listened and learned.

By trial and error, and a lot of quick thinking, she had taken control of the afternoon. They had learned about the amazing and growing railroad industry, and had heard details of her long and dusty trip across the plains. In between stories, she had rearranged them, using the scanty knowledge she had ascertained during her frustrating morning. Readers were in one group. Small beginners were in another. She would let the older ones help tutor the little ones. Most of the class had settled down. But in the back corner of the room, Jeb, nearly six feet tall, and the victor of both the recess schoolyard scuffles, still sat smirking and defiant.

"Tomorrow we will begin writing," she promised. "And if you are good, I will tell you about New York."

"Are there really buildings so tall they reach the sky?"

"I hear they put their outhouses right *inside* the house," smirked Jeb, in a loud, deep voice from the back of the room.

The class groaned in disbelief.

She let the silence that followed permeate the room. Heads swiveled from the front of the room, to the back, and then back again, expectantly.

"Jeb's right," she said, grinning. "Inside outhouses. They call them bathrooms. With something called a toilet for doing what's necessary, and also a bathtub for taking a bath. And water that comes right out of a pipe into the room. We'll talk about that, too."

There was a buzz of voices as the class reacted.

"More questions tomorrow. Now, it's time to end the day. But first I need a volunteer to be in charge of the school bell. Morning and afternoon."

Almost every hand in the room went up. Except Jeb's.

"Jeb? Could you do it?" she asked as if she hadn't noticed his lack of participation. "Could you be the one who's in charge of the bell?"

He gave her a startled look.

"I suppose," he grumbled, not meeting her eye.

"Aww," groaned several voices in the room. "He'll just make a mess of it. He makes a mess of everything."

"Nonsense. I can see that Jeb has strength, and that's what the job takes. He'll give it a try. Go ring, Jeb."

After a moment of hesitation, the tense young boy unfolded his gangly frame from the school bench and walked stiffly to the rope. Grabbing with two hands, he gave a hard yank, and the sound of the bell resounded through the air.

"Now *that* was a proper ring," Julie said primly to the class before her. "Thank you, Jeb. Nine o'clock tomorrow, please. Class dismissed."

They scrambled for the door. The tall boy was the last one to leave. He didn't say a word, and his long, stringy dark hair was falling forward, hiding his eyes, but it didn't disguise the surprised look of pride that had crept into his eyes.

Jack had come out to the schoolhouse at the end of the day to dismiss her. The scene he had observed in the morning was crazier than a cattle stampede, children hopping around, climbing on chairs, making more noise than a pig in heat. He had known it from the start. She hadn't looked like a proper schoolmarm, and he had known she couldn't do the job. But he had let those sparkly little eyes turn his head and cloud his judgement. He had let her stay, and now he had to make it right.

No matter how hard it ripped at his guts. It was his fault, and he had to fix it.

So he had ridden back out to the schoolhouse before dismissal time, and had tethered his horse under the spring shade of the big tree that sat beside the schoolhouse, to wait to talk to her. This time, he would not be deterred. He would send her back to wherever she had come from, and he was going to find a real schoolmarm for the children of Grey Eagle.

From his spot on the front porch, he was surprised he could hear her voice float out the open window. They were sitting, orderly like now, giving her their rapt attention. How had she done that? She was telling the children a story, and they were listening. Heck, within minutes, he was listening, too. She was recounting the history of the building of the railroad, the many hands who had dug and hammered each metal rail, the land fights, the competitions, the excitement of success.

She described her trip in detail, the rhythm of the train, the smell and bustle of each new city, the varying landscape as she had crossed the United States to the new state of Montana.

Like a magic spell, she had every student hanging on every word. Even the illiterate sheriff, he thought grudgingly.

He heard her close out the day with promises of tomorrow. He heard her assign Jeb Johnson to ring the bell. *Jeb Johnson?*

Jeb was the son of Helen Johnson, a widow lady who was a seamstress in town. A widow lady. He knew that first hand. Her husband, Jonas had been shot while holding up a stage a while back, and she'd been bringing up the boy alone since then. And Jeb . . . it was pretty much the definite opinion of the town in general that Jeb would be following right in his father's surly and violent footsteps as soon as he was old enough to be off on his own.

But when the class had exploded from the schoolhouse, he had seen Jeb at the rear. Smiling. Proud. Bellringer instead of gunslinger. Not a bad change, he had to admit to himself. How had she done that? Practically a miracle. Did he believe in miracles?

He stood up and mounted the steps to the schoolroom.

Chapter Seven

Jack White walked through the open door of the schoolhouse, looking around the room for Miss Julie Bright. He didn't see her at first. The afternoon sun was peeking in through the tall windows at the straight rows of benches and desks. He found her sitting in the back row, arms folded on the desk, head resting on her arms. She was crying.

He was filled with alarm. He didn't know much about females in general, and he didn't want to know anything in specific about crying ones. What was he supposed to do? He stood rooted to the spot.

She sensed, rather than heard, his presence. She pulled her head up, saw him, and quickly wiped her eyes, pulling herself upright.

"Why, Sheriff," she said a shade too brightly. "How nice of you to come visit."

She was going to pretend she hadn't been crying. That

was all right by him, for sure. He could pretend as well as the next guy.

"I came to talk to you about your day. I came by this morning."

Her face was a bit blotchy from crying (or not crying, as they were pretending), but now she blushed to a deep rose color. Nervously, she pushed her spectacles back up on her nose.

"Yes, well, I suppose I did see you, though in the rush of getting started, I didn't have time to converse."

The rush to get started? He had seen a boy catapult himself over a desk!

"I suppose you noticed . . ." she cleared her throat, "that things were a bit, ah, hectic."

"Hectic."

"A tad noisy."

"A tad."

She pursed her lips determinedly and stared at him defiantly.

Her back was stiff, and she certainly looked determined, but he could see the wetness around her eyes.

Oh, God, no more crying, pretend or not.

"Oh, all right," she conceded, looking up at the ceiling, and biting her lip. "It was miserable. I was miserable. It was hard to get started. But it got better. I promise. It got better."

That little chin was quivering now, but she was, as they say, keeping a stiff upper lip. For some stranger reason, he had to fight the urge to plant a kiss on that pointy little quivering chin. What was wrong with him? Was he here to kiss her or to fire her?

A voice spoke, and he was surprised to find it was his.

"It got a lot better. Especially about the train. They really listened to the train story. So did I."

The large brown eyes sparkled again, the chin stopped quivering, and she looked at him in amazement.

"You heard me? What were you doing, hiding outside the window?"

He blushed and grinned. "Exactly."

Julie just smiled brightly.

"Weren't they wonderful? They have so many questions. I can't wait for tomorrow. We'll learn all about New York, and learn to write our names. And we'll begin our arithmetic. It's vitally important that these children know arithmetic . . ."

"About tomorrow." He had a job to do, trains or no trains, New York or no New York. Quivering chins or no quivering chins.

"You'll come?" Her enthusiasm bubbled. "To tell the truth, I was so intimidated by this morning, I didn't know what to do. But I only had to get to know them, to learn what was important to them, and then it was all right. We moved right along, like a steam engine along the track, don't you think?"

A steam engine was right. He felt like there was one charging down the tracks, right at him. And he was being derailed again.

Fire her? He may be the sheriff, but he doubted there was a law man alive who could stand up to those big brown eyes. And it was important for the children to learn their arithmetic, wasn't it? Maybe he'd give her another chance.

"Are you sure you can keep them in their seats? Are

you sure you can handle this job?" His voice had taken on a mind of its own. He couldn't believe it. He was giving in again.

"Absolutely." She crossed her fingers behind her back. If she had to hog-tie them, she would keep them at their desks. And if she had to hog-tie herself, she would keep control of her emotions.

It was almost a relief when the big man had gone. Almost. She watched his giant horse gallop away, carrying him back toward the center of town. The square frame of his shoulders, and the outline of his huge hat were silhouetted against the cloudless sky.

Julie sat back down at the back desk, legs suddenly wobbly. She wouldn't allow herself to cry again. There had been nothing to cry about this afternoon, really. The afternoon had been a smashing success. She could have shed a few tears after the morning session she admitted to herself, had she not been so numbed with shock about the children's behavior. But it had all turned out well in the end, so tears were unnecessary. Her outburst had been the result of pent up tension and emotions, a silly display of weakness that she was not intending to repeat. She had to keep her wits about her.

The sheriff had had every intention of firing her. She could feel it in her bones. He had come back to the schoolhouse prepared to send her back to New York, on the tip of his boot if necessary. But he'd changed his mind. At least for now.

She pulled herself together and settled in at her desk at the front of the room, soon absorbed in her textbooks, planning lessons and activities to keep thirty-two active children learning and well behaved in the morning. Now she knew what it would take. The time flew by, and the sun began its descent in the Montana sky.

She was just beginning to think that the light was growing too dim for reading, when she thought she noticed a movement in one of the schoolroom windows. She turned her head and stared, but the window was empty. She crossed the room and looked outside. Everything was still and normal.

She was putting the heavy texts away when she again caught a glimpse of movement in the window. This time she darted to the window and looked out. Nothing.

Chiding herself for being nervous, she closed up the schoolroom and retired to her living quarters. With a warming fire burning in the wood stove, she put on a kettle for tea, and stirred the soup she had started in the morning before class. Soon the aroma of vegetables and spices filled the air.

While the soup cooked, she took a walk outside in the waning light, enjoying the quiet and the open expanse of land and sky everywhere she looked. She was definitely in love with Montana.

The barn beckoned her, and she walked over to inspect the wagon that sat idly under its roof. The wood was fresh and gleaming, the spoked wheels greased and ready to roll. Ready except for a horse. With hands on hips, she regarded the wagon. A horse would be her next project. She could only imagine what the sheriff would say about the idea that was forming in her head!

The hay bales had been neatly stacked when she had investigated the day before. Quizzically, she noticed that they had been moved, restacked in the corner, but away from the wall. That was odd. She had obviously missed the children playing near the barn during their recess. She sighed. More rules to iron out.

Evening was rapidly descending by the time she walked back to the schoolhouse. She climbed the steps, and put her hand on the door handle to open the door. It wouldn't turn.

That was odd. She was sure that she had left the door unlocked when she had stepped outside for some fresh air. She could envision the key where she had left it, hanging from the large hook right inside the door. She tried the door again. It was definitely locked. She had locked herself out of her own house.

Chiding herself that she was finally losing her mind, she looked around for a solution. Grumbling and talking under her breath, she hefted a few logs from the well-stacked woodpile that sat behind the schoolhouse, placing them stragically under the still open window. Putting one log atop the other, she scrambled up to the top, and hoisted one leg through the window, skirts flying. The other leg was next, with the rest of her body following rapidly with the momentum. She flew through the window, lost her balance and went crashing to the school-room floor.

Whoosh! The breath went out of her. It was like the mansion drain pipe all over again. She lay there for a minute staring at the far away ceiling while she caught her breath. At least she was safely inside, and didn't have to trek to town to get the sheriff to open the door. The embarrassment would have killed her.

She stood up, dusted off her skirt and went to check the door. The key still hung on the hook by the door. But the latch was definitely locked. And she knew that she had not locked it. Someone had turned the latch and pulled the door shut after she had gone out. But who?

Suddenly, the smell of burning food assailed her nostrils. Her soup! She darted across the schoolroom and into her kitchen, just in time to see the pot on the woodstove start to smoke. Slightly charred but still edible, she decided, reaching for a loaf of bread that had been left over from the town's party the night before. She'd solve the locked door mystery later. Right now, her stomach was growling, and dinner was more than done.

She sat at the table and began to eat hungrily. She paused for a minute, listening. Her imagination was working overtime. She kept thinking she was hearing the sound of distant laughter. Laughter? She might be losing her mind, but she would have to wait and lose it after supper! She dug into the soup with gusto.

The next week flew by for Julie. Each day was a challenge, but never as much of a disaster as that first day had been. She worked hard at planning lessons that would keep the big ones quiet, and lessons that would slowly help the little ones to learn their letters and numbers.

She put the remaining ink away, and had the children use the slates and chalk. That kept the Perkins twins, who seemed to have a penchant for spilling things, out of trouble. The Adams children, Jane's brother, Eric and sister, Emily were the most dependable, and were the quickest to learn. Jeb Johnson kept ringing the bell, and hadn't missed a day of school yet.

Day by day, lesson by lesson, the little schoolhouse was beginning to bustle with learning. Julie went to sleep each night exhausted, but proud. She still hadn't figured out how she had managed to lock herself out after her first day of school, but she was careful to see that it wasn't repeated. She wore the key to the schoolhouse on a string around her neck. She wasn't leaving anything to chance!

Jack White hadn't ridden out to check up on her since that first amazing day. On the one hand, she was glad to be out from under his scrutiny. But on the other hand, she had to admit to herself that she missed seeing his big hat, and hearing his big boots on the wooden steps. And then there were his eyes. But she wasn't going to let herself dwell on such foolishness.

Sunday morning dawned bright and sunny, and she put on her best dress. It was a green gingham check, with a wide white collar and a very full skirt. She thought for a moment about the satins and laces she had given away in New York, dresses that could turn so many people pea green with envy. There was no doubt about it. She preferred this one. It was simple and cheerful, and just right for going to church in Grey Eagle, which was what she planned to do. Jane Adams had invited her to attend with her family, and they had agreed to come by the schoolhouse in their wagon on the way to church to pick her up.

Though it was not at all too far to walk, going alone to church had not seemed like a comfortable thing to do, and so she appreciated Jane's friendly offer to accompany her into town.

She was tying her white bonnet on her head when the carriage arrived. She carefully locked the schoolhouse door behind her, returning the key to its place around her neck, and climbed into the already full Adams family wagon. There was a scramble to change seats, and before she knew it, she had Emily and Eric on each side of her, and had the bouncing two-year-old Michelle on her lap. Jane sat across from her with her mother, while her father sat in the front holding the reins.

"So glad to meet you, Miss Bright," said Mrs. Adams shyly. She and her husband were struggling farmers who harvested hay for livestock. "We're so glad you've come to teach, and so glad that you're teachin' *all* the children."

Julie smiled. "Call me Julie, Mrs. Adams. And of course I'm teaching *all* the children. At least all the ones that show up!"

"Mama grew up in Missouri, Julie, and her folks didn't have much money either. But in that town, the schoolmarm would only take on those that came from monied families, so she never got to learn. Then she married Papa and they settled here in Montana. So Emily and Eric will learn to read. There wasn't a school when I was young, so that's why I didn't get to go."

Julie's heart broke at the emotion in Jane's voice. She heard the hope and delight for her siblings, and the sadness at her own loss.

"You don't have to be a child to learn to read, Jane. You can learn any old time you put your mind to it. You're going to learn to read, Jane. I can teach you. I promise. You wait and see."

Jane's eyes were misty. "I told you she was something special, Mama," the young woman said softly.

Mrs. Adams nodded, not saying a word. But Julie could see the tears that were flowing down her cheeks, which she brushed away with work-worn hands.

I am in the right place, Julie thought with certainty to

herself, as the church came into view. In her lap, Michelle squirmed and giggled and flapped her arms like a seasoned entertainer. She was the first baby, Julie realized, that she had ever held in her arms. She held her close, and breathed in the sweet baby scent of her, mingled with the sun fresh smell of her clothes, and felt a strange surge of happiness. By the time the wagon rolled to a stop in front of the large wooden doors of the big white church, they were all smiling again.

The church was packed on the bright spring morning. Julie saw some familiar faces from the reception at the schoolhouse mixed in with the crowd. Each family seemed to have their own place to sit in the church, she noticed, as the congregation flowed in through the big wooden doors. She sat contentedly with the Adams family, toward the back of the church, watching every one arrive. Jane, now holding Michelle, sat on the aisle, with Julie at her side. Mrs. Adams sat on her other side.

A few minutes before the service was to begin, a tall, thin woman detached herself from one of the first pews and walked back to approach Julie. Julie recognized Mrs. Miriam Davis, wife of the wealthy owner of the Davis Brain Mill.

"Miss Bright," the woman said cheerfully. "How lovely to see you." She extended her hand, and Julie shook it with a smile.

"Come dear, and join us in the front. We have an appropriate seat for you," she said, her bonnet bobbing as she tilted her head toward the front.

"Well, thank you Mrs. Davis," Julie said. "But I've come with the Adams family and I'm perfectly fine sitting right here."

Beside her, she could feel Jane stiffen.

"Really," the matron continued. "That's not necessary. You belong up front with us."

Julie found her cheeks burning as she realized the meaning of the woman's words. For Jane. For her parents.

"Thank you, but I'm just fine where I am," she said softly, forcing a smile on her now stiffened lips. "This is right where I want to be."

There was a rustling sound in the church signifying that the service was about to begin. Mrs. Davis withdrew her hand, and squared her shoulders.

"I see," she said, her smile looking a little forced. "And it's time I returned to my place. Perhaps we will speak later." She turned on the heel of her finely laced shoe, and walked sedately back up the aisle to her waiting family, her back ramrod straight.

"Oh Julie," whispered Jane, clutching her hand. "You didn't have to do that. She'll be so mad. I guess you're supposed to be up there."

Julie squeezed her hand back. "Jane, I guess I'm supposed to be right where I want to be, and I choose to be right here. So there!"

With that, Michelle flung one of her chubby arms, and boxed Julie squarely in the jaw.

"Ouch!" she whispered, rubbing the spot. "That child has a definite future in a boxing ring." When they laughed, Mrs. Adams shot them a sobering look, and the preacher began leading the crowd in a hymn.

Behind them, in the last row of the church, where he stopped every Sunday to see the town gathered for their prayers, sat Sheriff Jack White, who had witnessed the whole interaction with a puzzled look on his face.

As the singing began, he stood, as he did every Sunday of every week, and quietly exited the church. Out in the sunshine, he returned his hat to his head, and strode down the street, leaving the little church behind.

In his years of living on the land, watching its rhythms and phases, Jack White had learned that he had a certain instinct about the natural course of events. He was darn good at predicting what was coming. Like a storm. He could sense the onset of a dangerous hailstorm, sometimes hours before other folk. There was a certain smell in the air. There was a certain greenish tinge to the sky. There was a certain prickly feeling in his skin. And a snowstorm. During the nightmare winters of '86 and '87, when so many folks had lost their cattle due to the never-ending piles of snow and ice that had been dumped on the plains of Montana, he had been able to predict the oncoming flakes, just by the smell of the cold, icy air. When it smelled like snow, it smelled like snow. He was always right.

He'd protected both folk and critters from lightning strikes, and been able to sense the oncoming rare flash flood when a sudden rain doused the plains, and turned usually dry creekbeds into instantly rushing rivers. He could tell when a mare was going to foal, he could tell when a stallion was ready to bolt. He could just tell when these things were going to happen.

On the range, these had been valuable insights. And nobody had taught him. Just like everything in life that he knew, he had taught himself.

A familiar blanket of shame descended, when he thought of the things he didn't know. Not just the reading, which was a big deal in itself. But also the church stuff. All the folks would gather together and sing songs that they had learned as little tykes, and say prayers that they'd been taught. Which counted him out, because he'd never learned any of those church things in his scant years as a child.

But he'd never let them know. He'd choke of shame first.

He'd almost been caught, that one time the preacher had asked him to read from the Bible. It was an honor, really, to be asked. It had been the day of the dedication of the new church. He had dared to go to church that day, and the town had been applauding him for his commitment and efforts in organizing the erecting of the church. He had been so proud that day.

But then the preacher had asked him if he'd like to come up front and read a passage from the Bible to the congregation, he'd thought his heart was going to stop beating on the spot.

"Nice thought, Preacher Bell," he'd said, hoping that no one got a look at his dang eye, which had begun twitching like a worm stuck on a hook. "But I've got some important law business that needs attendin' to right now, so I'm going to have to take my leave."

He'd left, and he'd never ever stayed long enough to get put on the spot again.

But he always stopped by. It was his town, his church, his folk. And he loved to see them gathered together.

Today, he had seen the schoolmarm sitting there, looking so pretty and fresh, with the Adams baby flapping all over her, and it had made his heart soar like an eagle. But then he had seen her turn away old man Davis' wife, which was a hard thing to do, as the woman nearly always got her way in this town, no matter how unkindly she could be. And he had seen the older woman's unhappy face as she had taken her leave, like a spiteful, hungry cat who's eyed a tasty morsel of a mouse.

Not that Julie Bright resembled a mouse in any way. He'd noticed her giggling with that nice Jane Adams from the hotel. She'd totally ignored the obvious displeasure of Miriam Davis. Then she'd pushed her spectacles back up on her nose and begun to sing with fervor.

And he'd run out the door with even more fervor.

And a sinking feeling in the pit of his stomach.

A storm was brewing in Grey Eagle. He could feel it right down to his bones. Every instinct was on alert. The forces of nature were about to bear down on them, and he didn't know what the result would be. Because this storm was going to be about human nature. And Julie Bright was right in the middle of it.

And there was not a thing he could do about it at this point, he knew. But he reckoned that nobody in Grey Eagle would be the same once the storm passed, least of all, him.

Chapter Eight

When class was dismissed the following Thursday, Julie took a minute to freshen up her face, and took a brush to her hair. The tendrils that tended to escape to frame her face during the course of the day were tamed and restyled to restore her proper appearance. She was going into town for the ladies tea at the hotel.

She made a face at herself in the little mirror in her room, as she put her bonnet on her head and tied it beneath her chin. She didn't look like Julietta Brightingham at all. She was getting used to the mousy drab appearance of her hair, though she missed her normal blond hair. And she certainly enjoyed the fact that she could wear her spectacles freely to enjoy seeing the world around her. She didn't miss the dictates of New York high society at all. Her mother had always banned her from wearing her spectacles in public. That had certainly curtailed her vision of the world.

She carefully locked the schoolhouse and rehung the

key around her neck, hiding it beneath her dress. She had decided to walk into town, instead of inquiring about a ride. It was a beautiful day, and she loved to walk.

Strolling down the main street on the way to the hotel, she studied the town of Grey Eagle. A new shoemaker was moving to town, and two men were struggling to hang a new wooden sign depicting a boot above the door of the newly finished building. From an upstairs window, evidently the living quarters for the new family, a woman stuck her head out and shrilly criticized their efforts.

"To the right, Clyde. It ain't straight!"

"Yes, Martha," said the smaller man, huffing and puffing.

"Lower, Clyde," she shrilled. "How many times to I have to say it?"

"You best quit your huffing now, Martha. You may be my sister, but I'm gonna drop this here end right on the walkway and head on home to supper," laughed the other man.

"You're a good for nothin' . . ."

"Ain't that your biscuits I smell burnin', woman?" said her husband from under his heavy load.

"Well, I never . . ." pouted the woman, but she pulled her head in the window and went to rescue the biscuits, leaving the two men laughing as they struggled with the sign.

"Good afternoon, Miss Bright," they said cheerfully, despite their load as she passed by.

"Good afternoon, gentlemen," she smiled brightly at them. "Wonderful sign!"

The men smiled proudly.

"But if I may say so, the missus is right. Lower *would*

look better! That way, it keeps the sun glare off the sign at this hour of the day."

"Well, I'll be . . ." said the shoemaker, lowering the sign thoughtfully.

"Women!" growled his brother-in-law, as he lowered the other end.

Julie was grinning broadly as she mounted the hotel steps. She stepped into the inviting lobby and was greeted by the hotel keeper.

"The ladies are awaiting you, my dear," he said, as she removed her bonnet. He led her to the main dining room, where a table of eight women sat properly at the table.

"So lovely to see you," said Olive Newby, the banker's wife. Beside her, she saw Miriam Davis and Bonnie Baker, the wife of the owner of the mercantile, and mother of Gloria, one of her older students. The oldest woman present was introduced as Sarah Blanding, the sister of the owner of the oldest ranch in the area, and the other ladies were wives of additional prominent ranchers.

"We're delighted that you have come to settle in Grey Eagle, Miss Bright," said Miriam Davis. The children are responding well to receiving a formal education. My MaryBeth is thrilled with going to the schoolhouse. We are extremely supportive of your work with the children."

Over her shoulder, Julie saw Jane enter the room carrying a large tray laden with crumpets and steaming pots of tea.

"Hello, Jane," she said brightly, happy to see her friend.

"Good day, Miss," said Jane deferentially, keeping her

head down as she carefully deposited the plates of goodies and poured the tea.

Julie flushed, seeing Jane's discomfiture.

"I'm sure my MaryBeth will prove to be one of your star pupils, Miss Bright," Mrs. Davis went on. "She is so enjoying the class."

"She's a delightful girl," remarked Julie kindly. "Each student is wonderful, as a matter of fact. I can see much progress already."

"Well, you'll learn, too, as you go along," sniffed Mrs. Davis. "Coming to a new town, such as you have, it's understandable that it takes some time to get to know who is who, and which children are most worth the effort."

Julie bristled, but tried not to show it.

"I find they are *all* worth the effort, Mrs. Davis. All children need to learn their numbers and letters to build a better life for themselves. They all deserve the chance, don't you think?"

Several of the women sighed, and one shook her head. "Take that Jeb Johnson, for instance," pouted Mrs. Newby sourly. "You are pouring good efforts after bad, if you ask me. The apple doesn't fall far from the tree. He's as much like his father as can be. He's up to no good as a child, and he'll be up to even worse when he's a man. Wasted efforts on that one, mark my words."

Julie's pulse was hammering now, angry at the unfairness she was hearing.

"Should a child be held accountable for the father's sins, Mrs. Newby?"

She thought of the tall lanky youth who had arrived every day to ring the school bell, getting more and more responsible in his school work with each class. He could write his name now, and had showed an amazing interest in learning about the concepts of plumbing that she had shared about life in New York. He had a quick mind, and a fast hand. He deserved to find his way in the world with a clean slate, just like everyone else.

"Wouldn't trust him as far as I could throw him, Miss Bright," said Mrs. Blanding of the Circle B ranch. "His father worked on the ranch for a while, years back, and he was nothing but trouble. A fighter who would never follow orders. My husband let him go. Had to."

"I wouldn't know about that, Mrs. Blanding. I only know about the boy I see in class each day. He has potential. I'd swear by that."

In the lobby of the hotel, behind her, the large doors had opened, and the sheriff had come in. He had moved toward the dining room, as he did each Thursday that the Ladies Tea was held, to pay his respects to them. As Julie's voice, sounding slightly perturbed, drifted toward him, he stopped and listened.

"Harummph, potential!" answered Mrs. Davis with a cutting voice. "He has the potential to be the next stage robber in the state of Montana, and that is all. People don't rise from their roots. Ignorant parents breed ignorant children. You can't change human nature. It's one thing to teach the children to read and write, it's another to expect them to rise above their station. They can't. They mustn't. You'd best be aware of that, Miss Bright."

Julie's crumpet felt stuck in her throat. Anger was pulsing through her veins.

Jane had been nervously pouring tea throughout the conversation, and at the woman's strident words, she faltered and missed the last cup, splashing a few drops onto the saucer.

"Clumsy girl!" exclaimed Mrs. Davis. "Mind yourself or you'll find yourself back on that dirt farm."

Jane looked ready to cry. She turned and left the room.

"You'll have to excuse me," said Julie through clenched teeth, standing up. Years of training by her mannerly mother, and her disciplined father kept her from throwing a tea cup, but only barely.

"Suddenly I feel positively ill. While we have much more to discuss on this topic, it's probably not a good time. Thank you for inviting me to join you."

She turned on her heel, bonnet in hand, and almost ran from the room, following Jane.

Sheriff White watched her go. The matron's comments had cut him to the core, remembering his own humble beginnings with shame. But he had also been mesmerized by the flashing brown eyes, the barely controlled temper that she had corralled with head erect, remaining polite. Her lips were tightly closed, when she had obviously wanted to open her mouth and flay the ladies of Grey Eagle with the sassy words that he had no doubt were on the tip of her tongue. He knew what those words could do. But she hadn't spoken.

He turned and left the hotel. The ladies would have to do without his polite welcome this month. He had things on his mind to sort out, not the least being a tiny little slip of an impudent schoolteacher who could stand up for Jeb Johnson and Jane Adams without losing her head, and who even gave *him* the idea that he had a chance for dignity in the world.

* * *

Julie had sprinted after Jane, and found her in the cloak room of the hotel, still dabbing her eyes.

"Oh Jane, you can't let them get to you like this. You're as good as anybody else, and they are a bunch of old biddies to treat you otherwise."

Jane sniffed.

"They're usually a bit full of themselves, but they've never been this horrid before. That Miriam Davis. She was actually mean."

"She's probably still mad that I chose to sit with you at church on Sunday."

Jane looked pensive. "You really think so? I'd like to have poured the tea right in her lap."

"Next time," Julie said, giggling. "You can practice so that your aim will get better."

Jane smiled. "I better get back to work, or I'll have more of a problem than just the hens pecking at me. Are you going back in?"

"Not today, Jane, my friend. I have to come up with a way to handle that group in the future. If they got me any angrier, I'd be dangerous. I happen to have excellent aim already."

"So I heard. From the stagecoach driver. When he was drinking at the hotel bar, he admitted it was you who knocked out the stagecoach robber. With a rock, no less."

Julie blushed. "No less. But it took me two shots. I must be losing my touch." She wound up her arm like a pitcher and Jane began to laugh.

"Oh, Julie, I'm so glad you've come to this town. You've no idea." She straightened her apron and started back to work. Julie felt flushed with pleasure at the compliment.

"Thanks, Jane," she said softly.

"Are you going back home then?"

"Not yet," Julie said resolutely. "I'm going to see a man about a horse."

Julie left the hotel and strode purposefully down the street to the livery at the far end of town. The sidewalks were quiet at this time of day. The shoppers were long gone and it was still too early for the ranchhands or mill-workers to arrive for the evening.

She could hear the clank of metal hitting metal as she neared the livery, and saw the broad back of Harvey Mills as he stood pounding hot metal on his anvil inside the door. She could smell the pungent odor of horses and hay. It reminded her of the many Saturday afternoons she had spent around stables while she had been taking riding lessons in the park.

"Good afternoon, Harvey," she called out over the hammering, and the big man lowered his hammer immediately. His thick muscular arms were glistening with sweat, though the spring air was far from hot.

"Why it's the pretty little schoolmarm. Howdy do, Miss Bright. It's sure good to see ya. What are you all doing at this fer end of town?"

"Came to see you and the horses, and the name is Julie, if you will."

"Is that so? You like horses, Miss Julie?"

"Better than some people I know," she retorted saucily.

The blacksmith put back his dark curly head and bellowed in laughter.

"Now if that ain't just the truth! Now as you're living

in the west, ma'am, we're gonna hafta get someone to learn you how to set a horse. All the folks out here can ride, and that should be you, too."

"Sitting a horse is one of my favorite things. I know how to ride. I've ridden for years."

He looked at her quizzically. "Is that just right? I coulda sweared I heard you was from the city."

"Guilty. But I rode. In the park. I had lessons. But I learned with an English saddle. My father . . ."

Her voice broke off suddenly. She had never mentioned her father to a soul.

He sensed her discomfort, and didn't seem to need to know its cause.

"That's just fine, ma'am. No explainin' necessary. I'm a man of few words myself."

"Thanks," she said softly. "But I need a horse. I want to get a horse that I can ride, and that can also pull the little wagon out at the schoolhouse."

He looked up at the ceiling thoughtfully. "Hmm. Let me think. You'll need a horse. And a saddle. But a western saddle. We don't have none of those sissy English contraptions here."

Julie smiled as her eyes wandered around the livery, now that they had adjusted to the dimness inside. She could see the stalls lined up before her. Three on one end held horses, and the tack and saddles for each were neatly stored in front of them. Then there were several empty stalls. At the far end, only one stall was occupied. Julie strained her eyes, and knew her hunch was correct.

A tall black head stared out at her from the dimness of the corner. Proudly, the wild black horse that had been ridden during the stagecoach robbery stared back at her, his dark eyes gleaming in his head.

"The Widow McGee mentioned she might want to part with Patches, her older pony. He's fourteen hands, large for a pony, and a little long in the tooth, but he'd be good safe transport to get you in and out of town no trouble. You want me to find out if . . ."

"How about that one?" she asked softly, motioning to the horse who pawed the ground and snorted with disgust, as if he knew she was talking about him.

"You mean Devil? The bandit's horse?" he asked incredulously.

"Devil's a good name for him," she said, not breaking eye contact with the huge beast. "And he's the one I want. He's for sale isn't he? How much?"

"Well, he may be for sale," the stocky man said in a flustered tone, "but not in God's green earth is there going to be a day I'd sell him to the likes of you. That beast is a killer."

"I'm sure he's a powerful horse."

"Powerful mean, you better know. The sheriff confiscated him, and I bought him off the town, as I always do. But this one, we might have to put him down. He's a beautiful thing, Miss Bright, but he's . . . well, it's like he's tetched in the head, if you get my meaning. No one can get close to him, ceptin' me, and it's not my favorite part of the day, if you know what I mean."

"You can't put an animal like that down, Harvey. Tell me you won't do that."

"Well, he's good for nothing, mean as he is. And it's a cost just keeping him."

"So what if I just kept him? You know, kept him out at the schoolhouse, out in the barn. Couldn't hurt anybody there, as the children aren't permitted near the barn. I have some money. I can pay for him and keep him up."

"Sounds like a blasted fool idea to me! And I can't take your money. It'll never work out and I'd feel like a mean cuss myself."

"Let me try it, then. You bring him out to the barn, and I'll keep him for a week, and if everything is all right, I'll pay you then. How much?"

She was trying to keep her voice businesslike and calm, but her heart was hammering in her chest.

"Twenty dollars is the going price. But I'll sell this one for ten. But in a week, if you haven't come to your senses by then. Or sooner."

She swallowed hard. Even the ten dollars would make a large dent in her stash of cash money. And there was no way that she would part with her mother's jewels. But she would scrimp, and live carefully, and stretch her teacher's salary. She would be all right.

"Deal," she said, holding out her hand. He took it.

"I guess," the blacksmith said without much enthusiasm. "Don't you get hurt now, or the sheriff will have my head. He'll probably kick me in the backside as it is. Excuse my plain talking, Miss Julie. I got carried away."

"You're excused. And if the sheriff has a problem, you just send him to me. If there is to be any backside kicking around here," she said with a twinkle in her eye, "I'll be the one to do it."

He smiled broadly. "Yes, ma'am."

"Can you bring him out tonight, Harvey? I'd just as soon get him settled."

"Right after supper, Miss Julie. Have you met my sister Lilly yet? She don't go out much. She's in a wheelchair. We live upstairs here. Maybe one day you could visit her?"

"I'll do that for certain, Harvey. You let her know that."

"Well, I'll bring Devil over tonight. I do believe there is hay out there. I'll bring some food and a few buckets. As long as you're *sure* you want to go through with this crazy plan?"

"I'm sure. I'll be waiting. Thanks! See you soon, Devil," she said to the big black horse.

He snorted in reply.

Harvey, the usually silent blacksmith watched her go, shaking his head. That woman sure has a way with words, he thought to himself. And a way of making him, who was usually so short on words, chatter like a danged magpie.

He had a sinking feeling that he'd better be putting together some more quick words to explain what he'd done, because when Sheriff Jack White got a whiff of what he'd agreed to, he'd be needing to do some quick talkin' and he knew there'd be hell to pay.

Chapter Nine

True to his word, Harvey arrived that evening on horseback, leading the errant Devil on a long rope behind him. He had placed the horse in a special halter, which held his head down and kept him from rearing up on his hind legs.

"This is a fool idea, if anybody was askin' me, which you ain't," admonished the worried blacksmith. "This here horse got a mind of his own, and he'd as soon as take a bite out of you or pound you into the dust as look at you."

Julie nodded somberly. "I can see that, Harvey. I promise I'll be careful. It just seems a shame to put a horse like that down. Maybe he'll calm down with a little time."

"And maybe it'll snow monkeys, Miss Julie," said Harvey under his breath. Julie laughed. "Thanks for your help."

"Like a partner in crime, that's what I am, Miss Julie," he said, kicking the dust with his well-worn boot.

They bolted the stall door securely. Devil immediately began to kick and snort.

He gave up his antics in a few minutes, and began to explore his new stall. When he found the well-filled food bucket, he snickered and began to eat.

"Let me know when you've had enough of this fella," Harvey called as he rode off into the darkening night.

"We'll be fine," she said in a confident tone as she waved.

Behind her, Devil began banging the stall door again.

"We'll get used to each other, Devil," she said in a low tone. "It'll be all right."

Emotions swirled as she left the unhappy horse for the night. She had done what she felt she had to do. She just hoped she hadn't bitten off more than she could chew.

She awakened in the morning to the sound of Devil banging on the stall door, the sound reverberating the quiet morning air. She dressed quickly, and by the time the sun had even begun to peak over the eastern horizon, she was on her way out the door to the barn with a pocket full of carrot pieces and a cut up apple.

Devil eyed her suspiciously when she entered the small barn.

"Good boy, that's a good boy," she said softly as she approached the snorting horse. His eyes shown like black marbles. She could see the anger there, but also something else.

"Hungry, Devil?"

She didn't dare open the stall door yet. She was daring, but she wasn't stark crazy. She filled a spare bucket with his food and lowered it over the side to the floor.

The horse eyed it suspiciously, but then bent his head to eat, devouring every morsel in the bucket.

"Still hungry fella?" she said softly, dropping a piece of carrot over the stall door, where it plunked with an echo into the empty bucket. The horse gobbled it up.

She got braver then, extending her hand, palm open, with a large piece of apple balanced in the center.

The horse snorted and backed up. He sniffed. He pawed the ground. He pulled his head up and then down, keeping a constant watch on her with his big, black eyes. She didn't move a muscle.

Several minutes passed, but it seemed like hours. Julie's arm was aching from being held outstretched, but she stubbornly didn't move. Silently, she stared back at the horse, and she waited.

When he finally moved, he moved like a flash. With no warning, his head whipped down, teeth bared, and he chomped the piece of apple out of her hand, swallowing it with a satisfied snort. She lowered her tired arm then, and found her hand was actually shaking. She held no illusions about the danger of what she had just done. The monstrous horse could have chomped her whole hand if he had chosen. But he hadn't.

"I'm your friend, Devil," she said softly to the horse that stared back at her. "We're going to come to an agreement, you and I. Take all the time you need."

Without another word, she dropped the remaining pieces of apple and carrot over the wall into the bucket. No sense tempting the fates more than once at a shot.

Swiftly, she turned and walked back to the schoolhouse, pausing only once to turn and look back at the big horse who watched her every move. "I'll be back after class," she called, as if he could understand her. Crazy as it was, she was drawn to the horse. She climbed the steps to the schoolhouse with shaky knees, getting ready for the arrival of the schoolchildren. It took all her efforts to focus on her classwork all day. Devil was absolutely quiet in his stall out behind the schoolhouse, a fact that she found more disconcerting than if he had been trying to bang the stall walls down with his gigantic hooves. There was a rare midday shower which kept the children in at recess time, and she kept busy organizing games for them in the close confines of the classroom, to give them a break from the long day working at their desks. And they were working hard.

Their progress brought her joy. In a few short weeks, the undisciplined hooligans who had bounded in the doorway on that first day had taken to learning like pigs to a mud hole. It was like they couldn't get enough. Already, many were reading and writing words on their slates, and their ability to understand number concepts made her both happy and proud.

Jeb rang the bell, signalling the end of recess. Instantly, the children hustled to their seats, faces turned toward her in anticipation. Julie read out loud to them every day after their recess time, and they settled quickly so as not to miss the next pages of *Moby-Dick* one of the books she had brought with her on her trek from New York. They had already finished *Uncle Tom's Cabin*, which had sparked a lot of questions and discussions, and she had marvelled at seeing their minds go into action. It wouldn't be long, she thought with a pleased sigh, before the older ones could read such a book for themselves.

And it also wouldn't be long until she was out of books. And supplies. She was going to have to face the sheriff about that, she thought, wrinkling her nose in frustration.

She started to read, taking them to the world of Captain Ahab and the great whale, and the afternoon began.

By the time the end of day bell sounded, they had finished reading, completed a new lesson in arithmetic, and had learned about the strange instrument that was the marvel of the east: the telephone. For children in a small isolated town where even the nearest telegraph office was a day's ride away on a fast horse, the idea of information traveling from building to building through wire was a puzzling one.

Julie ushered the last students out the door at the end of the day, anxious to rush to the barn to see Devil. A handful of carrots were stuffed in the pocket of her skirt.

She darted around the schoolhouse, her boots kicking up spring dirt as she hurried along.

The big black horse had been waiting for her. He gave a loud snort as she stepped into the small barn, blinking her eyes to adjust to the inside dimness after the late afternoon sun. Big black eyes blinked back at her suspiciously.

"How's Devil today?" she crooned softly, moving toward him. He snorted, shook his ferocious head, and backed up in the stall.

"Grumpy little Devil, aren't you?" she laughed, moving steadily, silently, toward the stall gate. With one hand she withdrew a large carrot, shaking the leafy green head of it in the air. "Anybody here lose a carrot?"

The horse stilled, and stared at her, eyes flashing. She swallowed hard, her pulse quickening with fear as she looked into his menacing eyes.

I could bite your head off, his gaze threatened. She swallowed hard.

But she didn't back down. She stepped up onto the first rail of the gate, balancing her weight on her booted feet as she leaned far over the gate. She stretched her arm out, holding the carrot, willing her arm to cease shaking.

"Here, boy," she said softly. "Come and get it. We're going to be friends, sooner or later, you and me."

She stood still, seconds passing that seemed like eternity. Finally, with a soft snort, the horse moved forward a few small steps, eyeing the carrot.

The horse came closer, and she watched him, her pulse hammering. Such a beautiful animal. And so spooked. Whatever had happened to him to make him so angry was a tragedy. She didn't fool herself that it would be an easy task to calm him down, but she was determined to try.

"Take the carrot, boy."

The big horse had stepped toward her, raising his proud head and looking directly at her where she teetered at the railing, reaching with the carrot. With a mighty sweep, he lowered his massive head and whipped the carrot out of her hand.

Thud!

At the same time, Julie was hit hard from behind, a flash of blue stunning her as giant arms grappled with her, plucking her from the railing with a low pitched growl.

"Urghh!"

She fell backward with the tug, flying through the air, and landing solidly on her posterior on the ground outside of the stall. Well, almost on the ground. Something, or as she quickly found out, someone, was underneath her.

As she caught her breath, and tried to figure out exactly what had happened, she discovered she was sitting plumb on top of the 6'6" horizontal sheriff. He was laying in the dust.

"Are you out of your fool mind? Are you some kind of walking hurricane? Are you just plain crazy?"

"I'm crazy?" she said in an irritated voice as she wiggled around to right herself, rising to her feet and dusting off her skirt. "What in God's green earth has come over you? Why did you do that?"

The sheriff didn't move. He just lay in the dirt, hat over his face where it had fallen, and kept talking.

"This is *my* fault. I brought you to this town. I let you stay. I could tell you didn't have the sense of a prairie dog the minute you stepped off that stagecoach. Now you've gone and taken over a wild killer of a horse, who would like nothing better than to eat your fist at the very least for his afternoon snack. And I find you one step away from falling right into his dang stall and getting trampled to death."

"I was giving the poor thing a carrot."

"Poor thing?" he yelled, suddenly leaping to his feet. "Poor thing? Do you know that this vicious beast has already bitten three people in this town? I swear I'm going to hog-tie that Harvey and use him for cougar bait for selling you this horse."

"You leave Harvey out of this. I bought this horse, and I'll take responsibility for him. Not Harvey. You want cougar bait, you talk to me!"

She stamped her foot angrily in the dirt, shaking a fist up into the face of the irate sheriff, which looked ridiculous, as she didn't even come up to his shoulder.

He couldn't help smiling. He couldn't help the warm curly feeling that came over him then, uninvited and unexpected. One minute, he was so absolutely mad, and the next? Well, he wanted to pick her up in his arms and give her a hug, to smell the flowery cleanness of her, to laugh at her bravery and her daring as she shook that little fist into his face. But he couldn't do that, he knew. She'd probably bite worse than the fool horse!

"Okay little lady, I'm talking to you. This horse isn't a pet. This horse isn't transportation. This horse is damaged goods. The bandit that owned him has been shipped off for trial, and the word is, he'll be spending the rest of his days behind bars, if he's lucky enough to escape hanging for his long list of crimes."

"So he needs an owner. Harvey said he was going to be put down."

His voice was soft. "Harvey was right. This horse was mistreated and brutalized in ways we'll probably never know, Julie. That bandit was an evil man. But now the horse is dangerous. You can't ignore that. And you can't keep him. This town would run me out on a rail if I let something happen to you."

To say nothing about how I'd feel myself, the nagging voice inside of him prodded.

"He's mine. He's getting a second chance. Everyone deserves a second chance, Sheriff. I promise I'll be careful, I'll take it slow. But I'm going to try."

He shook his head in frustration. And then he looked over her shoulder. She had been standing just a few feet from the stall, with her back to the gate. As she had been arguing in defence of the vicious black horse, he had stepped to the gate, now calm and quiet. Stretching his head as far forward as he could, he could just barely reach Julie's bare head. Jack almost jumped out of his skin in fear, when he realized the fiery look had gone from the beast's eyes. As Jack stared in open amazement, the horse nuzzled her hair gently.

She turned slowly, a big smile lighting her face.

"You hear that, you Devil? You like being the topic of conversation?"

She reached her hand into her apron pocket and pulled out two more carrots, calmly feeding them to the huge horse, who swished his tail in appreciation as he happily chomped down on them, one at a time.

Hesitantly, she reached out and patted his nose as if it were something she did every day.

"Good boy."

The horse stood quietly.

"I don't believe it." Jack said, shaking his head, and plopping his hat back where it belonged. "You win this round, Julie. But I want you to be careful, you hear? You take this thing slow, and I'll be here to help you when I can."

Julie was radiant. "Thanks, Sheriff. It'll work out, you'll see. Devil will be tame as toast before you know it."

They walked slowly away from the barn toward the

schoolhouse. Jack looked over his shoulder one more time. Devil stared back at him, the mean look back in his eyes, pawing the ground. *Keep your distance,* the horse seemed to say. He mounted his big red stallion and took off for town, giving the horse his head as he galloped along the plain. *What have I gotten myself into?* The wind raced by. In a matter of weeks, the order and stability of his life had been replaced by waves of unruly emotions and feelings.

Everything was complicated and confused since Julie Bright had arrived in Grey Eagle.

And yet? The feel of that soft body in his arms, even momentarily, as he had plucked her from that railing in fear made him feel alive. Then there was the sparkling look of those daring eyes, the angry little fist she shook to make her point. Even if he had a chance, no matter how crazy she made him, he knew he could never put her on that stage and send her away.

Chapter Ten

There was something about looking into Devil's eyes that made Julie shiver inside. But she didn't shiver with fear. The proud, high strung horse would stare her down each morning and night when she arrived with the obligatory offering of carrot and apple, taking the morsels with a head flung high with arrogance. She would look into his eyes then, and she would see the raw emotion he felt. He was trapped.

Julie knew firsthand the breathstealing feeling of not being free. Born to the gilded cage, but still able to escape on occasion to spread her curious wings, she had tolerated her controlled childhood. Her father had, she knew, had the best intentions, trying to raise his daughter into a position in New York society that he had spent his life envisioning.

But his values hadn't matched hers. The life he had wanted hadn't been right for her. But Julietta Brightingham had a stubborness of her own, and given the time, she had always thought that sooner or later, he would see her point of view.

Times were changing in the United States as the millenium drew near, and she had always been full of optimism that her father would eventually accept her need to live her own style of life.

But he had died. The thought of his sudden death raised a lump the size of a baseball in her throat, and she fought down the urge to cry. Had he known what his plans would mean to her? Had he even imagined the heartbreak that he had orchestrated for his daughter with his ridiculous will? To ease her mind she *had* to believe that hs decisions were based on a rare error of judgment, being unable to see the true nature of his greedy younger brother, her Uncle Edward.

The funny thing was, she had never had any illusions about her Uncle Edward. He had made her skin crawl since she had been a very little girl. Her instincts had made her wary of him, of his piercing eyes that had so often looked at her with a kind of envy, as if he resented her very being. Which evidently was true.

Julie swallowed the lump in her throat, and stuffed carrots and an apple in her apron pocket as she headed out to the barn for Devil's evening treat.

Trapped, that's what she had been. Trapped just like Devil.

And if she hadn't escaped when she had? Well, she'd be kicking in a few walls by now, too, she imagined.

The horse whinnied softly when she arrived, looking calmer than usual. With surprise, she saw that his stall was already cleaned, and his water bucket filled. Smiling, she thought of Harvey at the livery. He must have snuck out to the schoolhouse to do the chores, still smarting with guilt for letting her have the wild horse. The sheriff had given him quite a dressing down, so the town gossip mill had churned. But good old Harvey had stuck to his word.

Devil had been with her for three weeks, and he was still far from a dream horse, but she had made some progress. She climbed up on the rail, and for a rare instant, he allowed her to pet his arrogant nose while she fed him his apple.

The spring air felt cool and clear in the early evening, and she breathed in deeply. There were none of the multitude of street smells that she had grown up with in New York City.

Suddenly she was envisioning the brutal morning in New York when the truth of her predicament had become clear to her. Her father had been buried the day before. She had been summoned to Uncle Edward's law office on 5th Avenue, and had been ushered to his elegant conference room by his dour faced assistant Henri.

"Please be seated here, Miss Brightingham," the man had said with an affected sniff. "Mr. Edward will be with you shortly. May I get you tea?"

She had declined, which had turned out to be a good thing. She hadn't stayed long enough for tea, at least not to drink it. Although she *might* have thrown a cup or two if she had been given the chance.

Though her father had had business dealings with his younger brother Edward, Julietta had never spent more time in his presence than was necessary for propriety. The very fact that her father had involved him as a trustee in his will was repugnant to her. Quite frankly, his sneaky, mean spirited ways had always irked her.

Uncle Edward had arrived, and with him came a round faced man whose nearly bald head shone slightly in the lamp light. He was introduced as Leroy Allen.

"We'll get right down to business, dear Julietta," his voice had whined in his nasal way, and despite the endearment of "dear" in his greeting, Julietta instantly knew two things. The news he was bringing was not going to be good, and he was going to delight in telling her about it. Her skin crawled, but she sat sedately, gloved hands folded gracefully in her lap, and watched his beady eyes travel over her.

"You are, as you well know, dear Julietta, my dear departed brother James' only child, and therefore the heir to his not inconsiderable fortune."

Julietta nodded but did not speak.

"And this is both a great honor and a great responsibility. Your father showed great foresight in planning for your future. You realize that, child?"

The sniveling voice had risen half an octave, and Julietta regarded her uncle closely, noticing that small drops of sweat had broken out on his upper lip as he had been speaking.

The news was that bad? It was bad enough to make a man with no moral character break into a sweat. She braced herself. But she faced him straight on.

"And what planning would that be, Uncle Edward?"

"A trust, Julietta. The entire estate has been left in a trust, with you as the beneficiary."

"And what exactly does this mean, Uncle Edward?"

she had asked, not clear of the legalities of what he had been explaining.

"A trust. The money is held for you, managed for you, and then, if you have fulfilled the stipulations of the will, released to you when you reach the age of twenty-five."

"But that is almost a year away, Uncle Edward. How are things going to be taken care of in the meanwhile? The care of the house? The running of the company? And what are the stipulations?"

She was puzzled.

"There is nothing for you to worry your pretty little head over, dear Julietta. That is where I come in. Your father has wisely named me the trustee of the entire estate in the meanwhile. I will make all decisions for the company, see that the house is taken care of in its usual way, even provide you with a monthly stipend for the many things you enjoy."

Julie's mind was racing. She definitely smelled a rat. And the rat had beady eyes and was standing right in front of her.

"Until I turn twenty-five? The estate is turned over to me?"

Uncle Edward was clearly sweating now.

"In a matter of speaking, Julietta. Along with your husband, of course. You see, there is an additional stipulation in the will. As you know, your father was more than determined to guide you into society as a lady of position and wealth . . . a fact which you made quite clear wasn't popular with you. He was most distressed that you had avoided all of the eligible young men who he encouraged to court you in the last few seasons,

flaunting your spinster status and refusing to take anyone's bid for your hand seriously."

"Marriage is a serious thing, Uncle Edward, and not
something that I would rush into. And there has been no
one suitable. . . ."

"True. This is true. The young whippersnappers, still
wet behind the ears, were certainly not the correct match
for someone of your means, no matter what their social
standing. Your father and I had numerous conversations
on this matter. Which is why he included this stipulation."

"Which is?"

"I have arranged for your marriage, Julietta, following
your father's wishes."

"My *marriage?*" she bellowed. "My father told you to
arrange for my marriage?"

"Your father endowed me with the power to insist that
you behave in a proper, civilized way, as befits a lady of
your social standing. I have decided that this includes
marriage. And unless you follow my wishes, as trustee, I
have the power to control your inheritance in any way
that I deem in your best interest."

"*My* best interest?" she croaked, standing up abruptly.

"It is in your best interest to follow my directions,
young lady, if you ever wish to see a penny of your inheritance. Your father's idea was that having things han-
dled by a trustee for a year would give you the time to
settle yourself, to take your place in society. So you will
select a husband, prepare yourself for marriage, and follow my advice. As soon as you do this, you, along with
your acceptable husband, will assume control over the
inheritance.

"Now, it is my opinion that your father was far too liberal and not nearly assertive enough with you in his lifetime, which is why this stipulation needed to be designed at all. It is my belief that if you were inclined or able to select your own husband, you would have done so by now. In the spirit of saving precious time, I have taken the liberty of doing that for you. And so there it is. A portion of the estate will be released to Leroy at the time of engagement, as your dowry."

Julietta blinked, freezing where she stood. Then she turned her head to the chubby, balding, red-eyed man who had been sitting at the other end of the table, and who hadn't said as much as a word. His face was set in a guilty stare.

"Leroy Allen? You plan to marry me off to Leroy Allen?"

Disbelief shook her from her head to her toes. Her heart began to race. The idea of being married to such an old, simple man was ridiculous. Did he think he could force her to do it? Why? Why? And why did Leroy look so guilty?

It suddenly all became clear to her. Her uncle would release a large amount of the funds he controlled as her dowry, having persuaded Leroy Allen to take on the role of ardent if aging husband of the young reckless heiress.

During the engagement period, he would make sure that he took as much personal benefit as he could as trustee. And then, as her husband, Leroy would be making the decisions about Brightingham Shipping, right under Uncle Edward's sly thumb. Julietta would be left with no money or freedom and stuck in a loveless marriage before she reached the age of twenty-five. She would be stuck for the rest of her life.

But they simply couldn't make her do it. With or without the estate, she would not be penniless, she promised herself. For at her mother's death many years before, she had inherited her mother's jewels, which were tucked safely away in a trunk in her room.

He could not make her marry. If her father, in his ridiculous efforts to control her, had given his greedy younger brother the opportunity to ravish his estate, then so be it. But there must be a way she could fight. She would stand up for herself, in court, if necessary. She was the daughter of James Brightingham, and she could be as stubborn as a mule.

The door of the office opened and Henri reappeared.

"There is a message, sir, from the stables. It seems your horse has come up with a lame leg. They want to know if they should call the veterinarian. What shall I tell them, sir?"

Edward kept his gaze locked on Julietta.

"Have them shoot him," he said in a flat voice. "No need for an additional burden."

Henri shut the door without a word.

"You will think this over, Julietta. We will speak again. And in the meantime, we will be taking an inventory of your possessions, for your own security. For instance, I understand that there are some family jewels . . ."

"They are my mother's bequest, Uncle Edward. They have nothing to do with your trust."

"Of course. But as your closest male relative, and the one entrusted by your father to see to your welfare, we must be sure that everything is kept safely for you."

His words dripped like acid, and she felt her heart begin to pound again, despite her resolve.

"The servants have been directed to go over the house, securing any valuables so that they may be stored—safely."

"You may not have my mother's jewels."

"You will be rational about this, Julietta."

"I think not."

"You will obey my wishes, marry Mr. Allen, and do as I say, or you will not see a penny of the Brightingham money."

"There are worse things than being poor. I may see poverty, but some day you will see the inside of a jail cell for conspiring like this."

"I will never see the inside of a jail cell, Julietta. Your father, while an excellent business man, was weak willed and far too lenient with you, in my opinion. I will go to any length to get what I want in this situation. Any length. Do you understand me, young lady?"

His beady eyes had turned to ice, and a shiver of fear ran down her spine. But she would not show it.

She stood then, and exited the conference room on wobbly legs, but showing as much poise as she could muster. It had only taken her minutes then, to make the difficult decision about changing her life. She had run the sixteen blocks home to save her mother's jewels, and to plan her new life.

The house staff had looked at her nervously when she exploded through the door.

"What's going on miss?" her maid, Lydia, had wailed. "Mr. Edward has demanded that we gather your things, so that his accountants can make some sort of list. And they are searching for the jewelry."

Julietta paled. "Did they find it?" Her heart was hammering.

"No, ma'am. They did not."

Lydia paused for a long second, then went on in a whisper.

"But I did. It didn't seem right, those men wanting your mother's jewels. So I hid them. I thought that you should be the one to turn them over, if that was your wish. So I had the cook's son wrap them in an old horse blanket and hide them beneath the coal in the basement bin. You aren't mad, are you, miss?"

Julietta's laugh tinkled gaily through the foyer, and she hugged the girl who was about her age and size.

"Come, Lydia. I have many plans to make, and you can help me. You have the heart of an adventurer, and someday I will repay you greatly for this."

And so it had begun. With the help of the staff, she had swapped her clothes, and belongings, preparing to escape her uncle's devious plans. She had received miraculous help from Mrs. Mayberry, who was determined to give up her post in Montana when she heard of her favorite charge's unfortunate plight. Julietta would go in her place.

"Women are more free in the west," the wise woman had stated, staring her favorite past pupil in the eye. "They have built the frontier right alongside their men, know how to shoot, ride, chop wood. There are women doctors, and women who run businesses. There are strong minded, strong willed women in Montana, and you will find a place there. That was why I was daring to make the trip, even at my age. The sheriff in Grey Eagle seemed delighted that I was older, experienced. But I will stay here with my sister, and you will take off on this great adventure. Montana is a place for the young, for people building their lives. They need teachers."

Her words had not fallen on deaf ears. Julietta's mind had raced with the possibilities. Would she dare? Could she dare?

"I wouldn't have it any other way," the gray-haired woman had chuckled, handing her a glowing letter of recommendation. "I fibbed a bit, and said you had experience, but I'm not worried. Anyone who can stand up to your repulsively greedy uncle can tackle a school room full of children. Even frontier children."

And so the plans had been set. Julietta Brightingham had turned into Julie Bright, and she and her cherished jewels had crossed the mountains, and the plains, and had landed in Grey Eagle, Montana.

She had found her freedom here, she thought quietly, away from her father's control, her uncle's machinations, and society's expectations.

She watched the big black horse shake his head from side-to-side. She was no longer trapped. But Devil was.

She reached out a hand to the horse, and he backed up instinctively, afraid. She sighed. He had been her charge for three weeks. He would eat from her hand, he would let her touch him. But he was still wild, and angry, and trapped, and that was not going to change in the next week. Should she give him back to the livery? He would most probably be put down. No one in this wild, working west could afford to keep a horse that was uncontrollable. But to put him to sleep? Her stomach clenched at the thought. She just couldn't do it. He deserved a chance. He deserved to live free.

Without a pause, she raised her hand to the gate latch and unlocked the stall, stepping aside, and swinging the door open.

"Go, Devil," she whispered through a tear choked throat. "Be free. You have a better chance of making it on the prairie than you have in a stall, Go, be free."

The horse exploded from the stall, darting out into the waning sunlight, his coat gleaming, muscles rippling as he moved. Loose from confinement, he reared up on his back legs, a breathtaking, terrifying display of strength and power.

Julie gasped in awe.

His front hooves hit the dirt. He bolted forward in a gallop, ran about fifteen yards, and then stopped abruptly. He turned around and looked at her, where she stood slumped against the stall door. Devil tossed his head, made a loud whinny, and then took off like lightning.

At first she smiled, imagining that the big black horse had whinnied a slow, sincere, *thank you!*

And then she sat down in the sunbaked dirt, and began to cry softly. Through her tears, she wished the horse luck, missing him already, and realized that freedom sometimes has a painful price.

Chapter Eleven

For the next two days, Julie threw her energies into her school work with even greater vigor. She bustled around the wooden floor, up one aisle and down the other, instructing, correcting, rewarding and questioning.

The children would be taking a break from classes in a week's time, a necessity when planting time arrived at the same time that cows were dropping their calves. The older students were needed in the fields, and in the barns, and would return to their desks in the fall, after harvest, when the farm work slowed enough that every hand wasn't needed.

Julie was proud of their progress, and liked to tell them so. On the morning after she had let Devil escape, the word passed around as quick as lightning that he wasn't in his stall, and the students were ready to barrage her with questions. Her eyes were stinging as they began. But as she opened her mouth to speak to them, a deep voice interrupted from the back of the room.

106

"I think we all should leave Miss Bright alone," said Jeb Johnson, taking on an uncharacteristic roll of leadership. "If she wanted to talk about the big black horse, she woulda. He's gone, and that's that. No sense crying over spilt milk. Especially when it ain't our business."

She smiled weakly in gratitude to the lanky boy who had probably just made the longest speech he'd ever spouted in his life.

"Thank you, Jeb, for your kindness. Though it's better to say 'Isn't our business,' of course. Isn't our business is much better than ain't."

"Yes, ma'am." he said quietly, his eyes meeting hers.

He understood about the pain of failing with the horse, she realized.

You just can't save all the wild things, Miss Bright.

The look in his eyes showed wisdom far beyond his years. The horse wasn't brought up again.

Summer break and the end of the term arrived, and when Jeb rang the bell for the last time, there was a scurry for the door, the children's happy faces charging for freedom and sunshine. But there was also a feeling of sadness in a few faces as they ended the school term. The children of Grey Eagle had adapted well to learning and to the dedicated enthusiasm of their new teacher.

"See you in church, Miss Bright."

"Come stop by the mercantile. I'll be helping out."

"Maybe I'll train you a new horse," said Jeb, the last one to leave. "I know you miss that Devil."

Julie sighed. "Well, sooner or later, I hope I get one, Jed. Hopefully one that doesn't want to bite my head off."

"He waren't a bad horse, miss." The words came out low but clear. "He just didn't catch on to what caring was about. He was just too ornery."

Julie could feel her eyes tear up, and blinked several times.

"Well, all creatures can learn, Jeb Johnson. I just didn't get through to him in time."

Jeb nodded, wisdom in his eyes.

"You take care out here, Miss Bright. You need me, you know where to find me."

The long lanky boy clunked down the steps, his boot heels pounding the wood beneath his feet.

She watched his back as he started walking toward town, a wave of emotion making her feel proud of him. He had come a long way.

But suddenly she blinked. She squinted into the distance at his retreating figure. What was that under his arm?

It was big and rectangular and very dark green. And he was carrying it carefully, like it was a cherished possession.

And it was. But it was *her* possession. He was carrying her beloved copy of Shakespeare. The little stinker was stealing her book!

She couldn't help but giggle. Jed Johnson was stealing a book. He wanted to read. She felt no outrage. She felt only joy. She had taught the toughest kid in town to want to learn.

"Enjoy the book," she called gaily into the summer air. "And bring it back when you're done."

He didn't even turn around. He simply raised his left arm into the air, and waved it over his head, acknowledging her words. And he and the book disappeared into the sunset.

During the next few quiet days, Julie planted some vegetables in the little garden behind the schoolhouse, and some flowers in a half barrel out front. She wrote a letter to Mrs. Mayberry to tell her of her progress. She walked to town almost daily, stopping to talk to the merchants and shoppers, enjoying living in the little town and learning its ways.

Each Thursday, she had tea with the ladies in the hotel restaurant, glad that she had stood up for her beliefs. There were no more rude incidents, and the ladies of the town had seemed to accept her relationship with the Adams family, and had made no more disparaging remarks. At least not in her hearing.

Though she tried not to, she found herself scanning the horizon when she went to town, watching for the massive sheriff. But he was simply not to be seen when she was there. Though she missed seeing him, this also meant that he was *not* at her side, instructing her to leave anymore. She was grateful for that.

On Sundays, she was picked up by the Adams family, and joyfully sang in church with the bouncing baby perched on her lap, and her beloved friend Jane by her side.

She missed teaching her students, and looked excitedly to the days when school would begin again. She missed her sessions with the big black horse, and felt the sadness each time she saw the empty stall with its haybales neatly stacked. But basically she was content and happy.

Jane's father had delivered a load of wood to the back of the schoolhouse. He leaned an ax against the back wall.

"I'll have the boys come and split and stack this," the hard-working man grunted as he climbed back up into his wagon. "We'll get you ready for the winter here."

"Thank you!"

"Fall will be here before you know it. And winter won't be far behind. We get some serious snow out here in Montana, miss. Best be ready."

She picked up the ax after he had left, stood up one of the thick logs, swinging the ax with all her might, trying to split it. Her aim was good. Her arms were strong. She was, she reminded herself, the best baseball batter in Central Park.

Thunk. The axe bit into the wood, the reverberation jarring her arms and shoulders.

Her aim had been true. But the wood did not split. Instead, the ax stood proudly lodged in the log, where it was determined to stay. She pulled it. She kicked it. She tugged it. She wiggled it. It was stuck.

"Arrrrghhh!" She growled, frustrated, as her hair slipped from her bonnet and her face turned red from exertion.

Through her intense concentration, trying to ply the ax from the wood, a distant sound registered in her ears.

It was the sound of movement, and it was coming from the other side of the schoolhouse. Who was there? She tucked her hair back up into her bonnet, trying to muster some dignity before facing her visitor, and hoping that they had *not* seen her antics with the trapped ax.

She brushed her hands on her skirt, and calmly turned the corner of the schoolhouse. No carriage was there.

She continued around to the other side of the building.
And stopped dead in her tracks.

She did have a visitor.

But it was not one she expected.

Standing in front of the stall, calmly bending and
chewing a mouthful of grass, stood Devil.

He heard her approach, he heard her gasp.

He lifted his proud, ornery head, and looked her
straight in the eye.

Got any grain? the dark eyes seemed to say.

Once her breathing returned to normal, she walked
smoothly, calmly around the horse and into the small
stall. Taking the wooden bucket in hand, she lifted the lid
of the storage bin and dipped the bucket into the store of
grain. She placed it on the ground beside the horse.

"You look just fine, you black prince!" she whispered
as she passed. "A little thin but good."

She took the remaining bucket to the well, turning the
crank to bring the cool water up from its depths, and
then hauled the splashing bucket back and placed it in
front of the horse, like a peace offering.

His tail swished decisively. He raised his head from
the grain and looked into her eyes, then lowered his
snout to the water and drank noisily.

Julie's eyes were blurring with tears, and her heart
was pounding as she watched him there, surprised at the
joy she felt in seeing the stallion standing peacefully in
her yard.

He drank his fill, then raised his head and shook it vig-
orously, muscles rippling along his broad back. Then
smoothly, as if he hadn't a care in the world, he turned,
flicking his tail in the sunlight and sauntered toward the

stall. He stepped inside, turned around, and blinked his eyes, as if enjoying the reprieve from the bright hot sunlight in the shady stall.

Julie stared. She didn't approach him. She just watched as he settled in, his quivering muscles stilling, his head held at a normal height instead of his normally defiant stance.

"Leave them alone and they'll come home, wagging their tails behind them." The words of the old nursery rhyme echoed somewhere in her brain.

"Welcome home, big guy," she said softly, turning with a swish of her skirt and walking back to the schoolhouse on slightly wobbly knees. No halter, no closed gate for the stall. She just left him where he stood.

He whinnied to her back, and if she didn't know absolutely better, she would have sworn that he said, "Thank you."

The next day dawned, and before the sun was high in the sky, Julie had officially given up on the woodpile. Try as she might, she could *not* get the ax out of the log where it was wedged. Much as she hated it, she would have to wait for help.

Devil had been gone when she had checked the stall in the morning, but she filled the grain bucket and scooped up fresh water for him anyway.

She was rubbing her dusty, slightly blistered hands on the sides of her skirt when she heard his hoofs pounding toward the schoolhouse.

He appeared, in a shiny glare of black, and began lapping up water from the bucket. This time, she laughed.

"Out for your morning run?" she whispered, and walked slowly toward the horse. He let her approach.

She ran her hand down his flank, feeling the quivering and powerful muscles respond to her soft touch. He was quite a horse.

He turned his head to look at her, and she swallowed in surprise. He was wearing a halter. It was not a traditional halter, but a handmade one, consisting of a piece of rough rope that was tied to a metal bit, and then fastened with knots over his head. He didn't seem to mind it.

She ran her fingers over and under the rope, seeing that it was tied comfortably, not too tight, yet secure. Who had done such a thing? Who had been riding Devil?

She swallowed hard as an idea formed in her head. Would he let *her* ride him?

She patted his flank, and stood along his side, watching his head turn toward her. She knew that her plan was foolhardy. Dangerous. Ridiculous. But she couldn't help herself. More than anything in the world at that particular second, she wanted to be atop this great horse. She wanted to feel the pounding of his hooves and the wind in her hair.

In a flash, she overturned the bucket he had finished, and placed it by his side as a step. She put her hands up to his mane.

Would he startle? Would he leap away from her if she attempted to mount? Gingerly, she stood on tiptoe on top of the bucket, tied up her skirts, reached as high as she could, then made a leap in the air, landing on his back with a thump.

He froze. She froze. And then, as if by magic, he sensed that her presence was acceptable. And he took off.

She hung on with her knees, and kept her hands tangled in his mane. Her heart was pounding, as she moved with the motion of the horse, up and down, bent low over his neck, feeling the summer air rush past, hearing his powerful breathing.

Her skirts were flying as the scenery flew past. Rocks, grey in the distance, showed their changing colors in the sunlight as she approached them. Overhead, the sky was a cloudless turquoise blue.

"Good boy," she crooned into his strong neck, feeling the oneness with the horse, the freedom of flying over the prairie and toward the foothills.

She knew she was crazy. She had no control over the horse. She had no idea where he would take her. She had been lost once already on the prairie when dusk had settled its murky head. She could end up miles from the little schoolhouse, and be stranded for the night. But she didn't care. She wouldn't have missed the ride for the world.

They had gone miles, and had entered the foothills, weaving along rocky paths, with scrubby trees and tufts of grass amidst grey faced boulders. Devil seemed to know where he was going.

The smell of food reached her nostrils. How could that be?

The horse was slowing now, making his way along a path that wound up a hill, around a series of jagged rocks, and opened into a grassy clearing. The smell of food became stronger, mingling the fragrance of a wood fire.

The horse stopped. She saw movement in the clearing. She squinted into the sunshine, and her face broke into a smile. Two medium sized boys were sprawled in the grass, one on top of the other, wrestling each other as arms and legs flew. Their shiny dark hair was reflected in the sun's rays. Blackfoot Indian children, it was easy to surmise, by their rugged skin clothing, and also easy to surmise that the one on top was going to be the victor.

With a hoot, he pinned his companion, and leapt to his feet, laughing. His eyes scanned the horizon, and in that split second, saw Devil and his rider. He stood straight, nudging his brother with his moccasined foot. The second boy stood too, a carbon copy of his companion. They both stared at the horse.

The oldest child walked toward her.

He knows the horse, Julie thought, thinking of the rope halter, the solid knots that tied it.

A female voice floated to her ears.

Looking beyond the boys she spotted several animal pelt teepees, almost blending into the grey rocks that surrounded them. She saw the fire that had teased her nostrils, a full skirted woman standing at its edge.

Blackfoot tribe, she thought, taking in the peacefulness of the small camp. They were a hunting people who revered the land.

At that instant the woman stopped calling the boys, having spied her on Devil's back at the edge of the clearning.

Were they friendly? Was she in danger? The small camp seemed almost deserted. She straightened on the back of the horse, watching the boys as they watched the horse with dark eyes. They were much more interested in the horse than they were in her. The thought made her smile. The boys turned and called something over their shoulder to the native woman.

The woman stood quietly for a moment, then beckoned with her hand.

Come, her motion said.

It was Devil who made the decision. The giant horse began gently traversing the green waving grass. The boys ran along his side, laughing, and talking to the horse in their native tongue. She didn't understand a word of it. But she knew they knew the horse. They stopped just a few yards from the campfire. Julie threw her leg over the horse and smoothly slipped to the ground, nervously straightening her skirts after her landing.

"Teacher," the woman said quietly. "Welcome."

She was not old by any means, and had an inherent beauty in her well-carved features and dark smooth skin. Her long hair hung down her back in a thick plait. Her skirt was cotton calico and faded from much washing, and her simple tunic played gently around her hips as she moved. She wore mocassins like the boys.

The boys had instantly begun nuzzling the horse, which seemed perfectly acceptable by the giant stallion. This amazed Julie, even though she had seen changes in Devil herself since he had returned to the schoolhouse.

Now she knew why. She knew that these boys had been responsible for training the hostile horse.

She was encouraged by the word "teacher." Did this woman know English? She obviously knew who Julie was.

"I am Julie. From the schoolhouse. Teacher. Do you speak English?"

"I speak a little, learned from my husband, Joe Horse Lover. We are Blackfoot. I want the young ones to speak, too. They have told me how you are teacher of young ones. That is good."

The boys came to stand beside her, and as she looked at their identical size and features, she knew they were twins.

"I am Young Joe Son. I am the smart one."

The other laughed and shoved his brother.

"I am Bill Blue Sky. I am the one who is not crazy, like my brother." Another shove, and Julie smiled. Their eyes twinkled.

"I can see that you are perhaps both smart. And crazy. If one could not look into your eyes, it might be difficult to tell you apart. But I can tell."

The truth was, that Young Joe Son had a small scar on his upper forehead, which she suspected was the result of a bout with smallpox. It would take much longer than a quick glance to tell these two apart, but she instinctively knew that their individuality was vital to them.

They both nodded.

"The teacher is smart," their wise mother stated simply, reading her mind. "I am Spring Meadow. These are my sons."

"Julie Bright, ma'am." she offered her hand, and the woman looked surprised, but took it gently. Then her eyes moved to Devil, standing quietly nearby.

"Devil is my horse. Was my horse. He was very wild, and I let him go. A few days ago he returned, gentled and rideable. When I mounted him, he took me here. I have a feeling that he knows this place."

The woman nodded. "He has been here. He would not like to be fenced. You let him go?"

"Seemed the only thing to do."

Spring Meadow nodded again. "He is a wild creature.

But wild creatures can sometimes become tame with freedom. I think you know that. You will fence him again?"

Julie's face pursed in thought. "No, I don't think so. I think he will come and go as he pleases."

Spring Meadow's face alit in a broad smile. "It is the way of life, to be free. It is the way of my people. Come. I have food. Join us."

And so she did. She sat in the grass alongside the fragrant cooking fire, shared in the food offered by Spring Meadow and her active boys, and learned, as she listened to the halting English of all three, of the life of the Blackfoot. She learned of the proud hunting tribes that had once roamed the plains in great numbers, mostly on foot, and how their family was part of the Siksika branch of the Blackfoot.

She learned of their colorful history of hunting the buffalo, and how the wicked past winters, and the growing lack of buffalo had resulted in starvation or at least relocation for many of their people. The loss of the buffalo, along with a smallpox epidemic that had spread through the tribespeople like wildfire, had left only small numbers of Blackfoot, such as their own, struggling tribe.

As they talked, three other women emerged from the teepees, one with a baby strapped to her back, and joined them in their meal. Spring Meadow, it appeared, was the only one of the women who could speak English.

"My husband, Joe Horse Lover, and the other men of the tribe are off on a several day hunt. We pray that they will be successful."

"My father is a great horseman," Bill Blue Sky stated

proudly. "It is he who took the devil from the big black horse. He talks to horses. He teaches me to do this also. I was first to ride the magnificent one."

As if hearing his name, Devil snorted and pawed the ground.

"He is a magnificent one. I agree with you. And I am delighted that he can be ridden now."

"He is your horse. He returned to you. Will you keep him locked in the small house again? Blackfoot do not believe in holding creatures captive, but I know it is what the settlers do."

"That small house is called a stable. He has returned there, but I will not lock the door again. He may stay or go as he pleases."

A thought came to her mind. "You have come to the schoolhouse. You have cleaned the stall and cared for the horse. Am I right?" The boys nodded.

She smiled at the boys. "And you may ride him if he lets you."

Both boys leapt to their feet and whooped out loud. Together they sped toward the horse, shoving each other to get to Devil first. Together they flew through the air, and landed one in front of the other on his back.

"Gee!" called Young Joe Son, and they took off, hair blowing behind them, dark skin glistening in the sunlight.

"You are kind to my sons," said Spring Meadow quietly. "They have enjoyed their time with the big horse. My husband would be grateful to you, so let me say that for him. He is a strong man, who knows that times have changed for the Blackfoot. Always he tells us of stories where the Blackfoot and the settlers work and live together, that there is good in both worlds, and we must learn it. It is he who has taught us the English."

"He is a wise man," said Julie. "How old are the boys?"

"It is eleven years since their birth. Soon they will be men. I fear for them. Times have changed for the Blackfoot in this land."

Julie nodded. "It's my hope that some day we can all live together, Spring Meadow."

"I am glad that you have come to teach, Julie Bright. The settlers have great luck."

Julie frowned for a minute, thinking. "Can you read English, Spring Meadow? Can you write?"

The woman bowed her head. "No, Julie Bright. Even Joe Horse Lover has not been able to learn this to pass it on. It is his special wish."

Julie thought for a moment. She was fully aware of the majority of the settlers and their reluctance to accept the Blackfoot people into their society. She had no illusions of what a melee it would cause in town to ask Spring Meadow's children to join her class. And she was hired by the town. But they didn't own her. They didn't control what she did with her spare time.

She smiled conspiratorily. "Would you like to learn to read and write, Spring Meadow? I will teach you, and you will teach the boys. And Joe Horse Lover."

A laugh bubbled up on the woman's surprised face. Then she looked toward the sky and thought for a minute, concentration furrowing her forehead.

"Would this be possible, Julie Bright? Could you do this?"

She had written in dirt with a stick before. She had been teaching people their letters since she was a child in Central Park. Later, she would bring slates, and chalk, and a tablet and ink well. Today, she would use what nature provided on the prairie.

She took the stick and carefully wrote her letters in the dirt beside the campfire. The other women looked by intently, smiling and nodding.

"We'll start with names. That is most important."

"SPRING MEADOW" she wrote, etching the letters deeply into the soil. Then she handed Spring Meadow the stick.

The woman stood, stared down thoughtfully at the letters, and copied them exactly in the dirt right beneath Julie's letters.

When she was done, she stood and stared, in awe of what she saw.

"I have done this. I have written my name." When she turned to face Julie, there were tears running silently down her brown cheeks.

She turned to the women who watched, and made a statement in the Blackfoot Siksika tongue. The women nodded and smiled.

Julie took the stick back. "Here's your husband's name."

"JOE HORSE LOVER" she wrote.

"And here are the boys' names."

She wrote "YOUNG JOE SON." And then "BILL BLUE SKY."

"That's the whole family, Spring Meadow. You can teach them this, and I will come back and teach some more."

The distant clap of Devil's approaching hooves could be heard, and within seconds, the black horse and his cheerful load came back into sight.

"It is time for you to return to the schoolhouse before the night darkness settles in," said Spring Meadow, nodding her head toward the setting sun that was taking on a reddish glow in the sky.

"The big horse will take you there, I am certain, but in case he has a strong head, you want to be heading directly into the setting sun. That will bring you to the town of Grey Eagle."

The boys clamored off the horse, stopping abruptly as they saw the figures scratched in the dirt.

"It is what the settlers do in the schoolhouse," Young Joe Son exclaimed in wonder. "I have seen the young ones do this. We can learn this?"

Hearing the emotion in his voice touched her heart, and she felt a tightness in her throat at the sound of it. Mysteries can solve themselves, she knew suddenly, thinking of the time she had been locked out of her own schoolhouse, the feeling that someone was spying in the windows, watching her lessons.

"I will be back tomorrow," she stated simply. "And we will learn more."

Young Joe Son lowered his joined hands when she stood at the side of the horse. She put a foot into his palms, and with a single hoist, he gave her a lift onto Devil's back.

"Thank you, Julie Bright," he said with a smile, looking up at her.

"You are welcome, all of you."

"Come here, my sons," said Spring Meadow, brandishing her stick. "I am going to teach you to write your names." Then she laughed out loud. "And then tonight,

Julie Bright, I shall have the joy of teaching Joe Horse Lover. How good it will be to be the one to teach *him* for a change!"

"He will have a different wish by the time she is through with him!" laughed Bill Blue Sky, and the two boys ran to join their mother.

Julie smiled half way back to Grey Eagle and the little schoolhouse. Devil kept his nose pointing directly toward the setting sun.

An idea was taking place. She was remembering a phrase that she had heard Mrs. Mayberry say about illiteracy in New York. She had been discussing the immigrants that had been arriving almost daily by ship, destitute, full of hope, and unable to read.

"When you teach a man to read, you teach a man to read. But when you teach a woman to read, you teach a family to read."

She was deep in thought, hatching a plan, for the rest of the trip home.

Chapter Twelve

Maybe she's a witch. Jack sat on the front porch of the schoolhouse, rubbing his eyes in a bout of disbelief as he watched the wild horse gallop across the prairie toward him at full speed.

He had heard the story from Jeb Johnson about how Julie Bright had let the wild horse go rather than have it put down the way any logical thinking creature would have decided. He had pondered long and hard about that one, about how she had plunked down good money for that crazy horse, like money all but grew on trees, without a minute's hesitation, and then she had let the darn thing go free.

Harvey at the livery was feeling as guilty as an over-stuffed critter for taking her money and exposing her to danger with the beast (which he for certain should), though Jack had assured him that he knew that she was a tad on the stubborn side (which was a bit like saying that Emmy Lou Burgess was just a little bit pregnant) and that most probably she would have come back and stolen the dadburned horse if he hadn't sold it.

So he had adjusted to the shock of hearing the horse was gone. And now, right before his eyes, the horse was back. And as if that wasn't enough surprise in itself, perched right up on the back of the horse, pretty as you please, with her hair flying free and her sunbonnet hanging loose halfway down her back, (instead of up on her head protecting her face from freckling like every other woman in the town would keep it), was Julie Bright, the most aggravating schoolteacher in the state of Montana.

Now he didn't know what surprised him most. He had, like the rest of Grey Eagle, who had been gossiping about the black horse for weeks, been sure that it was gone forever. Seeing the horse was a surprise, for sure. But seeing the little sassy schoolmarm up on his back, no saddle in sight, sitting spread legged like a cowpoke, well that was doing a little something to his lower regions that he wasn't all that proud of.

What was it about this woman that made him feel so crazy?

He watched the thundering horse approach, with Julie lying low on his back, rising and falling with his motion as if she had been born to do it. Geez, that girl could ride!

As she neared the schoolhouse, he could see that she had her eyes shut and an ecstatic smile upon her face, nose turned toward the sun, fingers gracefully entwined in the giant horse's mane. She didn't even see him as they galloped past.

The horse came to a stop in front of the stable. He stepped around the schoolhouse to see her dismount easily, though her skirts were flying, and he got a glimpse of white ruffly pantaloons that gave him another twist in his lower stomach. She seemed so alive, so energetic, so in tune with the horse. He swallowed hard.

She immediately picked up an overturned bucket and went toward the well.

"Howdy, Miss Bright," he said in the friendliest tone he could muster, hoping that his devilish man thoughts weren't showing through.

She jumped at his voice, then turned and smiled. Was it possible she was blushing?

"Sheriff White! How nice to see you."

She kept moving toward the well and he joined her there. He placed his big hand next to hers on the well crank, and felt like he was receiving another kick in the groin.

They turned the crank together. She didn't seem to mind his help, but she didn't stand back and allow him to do it for her, either.

They put the filled bucket in front of Devil, who was standing calmly, waiting. Jack looked at the horse through narrowed eyes.

"That can't be the same horse."

"The same."

He shook his head.

"If I didn't see it with my own eyes, I wouldn't believe it. To tell the truth, I *do* see it with my own eyes, and I'm not at all sure I believe it anyway. Maybe I been drinking too much corn whiskey and I'm not seeing right."

"Are you a man who drinks too much corn whiskey, Sheriff White?" she asked softly.

"No, ma'am," he grinned. "Not that I know of. But there's got to be an explanation."

She had picked up a brush now, and was gently going over the broad back of the horse. Jack picked up a brush, too.

"Think he'd let me do this?" he said, holding up the brush.

He was envisioning the wild stallion in the livery stall that was about ready to take off the arm of any man who came close. And yet, here was this pipsqueek of a woman running her tiny little hands all over him. And with no fear.

"Ask him," she giggled. "That seems to be the trick with Devil. He likes to be free to choose."

Jack played along, raising the brush in front of Devil's nose, and hoping, just for a split second, that the horse didn't bare its teeth and take a bite of him.

He brushed the horse, running the bristles over the fine, taut muscles that sometimes shivered under his hand. Devil liked the contact, he could tell, once he had let down his guard and let people close enough to touch.

Together they worked on the horse, standing close. He felt peaceful. How long had it been since he had felt such peace? He couldn't even remember. Seemed like he was forever in a state of worry and planning, wanting this town to grow and thrive, and worrying about the problems that would come because of it. He stood there, beside Julie Bright, brushing a horse, and he felt that all was right with the world, new and hopeful, like life was all right with its ups and downs. Did brushing a horse do that?

Or was it Julie Bright? He was watching the way her small strong arms moved over the horse, standing on tip-toe when she needed to, cooing softly to the horse as she worked.

What would it be like to have those small arms moving over *him,* to have her soft, generous touch on *him,* cooing in *his* ears? He pushed the thoughts away, chiding himself for thinking like a beast just because he was around an attractive and lively woman.

He looked at her. Her hair was flying every which way. Her skirts were dusty and rumpled from riding the horse. Her face was slightly pink from the sun, shiny from perspiration from exertion during her ride. Her hands were filthy and there was a slight smudge of god knows what on her nose. And she was the most beautiful thing that he had ever seen in his life.

"And you are crazy. Absolutely crazy," he chided himself, glad that she was not a mind reader who could tell his outlandish thoughts.

She is obstinant, unladylike, stubborn, on the one hand. And on the other hand, she makes no *hesitation in letting folks know how important education is, that reading and writing make a person a success.*

He cringed at the idea of her looking at him in another way, knowing that he was no more than an illiterate, stupid cowpoke who couldn't even write his own name. The shame of that was enough to make his feeling of peace a thing of the past. Nothing like the vision of her face when and if she learned the truth about him.

No, cowboy, keep your thoughts right where they belong, and not on the pretty little schoolteacher.

They finished with the horse in silence. The horse was standing still nearby, loose in the prairie grass.

"Aren't you going to put him in the stall?"

The stall gate stood wide open.

"Well, the truth is, if he wanted to be in the stall, he would be. Right now he wants to eat grass. So I let him."

He shook his head in wonder.

"It's a freedom thing, Sheriff, and it's all right with me. If he stays he stays, and if he goes he goes. Right now he stays. That's how the Blackfoot feel about the earth's creatures too, and I find it works with Devil."

"What do you know about the Blackfoot, Julie Bright? They can be a dangerous people."

He thought of her galloping across the prairie by herself, where small bands of Blackfoot Siksika roamed still, their tribes devastated in the past by famine and disease.

She looked pensive. "I'm sure some are still a warring people. But I have met some that are not."

They entered the schoolhouse, and went to her back quarters where she put a large pot of water on for tea. As she arranged cups and spoons on the table, she told him about Devil, and the small band she had met in the foothills. For some unknown reason, she did not tell him about planning to teach them to read and write.

"You be careful, Julie," he said in a gruff voice. "Things are not always what they seem. And the townspeople, well they are not necessarily accepting or friendly to the native peoples. And some have strong reason not to be."

He thought of scenes he had seen in his early days, of finding homesteads that had been attacked, inhabitants slaughtered and scalped. He thought of whole tribes that he had seen wiped out by soldiers, of the devastation of young children who had died of the pox. The beauty of

Montana could sometimes mask the ugliness of the pain and loss that its history also contained.

But how could one explain that to this headstrong young woman from New York? Time would teach her, and he hoped it would be in a gentle way.

He sighed and kept quiet.

She poured them each a mug of tea.

"It's good to see you, Sheriff. Seems like it's been moons since our paths have crossed. Is there a specific reason for this visit?" She cut right to the chase of things.

He felt on safe ground again.

"Well, yes, ma'am. I'm here at the request of the ladies at church. Seems that many of them want to start a Ladies Auxiliary that would meet once a week and they are hoping that you will cotton to the idea. Seems it would be a little, well, broader than the group that you join for tea at the hotel."

She giggled.

The sound of it made his heart race.

"You mean a group for *all* the ladies, no matter *where* they sit in church? Is that what you mean?"

He smiled. "Well yes, that's the general idea."

"Well, you can tell them that I love the idea and I will be glad to take part in it. When would we meet?"

"It seems it's to be announced at church this Sunday at the morning service, that the ladies could meet that evening and make the decision about what they want to do."

"Sounds wonderful. I shall be there. It's a good idea."

"Well," he said, running his hand through his hair thoughtfully as she placed a mug of tea before him. "I'm not sure what kind of idea it is. Seems to me that the ladies have enough to do with feeding their families and doing the washing and keeping track of their houses and little ones."

She huffed back at him. "Women can do that and more, Sheriff. We need friendships, and to learn new things, and to have a world beyond our families."

"Whoa, little lady," he chuckled, putting up his hand. "You are arguing with the wrong cowboy. I'm all for trying new things if it is good for the town. That's why I'm here. But I sure see why they want you on their committee! You're like one of them fighting soldiers that Shakespeare fellow wrote about who would fight to the death for a cause."

"Ah," she said, smiling brightly. "You like Shakespeare? You've read Shakespeare? Which play was your favorite?"

She was obviously impressed.

He was obviously distressed.

He stood quickly and grabbed his hat off the bench beside him. "No, no, I don't have a favorite, I don't like to read him. Not at all. Just heard the story, that's all. I'm talking off the top of my head, as usual."

His hands were clammy and he felt sure he was going to start stammering like a boy caught with his hand in the cookie jar at any minute. What had come over him, making a crack like that? Just because Jeb Johnson had been reading him and Marcus the story of "my kingdom for a horse," didn't mean he had a brain in his head and there was no use pretending. He felt shame to the core.

"Sheriff, you're leaving?" It seemed to happen so quickly. One minute they were talking, the next the big man was almost out the door. "Your tea."

He looked down at the mug. He looked over at her questioning face. And he wasn't ready by a long shot to answer any questions that she might have a right to ask. He had seen clearly the respect she would have had for him if he was a man who could and did read things written by that Shakespeare fellow. And he could imagine the look if she knew the truth. Besides, he didn't like tea much anyway, to tell the truth.

"Got to get back to town," he said gruffly. "All of a sudden I realized how long I was away."

And how good it felt. His mine echoed.

She stood, still puzzled.

"Well, certainly. That's fine. Thanks for coming. And I guess I will be seeing you again soon."

He banged the school door behind him.

Not if I can get out of the way fast enough, his mind rattled as he strode to his horse. He knew well enough to avoid danger.

Julie stood looking at the closed door after he left and realized how empty the room felt when he was gone.

Chapter Thirteen

Julie climbed into the wagon with Jane's family on Sunday morning with a smile. The tradition of travelling to church with the active Adams family had become very important to her.

On this particular day, the conversation was centered on the announcement that would be made about the new Ladies Auxiliary meetings, what projects they would do, and what this might mean to the ladies of the town.

After church, the minister announced the meeting would take place after supper in the church, and there was quite a buzz as the congregation was dismissed and families headed back home.

"You are mighty quiet," Jane said to her as she was almost back to her schoolhouse door. "I don't think for a minute you are thinking about organizing a quilting bee, or having a pie bake-off. I have a feeling that something is on your mind."

Julie nodded. "But I'm not ready to talk about it yet.

I'll talk about it tonight." An idea was forming in her mind, ideas that had grown by seeds planted on her first visit to the small Blackfoot camp.

She had been back to the camp twice during the week, and the Indian family was now working on the entire alphabet, and had started writing numbers, too. She had demonstrated hopscotch to the boys, who had taken to it as quickly and enthuiastically as the children she had taught in Central park. It seems like another lifetime ago, when she had stood beneath those gracious New York trees and etched blocks and numbers in the dirt there.

As the wagon pulled away with its noisy load, she sauntered around the side of the schoolhouse to see if Devil, the come-and-go-as-you-please horse was on the premises. He was not.

But beside the schoolhouse, something caught her eye. She had left the pile of thick logs the way they had been scattered, still with the axe stuck defiantly in the largest one. But now, the logs, all neatly split, had been stacked with mathematical precision behind the schoolhouse, and the axe rested safely leaning against the pile.

Who had done this? She was touched at the thoughtfulness, and walked with curiosity over to the pile. Sitting on its very top was a beautiful, beaded pair of Indian moccasins, made of the distinctive black skin that had been the trademark of the Blackfoot Siksika band for many generations.

Her heart swelled with gratitude and delight. A gift from Joe Horse Lover and his family. She thought of Sheriff White and his well meant warnings about the Blackfoot, dismissing them as prejudice and unfair.

She hugged the lovely moccasins to her breast, and went happily into her schoolhouse.

Julie walked to town for the meeting at the church. The sun had started its descent down to the horizon, taking on the reddish orange glow of summer evening. The prairie around her was peaceful and quiet and she made the trek easily.

She had only seen the sheriff from a distance at the morning church services, and when she wondered if she would see him on this visit, it was almost as though she had conjured him up. She saw his silhouette in the distance, easily recognizable with his broad shoulders, his large hat, and his large horse, and saw that he had just dismounted in front of the hotel. As she walked past, he was standing with one foot on the porch steps, speaking to a stagecoach driver who had arrived in town and was heading for the hotel for a respite.

"Miss Bright," he said politely, tipping his big brimmed hat. Something flipflopped in her stomach, but she pushed the feeling away.

"Good evening, Sheriff," she said primly, not intending to stop.

"Hold up there a minute, if you will. The stage has just arrived, and seems there's some mail for you from back east."

She was sure the panic showed bright and clear on her face.

Mail? She froze to the spot, her feet feeling planted.

"And of course you remember your stagecoach driver. He was the lucky man who drove the stage on your trip to Grey Eagle."

She lifted her eyes and looked at the gray-haired man, remembering. He was blushing to the roots of his sideburns.

"I tole the sheriff the truth, missy," he said miserably. "I was sure it would come out in that varmints trial, that I wasn't the one who nailed him to the ground, that it was you and that rock."

Men and their pride! She saw his misery and it touched her.

"Well, doesn't mean much, one way or another, does it? The fact that it took two of us to bring him down just shows for sure how good it is that he's not out there tormenting more honest folks."

The man raised his head a little.

"Well, yeah, I suppose."

"You suppose right." She nodded primly.

Jack stood by without saying a word.

"I'm going to go get me some dinner before heading back." He tipped his hat. "You are a kind and nice lady, miss. And probably the bravest little thing that I have ever seen. I swear I don't think you're afraid of anything."

He plodded up the steps toward the hotel.

"Except maybe a letter."

Jack's quiet words pierced the evening air.

She swallowed hard.

He held out a small, white envelope, but he was still too far away for her to reach it without stepping toward him, which she was not about to do.

A letter. Who had written her? Had someone found her? Was her peace and her new happy life going to crumble around her feet?

He watched her quietly, wondering. She was obviously afraid. The little woman who could slay bandits with a fist sized rock, who could fraternize with Blackfoot without turning a hair, who could mount the wildest stallion he himself had ever seen and ride bareback over the prairie like she had been born there . . . she was afraid of a little white envelope.

She watched him, watching her. He watched her, watching him. The standoff ended. She stepped toward him, and he stepped toward her in the same instant. She took the letter. She glanced quickly at the address, and her blood, which had literally felt frozen in her veins for the past minute, began to flow again, its heat caressing her and letting her breathe again. The return address stated Mrs. Mabel Mayberry. Her governess. Her friend.

She was still safe, and after the moment of panic had passed, she felt a wave of nostalgia, like she held her past, a link to her childhood in her hand.

He saw these changes go through her body, and it unsettled him. He felt like he knew so much about her, seeing her in action and hearing her affect upon his town. And yet, in that instant, her realized that he knew so little. And he didn't like that. Not a bit.

She looked down at the envelope. The edges of the seal were rumpled, as if it had been opened and then closed again.

She looked back up at him, wide eyed.

"What's this?" she said, eyes flashing, the anxiety returning as to what was in the letter, what damaging secrets it might hold. "This letter has been opened! Sheriff, did you read my mail?"

He sucked breath deep down into his lungs. This process made him seem even larger than he was, which was pretty large to start! For a passing minute, she thought he might explode.

And then, in a way, he did.

"Tarnation! You must be crazy as a loon, woman!" He grabbed his hat in his hand and slapped it hard across his thigh. "I did not read your mail! Why on God's green earth would you think I'd read your mail?"

And with that, he spun on the heel of his boot and stomped off across the street toward the sheriff's office, covering the broad distance in a few giant strides, muttering angrily under his breath the whole way.

Read her precious mail? Did he read her letter? Not only was he not inclined to snoop and do underhanded things, not only did he resent the fact that she just thought he might want to do such a low down thing, but he couldn't. He couldn't have read that blasted letter if his life had depended on it. Shame fell over him like a heavy blanket. He'd rather go to his grave than admit that fact to that sassy woman.

Julie had tucked the letter into the bodice of her dress, keeping it close to her heart, deciding to wait until she was safely tucked in at home to read Mrs. Mayberry's words.

Having it close to her felt good, like she was connected with her past.

She watched the tall, now angry sheriff stride away, and let her fears pass. His reaction had been immediate and real. She did *not* think that he had read the letter, though she was a bit puzzled that he had looked mad enough to spit at her question.

When she stepped into the church, many of the

women had already arrived, and were seated and chatting expectantly, enjoying their time out and without their family responsibilities. She looked around and saw many familiar faces, and responded to Jane's wave to draw her to the far side of the room to sit. There were woman of all ages and sizes and they listened expectantly as a tall slim woman, Harriet Roberts stood in front of them.

"Ladies, this is the first meeting of the Grey Eagle Women's Auxiliary. And we have some planning to do. In other towns, I hear the women's group are doing many interestin' things. We could start a quilting bee or two. We could have our first annual pie baking contest."

"How about making a plan to do our canning together this fall? We could swap and share what we have too much of, and cut down on the work," said a portly, gray-haired woman from that back of the group.

"Sounds like a good idea," Harriet nodded.

"How about a clothes swap? My little ones are growing so fast, and I don't have any more babies. I'd love to give away the things for a young one, and pick up some pants for these boys that just keep growing!"

An appreciative murmur went through the group.

"All great suggestions. Any more?"

Next to her, Jane Adams raised her hand and was recognized.

She stood shyly.

"These are all wonderful ideas. I think we can do many of them in the course of a year. But I have an idea that we might want to look at. This is something I've been wishing for a long time."

She turned and looked at Julie, then turned back to the crowd.

"Your children, and my brothers and sisters, are the luckiest kids alive, in my opinion. They get to go to school. I'm really glad for them. And some day, when I have little ones, I'll be glad for them, too. But right now, I'm kind of sad for me. You see, I really want to learn to read."

There was a hush over the crowd.

Jane turned red.

"Well, maybe that's not a good idea. It's just that it's something that's important to me. And I thought, if Julie could help, and if some of the other ladies knew their letters, we could help each other get started. I really want to learn to read."

She sat down, staring straight ahead.

Julie reached over and touched her hand, squeezing it gently, and watched the crowd.

"Well, um," stammered Mrs. Roberts.

Bonnie Baker from the mercantile stood up. "I'm not too proud to admit it. Jane is right. I see what my son is learning. If he can learn it, I can, too. If Miss Bright don't mind some more students."

"Lilly?" Mrs. Roberts called on the pale thin woman who sat in her wheelchair, who had raised her thin hand in the air to be recognized.

"I dream of this, Miz Roberts. I dream of being able to pass the time reading some of them stories I heard about. Maybe I would even write one, too, if I knew my letters."

Julie felt as if her heart would burst with feeling. This

was exactly what she had been thinking. Her eyes were filled, and she realized the gift she had been given even as a child, the ability to read.

"I could write letters to my son in California."

"I would read a newspaper and see what folks thought about this and that."

"I'm eighty-two years all," squeeked Bessie Borden from her seat beside her rancher granddaughter. "I'm afraid I'm too old to learn to read. I don't have much time left, I reckon."

In the lantern lit church, with forty-two sets of eyes staring at her, filled with hope, and fear, and doubt and excitement, Julie smiled and stood up.

"Well, Miss Bessie, I don't know for certain how much time any of us has. So we won't waste any. Class will begin next Sunday night at this time. Get ready to learn to read. And anyone who already knows how to read should let me know, and you can help teach."

The place buzzed with excitement.

"Can we still have the pie baking contest?" whined a dark-haired woman from the front row.

Julie laughed. "I don't see why we can't do both. And by the time we have the contest, the winner will be able to write down their famous recipe, and everyone will be able to read it."

The room echoed with laughter, as Harriet Roberts brought the first meeting of the Grey Eagle Women's Auxillary to a close.

Women! Sheriff White thought as he watched the ladies of Grey Eagle leave their first Sunday night meeting at the church. Who could understand them? They sounded and looked happy as buzzards on a side of beef as they yelled good-bye to each other and meandered to waiting wagons and carts parked along the side of the church building, some driven by waiting husbands or sons, some taking the reins themselves.

He watched Julie Bright climb into the Adams wagon with relief. He knew she had walked to town with the sun still up in the sky, but he didn't like the feeling of her making the hike back out to the schoolhouse in the dark of night.

She might state that she had no fear of the Blackfoot Indians, but the truth was, she hadn't been here long enough to understand the meanness that drought and blizzard and smallpox epidemic could do to a people who had lost a lot of their way of life. To say nothing of their land, as the settlers had come.

No, it just wasn't worth the risk, having her out on the prairie by herself. Even is she didn't know it. Even if he had to drive her. Which he didn't. Because, like usual, she was taking care of herself.

He grunted, as he watched the crowd disperse in an orderly, if female, manner.

It got quiet. He stood on the porch, watching his town go to sleep peacefully for the night. He loved this town. He loved watching it grow. He loved seeing the people come to expect their lives to be orderly, and safe, and productive. It was an amazing thing, watching a town grow up out of nothing. Grey Eagle had been just a prairie only a few years ago.

And then the mine had been built. And the Davis

Grain Mill and the Davis family who owned it had moved here to run it. And people had come to work it. And the Newby family, big in banking in California, had arrived on the scene to open a thriving branch. And people had built houses. And a hotel. And a church. And now a school. Ranchers had appreciated the general store, and the church.

People had come to work, to live, to be a part of life in Grey Eagle. They had come from the east, from the west, and from everything in between. Nobody asked too many questions about people's past. This was a fact that made him extremely grateful, not particularly wanting to expose his checkered and desperate youth himself.

No, people came to Grey Eagle to begin a new life, and they should have the right to do that. Only today, a new young man had arrived on the stagecoach, and was spending the night in the hotel. He was looking for work, and had that eager look in his eye. Seems like every day, a new soul showed up to make a new life. The town just kept growing, with folks coming from who knows where or why. People didn't just up and leave where they were if it was absolutely great. They moved because they needed a change. So it wasn't good to ask too many questions he had learned.

Jack sighed deeply, taking in the summer night air. He pushed his hat back on his head.

He thought of Julie's face when he had handed her that letter. Like it was about to up and bite her like a two bit rattler. But why? What kind of life had she left behind, he wondered?

It was none of his business, he reckoned, and best left alone. He turned and headed for home for the night.

Monday morning dawned sunny and bright. Devil was back, Julie saw happily, as soon as she was awake. She gathered up her teaching supplies and put them into a burlap sack, cinched shut with a long, thin rope. Dressed for riding in her brown dress that had become her "uniform" for traveling to and from the small Blackfoot camp, and with her new moccasins on her feet, she went out the schoolhouse door and whistled for the horse.

Almost prancing, he appeared in front of the schoolhouse steps, appearing almost delighted to be going on an excursion. She laughed to herself as she hung the bag of supplies around his thick neck, and standing on the second step of the schoolhouse porch, literally flung herself up onto his high back.

With a majestic leap, they took off across the prairie. Julie pulled the ties of her bonnet tight, hair tucked up inside, and rode low on the horse, as his forceful hooves galloped across the prairie and headed for the foothills.

"This is the life," she thought as they gobbled up the miles. Sun and fresh air and freedom. Freedom.

Tucked in her bodice, she carried the letter that she had received the night before from Mrs. Mayberry.

She had read the letter as soon as she had reached home, huddled around the lantern at her table, savoring a cup of tea, and letting her eyes fill with tears and her heart fill with warmth as she read the loving words of her old governess.

My dear Julietta,

The mail system being what it is, it will probably be an eternity before you receive this. Indeed, it may never even arrive, but I felt it worth the effort. I find myself thinking of you daily out on those plains in Montana, and hope that you are well.

Life is content here. I remain at my sister's home, and have the joy of caring for my niece's two children many days while their mother assists with church work.

I do hope that this letter finds you in great health and good spirits. I am certain that you have become a most excellent teacher, and delight in the thought that you are guiding young minds in this new town in my stead. It is a place for the young, I feel.

Your presence is missed, and the newspapers continue to carry advertisements as to a reward for information leading to your location. Gossip ranges from fear that you were abducted and held for ransom (though of course no ransom has been demanded) to speculation that you have run off with a most unsuitable gentleman. There has also been fear that you were the victim of unfortunate circumstances and are deceased and lying in a ditch somewhere. I am at peace knowing that none of these things is true.

However, I must warn you that the search fervor

has not yet died down. Your uncle has added to the rather substantial reward for information leading to your return. Be vigilant, Julietta, and be wary of alerting anyone to your past.

I would rejoice in hearing from you, my beloved student, when you have the chance, and if you ever need anything, please do not hesitate to ask me if you feel I can be of help.

Fondly, Mrs. Mabel Mayberry

She touched the bodice of her dress, thinking of the warmth she felt when she thought of her old governess. Her words took her back to her old life, but not only to the kindness of the woman who had understood her. The letter also brought back memories of the rest of her life. The frustrations, the criticisms, the unacceptable demands of her uncle flitted through her mind, too, stirred up like a dust storm on the prairie, swirling around her brain. Some day, she would have to face her past. But for now, she would take Mrs. Mayberry's warning to heart, and she would protect her identity in this new life that she had made for herself.

Mostly, she thought, as she bent low on the back of her large black stallion, and felt his thundering hooves pounding the ground beneath her as they ate up the miles, she would enjoy the feeling of being free.

She arrived at the camp of the Blackfoot band in short order, and found the boys and their mother ready to welcome her, and eager for their lesson.

Devil didn't gallop on the way home, which was fine with Julie. The sun was high in the sky, and cloudless, blue like sapphires, and looking like it could go on forever. Which it practically did.

A short while into the trip, Devil pulled toward the right, heading eastward, and she gave him the lead. Exploring on a sleepy sunny afternoon seemed just fine.

They headed toward a rocky area that seemed to jut up out of the flat land, and halfway up the elevation, she could see scraggly trees jutting their evergreen heads toward the sun.

She was wearing her bonnet, the sun was beating hot upon her. Shade, she thought easily, might make for a good respite.

She let the horse lead the way, climbing up the rocky path, winding around the jutting abutments, higher and higher, until the trees were close enough to touch.

She breathed in deeply, loving the hot summer air. It was quiet all around.

At first, she thought it was a mirage when she saw it. She rounded a bend, and the sparkle caught her eye, like a flash of reflection off glass, blue and intense and bright.

It was a pond. Hidden and calm, fed by some underground stream that dared to rise to the surface out here in the wilderness, the sunlight splashed down into the water, turning it the same sapphire blue as the sky. She sucked in her breath in wonder.

It was beautiful. It was deserted. It was inviting.

She only hesitated a minute. Then she slid off Devil's back, landing on the grassy path with a soft thud as her moccasins made contact.

She came to the edge of the pond, and looked down into the clear water with a sigh. Fed by a hidden underground stream somewhere, the water ripped slightly. Flashes like diamonds glistened as the sun reflected.

The moccasins and stockings were off before she even knew it. Then the bonnet. She plopped down on a giant rock at the water's edge, and stuck her toes into the water. It was cold. And wet. And wonderful.

She sighed, staring down at the ripples made by her happy feet. This was heaven, and she wasn't going to miss it. After all, she was *miles* from civilization. There was no one around but Julie and her horse.

She stood again with resolve. She pulled her sturdy traveling dress over her head. She scrunched up her face in thought for a minute, before eliminating even her bloomers, and standing practically naked in her cotton sheath. With one hand, she removed the clip that had anchored her hair. It tumbled down.

She felt the hot sun as it caressed her shoulders.

She looked at the water below, a thousand memories flooding her mind. Children, in Central Park, so very long ago, giggling and playing happily in the cool water of the stream that flowed through, swimming with glee. Her governess at the time turning up her nose at them, aghast that little ones could be so free to frolic. Julietta Brightingham had never been swimming.

"A lady should *not* do such things, Julietta Brightingham," she had admonished.

Julie had disagreed *then*, and she disagreed now. Without another second of hesitation, she held her nose tightly, closed her eyes, and hopped right off the side of the rock toward the water several feet below.

It was deeper than it looked. It was also colder than it looked. She splashed into the water, the cool wet closing over her head, shocking her system so much at first she thought her heart would stop.

But then, thankfully, her feet touched bottom, and she pushed upward, her head breaking the surface as she sputtered and gasped for air.

Standing on tiptoe, she could just keep her head out of the water. The rocks at the bottom of the pool were slippery and smooth. As her body adjusted to the temperature, she took a few tentative steps, feeling the water swirl around her as she moved. She had never felt anything like it before, this weightless feeling as she bounced along. The pond was small, it was not far to the other side, where the rocks were even higher.

Bravely, she lifted her feet off the bottom, and tried to float. Flustered, she kicked her feet, and pumped her arms. She was going nowhere fast, that was for sure. Her head went under water and she sucked in a mouthful of pond. Coughing, sputtering, she tried again. And again.

Finally, she was proud of the little paddle stroke she developed, laying on her stomach, pulling her head back and flapping her arms in front of her as evenly as she could. Her feet kept sinking, and she would quickly get out of breath, but inch by inch, she crossed the pool.

Refreshed from the heat, but with tired arms and legs, she pulled herself out of the pool, climbing up onto her rock carefully, the chemise sticking to her body like a glove, her hair a tangled mass over her shoulder.

The rock was warm from the sun. It felt glorious on her cooled skin. She stretched out on it, sun beating down on her, and took a few deep breaths.

Happy. Was this what it felt like to be happy? There was a warm glow deep in her stomach, a feeling of well being in her soul. This was her new life, and she loved it. She was still, and reveled in the peace.

Until she saw her hair.

Her hair. Instinctively, as she lay there, her fingers had begun to try to untangle the long strands that had snarled during her swim. She had pulled her hair over her left shoulder to work on it. And then she saw it. She was blond.

Since leaving New York and her heiress life, she had been vigilant about coloring her hair, each time she had washed it in the privacy of her own living quarters. She had hidden the eyecatching cornsilk blondeness of her long tresses with the horrible potion that cook had found for her. The long swim in the cool mountain pool had totally stripped it clean.

Her fingers finished untangling, and she sighed. She would anchor and tuck the tresses into her bonnet when she redressed, and when she got back to the school-house, douse her hair back to mousy brown.

The shining blond strands lay softly over her shoulder, curling as they began to dry in the sun. For now, she would just enjoy being who she was.

Chapter Fourteen

As Sheriff, Jack didn't go off and explore this land too often anymore, far from his town, far from anything that needed his attention. But on this particular day, he had been drawn, drawn by the blue sky, the bright sun, and some unknown spirit that beckoned him out into the foothills, meandering up and down mountain paths.

Jack's horse was surefooted and steady as he climbed the rocks. In not too long a time, it would be necessary to head back to town. But for now, he was enjoying the sights, and his horse was enjoying large mouthfuls of lush green grass along the path.

Must be a stream nearby, his land-minded thoughts told him. Lots of greenery up here. Mighty pretty.

Then he turned the corner on the path. And saw the pond. And saw the girl. It was as if his mind and his body had received a lightning jolt.

He stopped, staying at a distance, not quite believing what he was seeing.

At first, he thought it was an angel. He had heard stories like that, of people close to death who swore on the Holy Book that they had seen a heavenly being, or been rescued by one or some such thing. But he had never quite believed it.

He squinted his eyes, coming to believe that the sight in front of him was a human angel. A woman. And she was plum near naked. His throat was so tight, he thought he was about to swallow his tongue.

Even at this distance, he could see that she was beautiful. She was wearing some white flowing thing that gently curved around her body as she moved, clinging in all the right places, as she moved, just the way a man's hands would like to do.

She was a tiny thing, but curvy, and she was practically bare right down to her toes. Her back was to him.

It was her hair that stunned him.

It was long and flowing, laying softly on her shoulders, and shining in the bright light, so pale it was almost white, kissed by the sun.

Who was this angel hidden by this secret pond? He swore he knew every single person who had settled or even moved through this territory, and he had *never*, ever seen that hair. It was something that a man would remember.

He watched her back as she looked out over the pond, willing her to turn around in the distance so he could at least see her face. He couldn't call out to her. She was probably have a fit, half dressed as she was, and think he was some kind of a madman. How did she get there? Was she alone? He would wait and he would find out.

He slid off his horse, moving to a tree to tie the bridle.

He walked back to the opening between the rocks, where he had a clear view of the pond.

She was gone.

He blinked his eyes. Rubbed them. Got back on the horse to see if he needed greater height to see the rock where she had sat. The rock was still there. And she wasn't. She was gone.

He was baffled, frustrated, and determined. He moved with his horse down the path now, stepping around the rocks in the way and finding his way to the edge of the pond. He listened, and heard no one. He stared at the empty space. Had he gone plum insane?

His sharp eyes combed the ground, looking for evidence that she had been there, that she had been real. In the crack of a rock, he found a small blue bead.

He was more puzzled than ever. Blackfoot? He knew the intricate bead work done by the tribe. But they did not now, or *ever* as he knew it, have a blond angel in their band. He must be going plumb crazy.

Frustrated, he climbed on his horse, and headed for home.

Totally unaware that she had been watched, Julie had gathered her things as she left the rocks, climbing to the small rocky path she had followed down to the water. She found Devil resting quietly in a grove of greenery nestled between the boulders, chomping happily on grass.

The black horse lifted his head and make a slight noise before moving toward her, almost as if he had been expecting her. She smiled.

She climbed up onto his broad back, and stuffed her still damp hair back up into its confining bonnet. Her chemise had dried in the sun on the rocks, her dress was back in place, feeling stifling and hot. At least the moccasins she wore on her feet were cool.

Her heels gently nudged the horse, who took off like an eagle in flight. She lay low on his back, her cheek against his mane, reveling in the speed and smoothness of his gallop as they tore up the prairie and headed for Grey Eagle and the little schoolhouse. Miles flew by.

She had loved the little pond and its clear cool water. She had loved her sensuous swim in its depths. What would she have done if the horse had gone off?

Her logical side was warning her to be more careful. Her carefree side was laughing joyously. She had known the horse would be there. They were a team, she and the black horse Devil. She would remember that hidden pond, and she would return.

Julie sighed as she wrapped the damp tendrils of her hair in a large towel. The blond hair was gone. The smelly, awful hair dye had done its mousy trick. She was sick and tired of the charade, but she saw no way out of it. Every week, when she washed her hair, she had doused her head with the disgusting color for her disguise.

She sighed. How lies and deceit multiply and complicate things. If she stopped coloring her hair, it would bring questions as to why she had changed her appearance to start with.

Hair drying, and with a cup of tea at hand, she settled down to answer the letter of her dear friend in New York. She would give her the news, and send a list of supplies that could be sent to her, including a replacement bottle of hair dye.

She told her of the wide open spaces, the fresh, clean air. The smell of sawdust in the air as the town of Grey Eagle rose from the prairie, getting bigger and stronger each day.

She told of her students, her initial trials, her successes, her failures. She listed some books that she wished she could have for her lessons as they began again in the fall.

She told her about the giant sheriff, his hesitancy to believe in her, and the way that he mysteriously made her knees go weak at times.

She explained about tutoring the Blackfoot family, the need for education and acceptance in the west, and the simple fact that she felt she had found her life's work.

When she was done, the sun was long gone from the sky, and her small lantern was making shadows on the wall. Before folding the letter and placing it in the envelope, she slipped to her bed, and pulled the small wrapped package out from beneath her mattress. Her mother's jewels. Gingerly, she retrieved a small gold ring with a blue stone, then wrapped the rest, staring at them warily. She needed a better hiding place to keep the jewels safe. They were all she had. She came up with a plan.

Then she wrapped the ring in a wad of cotton, and enclosed it in the envelope before sealing it.

"Enclosed please find a ring that you may sell to cover the cost of the supplies I have requested. Again, your help and belief in me have made my new life possible, and I thank you from the bottom of my heart."

She sighed, and left the letter on the table to take

into town for the morning stagecoach that was heading east.

Hank Smith (who was new to his name, since he had just made it up) swung his feet over the side of the bed, pulled on his clothes like a man with a mission, and stared sullenly at himself in the oval shaped mirror over the basin table in his hotel room.

Well-worn shirt. Well-worn pants. Scuffed boots that had seen a lot of prairie dust and had nudged the side of many a horse. He snickered. Well-worn, but sure not by him.

He touched his hand to the brim of his hat in salute to the unknown cowboy who had unknowingly provided his ensemble, the tall blond youth he had met during his stop in Chicago on his way west. The sorrowful young man had been heading back east to his family for a funeral. Such a loss.

He snickered into the mirror, and the unfamiliar cowboy with his face snickered back at him. By the time the sad eyed young man had discovered that he had suffered yet another loss, Hank had been on the west bound train with the cowboy's duffle bag. The hat he had acquired in a poker game on the train.

He looked out the hotel window at the sleepy little town in the early morning light. It had been easy. He had just staked out the Brightingham's old governess until she had finally sent a letter. Easy as pie, and then had followed that letter right to Grey Eagle, Montana. He'd just arrived, and already he couldn't wait to leave.

He'd get a ride out to one of the ranches he heard tell about and hire on as a hand so he could get the lay of the land. They were eager, he'd seen right away, to welcome new blood into the community. They'd been delighted that he'd landed in their town, like so many other wandering cowboys and more than helpful to assist him in getting set up for work. Which suited him just fine.

She was here. He'd seen that right away, even if her disguise was pretty convincing. Julietta Brightingham, heir to the Brightingham fortune, didn't look one lick like the impressive picture her uncle had provided.

Well, we all change when we come west, he laughed, looking again at his reflection, his dark eyes and dark hair contrasting with his white smile.

He had his orders, and he was willing to carry them out. But first he was going to scope out the situation. She was a cute little piece, even with those wiry glasses and God awful boots. And by herself, she was worth even more than the generous sum that her uncle was willing to pay him to solve his "little problem." So first, he would lay low, and check out the little secret heiress-schoolteacher, and make sure that he wouldn't make out better taking her for his own.

And if that didn't work out, he would do what he had been paid to do. He would find the jewels. And then he would kill her.

"Try the Circle B Ranch," the owl-faced man at the hotel desk suggested. "They are looking for new hands right about now, I know for a fact. Mike," he called to an old man who was leaving the hotel dining room, "you going out to the ranch? Want to give this new young man a ride?"

It was as easy as that.

* * *

Sunday nights were becoming quite an event in Grey Eagle. Promptly at 7 P.M., the wagons and carriages would start pulling up to the church with the ladies of the town, and the number had tripled since the first night that the "learn to read" plan had been hatched. All ages, all types, and with a wide variety of abilities, the woman chattered happily as they found their place in the section of the church they had been assigned to. Several residents, including Olive Newby and Bonnie Baker, who already knew how to read, had volunteered to assist, and each week, three classes at different levels took place, with Julie supervising and teaching the beginning level class. It was organized pandemonium, and spirits ran high. At nine, the teaching stopped, baskets were opened, and homemade refreshments were passed around as the chatter increased. Talk turned to recipes, and clothing swaps, and local gossip.

Julie rested quietly on the front pew of the church during this social time, exhausted from the efforts of the night, but amazed and satisfied by the results. After only three weeks of lessons, the success was phenomenal.

The women learned, and then took the lessons home to share at home the best they could. She heard the funny stories of their first attempts. It seemed the men of Grey Eagle were not as inclined to buckle down to study.

There was laughter and cheerful banter as they tidied up and headed out to go home.

Jack had been making it a habit to loiter around the door of the church during these sessions, on the pretext that he was keeping the crowd safe and in order. But truth be told, he had been hoping to glean a bit from the lessons without looking too obvious.

When a group of husbands sauntered over, seeing him on the church porch, he saw trouble in their eyes.

"We got to stop this nonsense, Sheriff White. This Sunday night trouble making's got to stop?"

"Don't see that there's trouble making, Paul. The ladies are working real hard in there."

"But for what? This is filling their heads with all kinds of bad ideas. We got enough work to do on the ranch. We can't have our women lollygagging around with books instead of doing chores."

"You all look fed and clothed," Jack chuckled. "Don't hurt to have them learn to read."

Amos Brand blushed. "But they want *us* to learn, too. My Molly's making me write my name, and practice reading words from the Bible. This is awful."

Jack looked at him thoughtfully. "Don't hurt a man to read the Bible, Amos." He felt the anxiety grow like a weed in his gut. How he wished *he* had a way to learn to read without facing the shame.

"But this is a pain, Sheriff. Like today, instead of having our normal big Sunday dinner, we had some kind of dadburned stew Molly had made up yesterday, so as she could get out of the house in a timely way tonight. It ain't fair, Sheriff, it just ain't fair."

The other men grunted agreement. Jack laughed.

"Well not much you can do, as I see it. Might as well learn your letters and get it over with."

More grumbling was heard.

"Well, maybe we should just put our foot down," Amos stated harshly, sticking out his chin. "No more lessons."

The men cheered.

The door of the church opened, and the women began streaming out into the night summer air.

"I wouldn't do that if I was you," Jack said under his breath. He had seen the women's enthusiasm. He had sensed their dedication. And he understood how much they wanted to learn to read.

"All right, men," said Amos under his breath. "We're not having that little schoolteacher interfere with our lives. Time for us to take back control of our families."

Jack shook his head and watched the men break up to meet their wives, sisters and mothers. Trouble was brewing in Grey Eagle, and Julie Bright was right smack in the middle of it.

The next Sunday night, many of the women of Grey Eagle arrived with tight faces. A few were late. A few were missing.

"Those mule stubborn men," one exclaimed as she bustled to her seat. "They think this book learning is a waste of time. They think all we're good for is cooking and cleaning and taking up after the children."

"Well, this is important," another said. "I hate it when men think they have all the answers and all power. We're just asking for a little thing here. You'd think they'd go along with it. But this is probably going to be my last lesson. I never have been able to get my way with Herbert when he dug his boots in."

Julie sighed. "Men. They don't always know what's good for them. Sometimes we just have to stand up for what's right."

Mrs. Newby stepped forward, her hat bobbing as she walked. "Julie's right. We have to stand up here. But it's nothing new, ladies."

She took her place in the front of the group, pounding her fist upon the pulpit. "Sometimes what we want has been a struggle through the ages. But some women have been strong enough to do it."

The crowd murmured assent.

"Like in the Greek play, *Lysistrata*." She went on. "The women were upset. Their husbands would not stop going to war. The women *knew* there was a better way. And so they joined together and said . . ."

Every eye in the church was upon her.

"They wouldn't give their husbands certain . . . well . . . certain rights. Unless they were willing to work toward peace."

"Certain rights?" stammered Miriam Davis. "You mean marital rights?"

"That's exactly what they said," Olive Newby laughed. "Caused quite a ruckus, it did! And that play was written by the Greeks around 400 BC. And here we are, *still* trying to get men to accept a better way of life."

All eyes turned to Julie. "Is that right, Miss Bright? Is there a Greek play like that? Did it work?"

Julie blushed. "Well, yes, *Lysistrata* is a very famous play. Mrs. Newby is quite right. Caused quite a stir. It's a little, well, bawdy."

"Bawdy is as bawdy does, Miss Bright. It's a famous play. A Classic. I read it in finishing school in San Francisco. I think we should read it."

She looked at Julie's bulging book sachel by her side.

"You got Greek classics in there?"

Julie stared at her. "Well, yes, of course . . ."

"How about if you read it to us, Miss Bright? It would be quite . . . um, educational!"

Julie had a sinking feeling in the pit of her stomach as she opened her leather bound and cherished book of Greek plays. She had *dreamed* of making these hardworking women interested in the classics. Like Shakespeare, and Charles Dickens. She had *not* thought of Aristophanes' *Lysistrata*.

"*Go* ahead, Miss Bright! Read some to us!"

There was not even a whisper as she introduced the characters, gave the listeners a little historical background, and then began the play.

Their attention was rapt. After a few pages, she put down the book. "Well, that's enough of that for tonight. This is only one of many wonderful classics that I hope we can all enjoy together. But we have our own reading lessons to attend to now."

The room remained silent. Finally one woman spoke.

"Well those Greek ladies had the right idea. And I feel pretty strongly about these classes being important. That's just what I'm going to say if Herbert puts his foot down about my learning to read and write."

There was a murmur in the crowd.

Julie coughed, embarrassed. "Well, let's hope it doesn't come to that. That's a little extreme, don't you think? You can just explain how important it is to learn to read." She put the book back in her sachel, and began the instructions for the weekly lesson.

By the back door of the church, where he liked to hover to glean all he could from the lessons going on for the women, Sheriff White took off his hat and ran a troubled hand through his hair.

He sighed. Trouble was brewing between the men and

the women. If he were a betting man, which he wasn't, he would put his money on the women. In his opinion, there were going to be a lot of frustrated cowboys in this neck of the woods.

Of course, he was right. But the women were determined to keep to their course of action. It took exactly one uncomfortable week for the men of Grey Eagle to see the wisdom of going along with their wives desire to learn to read. The reading lessons went on. And life went back to normal.

And Jack sat outside the door each and every Sunday night, gleaning what he could.

Officially, he was there to protect the women's rights as they persisted in their "tomfoolery," but unofficially, he was as determined as the ladies of Grey Eagle to learn his letters and protect his pride.

Chapter Fifteen

The sound of fiddling filled the fall air, the barn floor reverberating as boots stomped, and ladies skirts swirled. It was Founder's Day, an important time in Grey Eagle. The hay harvest was baled and stored, and Monday morning, the school children would begin their new school term. Tonight was a night for celebration.

Jane's eyes sparkled as she stood with Julie.

"Every eligible man in this part of the state is here tonight, Julie! Let's go find us a husband!"

Julie laughed. "I don't know about that, Jane. I'm not sure that's in the cards for me." The thought of her uncle, and his horrible plan for her forced marriage flashed through her mind. "But I sure do love to dance!"

At that instant a young cowpoke had pulled her onto the dance floor, and twirled her around.

There was stomping and whooping, as colorful skirts flounced, and carefully polished boots pounded out the beat as the fiddlers feverishly played. The dance floor was packed, by the young and the old, and spirits were high.

It was impossible to miss the sheriff, Julie thought, as her breath caught at the sight of his impressive hat rising high above the crowd when he arrived. She had danced with an assistant banker, a shop keeper, and someone's aged grandfather. But Jack had not asked her to dance.

She saw him dance with some of the town's matrons. She saw him dance with some of the local young ladies who looked at him with dreamy eyes. But he totally ignored her.

Toward the end of the evening, a handsome muscular cowboy bowed in front of her, claiming her hand for a waltz. She gave a quick glance over her shoulder, to see Jack leading Jane's mother to the dance floor. He looked in her direction, and then quickly looked away. Julie's heart dropped. He simply wanted nothing to do with her.

"Yes, I'd love to dance," she said to the handsome cowboy, who looked at her with deep black eyes, and took her into his arms.

The hours of dance lesson torture she had endured as a teenager came in handy as she was whirled around the floor in a waltz. Compared to many of the enthusiastic cowboys, her partner's steps were smooth and graceful. Julie relaxed, and decided to enjoy the dance.

"You are a beautiful young lady," he said softly into her ear. "I have been wanting all evening to meet you. I am Hank Smith, and I've been working at the Circle B Ranch, until I get established enough to get my own spread here." His hand gently squeezed hers.

She smiled kindly. "That is wonderful. It's a lovely town."

"A place to settle with a beautiful woman," he said with a smile, and she felt his hand tighten on her waist.

Sadness settled over her. She thought of Jane's husband-seeking comments. He was a handsome, hard-working young man, and would probably make someone a wonderful husband. But not her.

She looked across the dance floor at the tall head in the big hat that was waltzing with much less grace and style, and had to sigh. There was just something about that man (and it definitely was not his rhythm on the dance floor) that made her heart soar. He turned then, and for an instant their eyes met. Was that a flash of sadness she saw on his face? Or was she just acknowledging her own feelings? Instantly, the look was gone.

"Enchanting, Miss Bright," said her partner as the fiddlers finished their set for the evening. "May I call on you some time out at the schoolhouse? I sure would like to get to know you better."

She gave him a kindly smile, but decided to tell him the truth. "I enjoyed the dance, Mr. Smith, but if the visit you are suggesting has to do with courting, I must be fair and honest. I am not a woman who is looking for a husband. My teaching job is my life, and that's enough for me."

His eyes narrowed a bit, as if puzzled, then he spoke. "Well, perhaps you will change your mind. I have certainly enjoyed meeting you. May I see you home?"

"No, thank you," she smiled, pulling her hand gently from his grasp. "I am fine."

He tipped his hat then, and make a stiff little bow before turning and disappearing into the crowd that was now scurrying to end the evening.

Julie watched the hugging, handshakes, and bustle as people said their good-byes. A feeling of loneliness drifted over her, as she left the lantern lighted barn and stepped out the door to the quiet darkness of the night.

"Alone?"

The deep soft voice made her jump visibly. As her eyes adjusted and she saw the big sheriff leaning on a fence post outside the barn. Her heart settled from the initial shock of being startled, but then began to beat in a different way, the way it always seemed to do when the lawman was around.

"Sheriff Jack," she said quietly, willing her pulse to return to normal. "I hope you enjoyed the dance."

"Not as much as you evidently did, Miss Bright. You danced every dance."

But none with you, the little voice inside her head said sadly.

"You seemed to do your share, too. I love to dance. It was a great event."

"And none of your obvious admirers offered to see you home? I am most surprised. You seemed to have them all mesmerized."

Was he making fun of her?

"I opted to walk myself. I like to walk in the night."

"I like a good hike in the moonlight myself," he said, as he stood up to his full height. "Come, I will walk with you."

Her heart soared at his words, but her spirit revolted at the thought he felt sorry for her.

"It's perfectly all right, Sheriff. I am fine on my own."

"I'm sure you are. But I'm lonely, and I want to walk. So you will be keeping me company, Miss Bright."

He matched his step to hers, and she couldn't argue. Besides, she liked having him by her side, though she would rather die than admit it out loud.

"You kick up quite a heel, Miss Bright, if I do say so. Where'd you learn to dance like that?"

"Oh, here and there, I suppose." She was instantly wary.

"A bit prickly about your past for some reason, Miss Bright? Whenever I bring up the subject, you turn skittish."

"Maybe you turn a mite nosy, Sheriff White. Did that thought ever occur to you?"

"And now we're back on formal name basis, I see. I thought we were friends."

She stopped, turned, and looked directly up into his eyes.

"Friends? Why you didn't even ask me to dance one single dance all evening!"

Then she gasped, throwing a hand over her mouth, eyes wide. What had come over her?

"Well, well, Julie Bright," he said in a soft voice, pushing his hat back on his head, then stroking his chin as if he was deep in thought. "Didn't figure you wanted or needed the likes of me asking for your dancing hand. Seemed to me like you needed to beat the suitors off with a stick the whole night."

She grimaced, wanting to reclaim her lost pride. She had literally admitted she had wanted him to ask her to dance.

"Suitors, suitors. Not for me. I'm not looking for any

husband here in Grey Eagle, Jack White. I just wanted to dance."

He looked sad. And changed the subject.

"Ready for the new term to begin? I hear tell the youngsters are yapping at the bit to get back into school. That must make you happy."

She laughed. It did make her happy. "I'm as ready as I've ever been. Except I'm waiting for some school supplies to come from the east. Thought they'd be here by now."

"If they come on the stagecoach tomorrow, I'll get them out to you. You got what you need to get started?"

"Yes, I'm fine. I've got the books I brought with me, and enough slates for the four new students who are starting."

"Four?" Jack's ears perked up. He prided himself on knowing everything that was going on in the territory.

"I only know about two new arrivals."

Julie smiled.

"That's because the other two were already here. Before the rest, as a matter of fact. And they are eager and ready to learn. I've been tutoring them. It's Young Joe Son and Bill Blue Sky, the Blackfoot sons of Joe Horse Lover."

He drew in his breath and stared at her.

"You want to have them come to the schoolhouse? To sit and learn with the settler children? Blackfoot children? Are you a mite crazy?"

She stuck out her chin.

He knew that look.

"There are probably those who think so. But I'm right.

Don't you think they belong in school? Do you think I'm crazy?"

"That's two separate questions, Julie Bright. Yes, probably they belong in school. And yes, you are crazy."

He looked at her serious little face, determination glowing. How could he explain to her the fear, the anger, the resentment that the townsfolk would feel when they heard this? But how could he disagree with her, knowing how learning to read and write were so important?

"There will be a lot said about this. Some might even pull their families out of school. The prejudice runs deep here, Julie."

"With you? Will you stand behind me?"

"They will fight it. They will fight you."

They had reached the schoolhouse, where the porch lantern still burned brightly from the post where she had hung it.

She clenched her fists. "Then let them fight. I teach all children. I'm not afraid."

He sighed. *One problem gets settled and she's cooking up a new one.* That's how it seemed to be with Julie Bright.

"You better go change that party dress, get some sleep, and get ready for school. Those kids are going to wonder if you've been up all night."

She laughed, her spirits growing at the thought of the kids.

"Ah, the first day of the new term. It will be exciting."

Yes it will, he thought, rolling his eyes, as he began his hike back to town. He took one last glance back at the schoolhouse, with its aggravating yet adorable schoolteacher standing on the porch. She had been courted by every handsome young man in the territory, and had turned his world and his heart upside down. And now she was going to allow Blackfoot children into the schoolhouse. Yes, it was going to be exciting.

Chapter Sixteen

As the sun climbed into the Montana sky, the children began arriving, and Julie Bright, dressed in teacher garb, was waiting for them.

Standing on the wooden porch with hands on hips, she felt the quivers of excitement at the first day of school, same as her young charges. They climbed out of wagons and off horses and climbed the schoolhouse steps with varying degrees of confidence and trepidation.

"Can I pick my bench, Miss Bright?"

"If you say *may* I," she laughed. "Ben, stop hitting Bradley in his writing arm. He is going to need it."

"Mary Frances, your hair is so long! Will you sit with me at recess?"

"What are we learning today?"

It was a far cry from her first day in the classroom when she had arrived. She smiled at the thought, as she greeted two new pupils who were introduced by their neighbor.

"My," she said softly. "You are big enough to come to

school now. Let's get you a bench by the front so you can get settled."

The day had begun.

The benches began to fill, slates were passed out, and the chatter quieted as Julie stepped to the front of the room.

"We are beginning a new school year here in Grey Eagle, and I can tell already how much you have grown over this break."

The door opened and Jeb strode in, looking, Julie thought, at least a head taller than he had when he left.

"Morning, Miss Bright," he said in a voice that had changed at least an octave.

The girls giggled.

"I'm sorry I'm late. I have me a part time job. But starting tomorrow I'll be on time. To ring the bell." He paused. "I can still ring the bell?"

She smiled broadly. "I'm counting on it, Jeb. Beginning and end of school. And at recess."

He seemed to stand even a little taller as he made his way down the rows of benches to the back of the room.

"We are going to have some changes here this year, some new students."

There was an expectant rustle in the classroom, and everyone looked at the twins who sat at the front.

"We have Mickey and Walt, who will begin their studies today. But we also have two other new students who will be joining us."

"From new families? Are they ranchers, Miss Bright?" asked Louisa with a thoughtful look on her face, trying to remember if she had heard of new settlers around the town.

"Not new families, Louisa. Their families have been here far longer than any of ours. But this will be their first time at the schoolhouse."

There was a rumble of curiosity.

"Their names are Joe Young Son and Bill Blue Sky. They are from the Blackfoot tribe that lives up in the hills.

"Indians?" Louisa shrieked, standing up. "You are not saying that you are letting Indians into this schoolhouse?"

There was terror on her face, and it was mirrored in the faces of all the children around here.

There was silence after her outburst, and Julie could feel every set of eyes upon her. She could feel the prejudice, the fear, the outrage, that had been bred into them.

She stood tall. "They are Blackfoot children, and they want to learn. Montana is a state now. Even though there has been a history of fighting and strife in the past, the present, and hopefully the future will be different. I'd like you to give them a chance."

"My mama's likely to take a fit, Miss Bright," said Josie, a tiny blond from the back of the room. We lost kin in fights with the Blackfoot, before I was born. And Mr. Mills, the blacksmith, his sister Lilly is spending her life in a wheelchair because of being on a stagecoach that was attacked by Blackfoot years ago." Her eyes were large and bright with tears.

"I'm scared, Miss Bright."

Julie spread her arms, as if to encompass the whole group.

"Please," she said softly. "Believe me when I say you are safe, and that these are wonderful boys. Can we just try to accept people for what they are, and get to know them? It's the way to end fighting, you know."

The younger ones looked up at her with hope and trust in their eyes. The older ones stared with cynicism and disgust.

Julie sighed. It was not going to be easy.

Almost as if on cue, there was the pounding of hooves outside the schoolhouse door, as Devil came to a halt and the two boys slid off his bare back.

Silently, stealthily, they stepped up the schoolhouse steps. Julie met them at the door.

"Morning boys," she said in a businesslike tone. "You are late. Try to be here on time tomorrow."

"Yes, ma'am," they said in unison, heads held high, but their eyes belied the apprehension they felt.

"This is Joe and this is Bill," she said to the stone silent class.

"Take the bench in the back, across from Jeb, and we'll get started."

You could have heard a pin drop.

The morning lessons began, and in the flurry of grouping, testing, and reviewing arithmetic skills and the alphabet sounds and letters, normalcy returned.

At noon time, Julie nodded to Jeb, who rang the bell for lunch recess.

Students of all sizes scurried out the door with their lunch pails, congregating in small groups under trees, and in the grass.

Joe and Bill, heads down, headed over toward the stall, where Devil sat calmly munching grass. No other students approached them.

Julie watched from the window as the group scattered. This would take time. She had to let it go. And pray for a miracle. She wanted these boys in her class, and she wanted these children to look at human beings in a different way. This was the tip of the iceberg, she knew. When they went home and reported to their parents about what had gone on, the backlash would be tremendous, she knew. But it was worth it. Though a miracle wouldn't hurt.

Jeb had hovered in the classroom.

"Ain't going to be easy, Miss Bright." he said in his new deep voice. "Folks around here have their minds made up. Stories of the Blackfoot disasters have been tossed around like folktales in a book. People see them as monsters. Ain't easy to change that."

"Isn't, not ain't," she said automatically, staring out the window. "And speaking of books," she said, squinting her eyes at the tall youth, "what did you do with my Shakespeare volume?"

He grinned. "It's safe. I read it, is all. He writes kinda funny, but his stories are good. And I'm reading them out loud to the sheriff. Figure if I can keep on his good side, he won't be so likely to arrest me."

She laughed. "Best you just keep out of trouble. That will keep you out of jail faster."

His words struck a cord though, and made her think. Reading out loud to Sheriff Jack?

"You best go eat, young man," she said, shooing him out the door. "Won't be but a split second and we'll be back in here again and working."

She looked out the window. Two of the boys had begun throwing rocks at Joe and Bill. She sighed, ready to enter the step in. "Well, I best put an end to that."

"No, Miss Bright. You stay here. You treat them like sissies and they'll never live it down. They fight back, and they're done for good. Let me take care of it."

She stared up into his lanky height, evaluating his words. "You're going to help me?"

"Least I can do. For stealing your Shakespeare book. Though it ain't stole really. I'm just borrowing. I'll bring it back. I heard of that, you know. That there are places that you can go and borrow books, then take them back so everybody can read them. Named after a berry of some kind."

She closed her eyes in thought. "Berry? Oh, Library, that's what you mean. Yes, those are wonderful."

"Ouch!" she heard from outside.

Squeals filled the air, a crowd was gathering, watching the rocks fly.

"I'll stop it, Miss Bright, if you trust me."

She stared for one split second. "Yes, I trust you. Though I wonder why you want to help."

He nodded. "I may not be Blackfoot, but I know the feeling of having folks make their mind up about you before they even know you. It ain't fair."

Jeb struck a pose. "My kingdom for a horse," he cried, as he lunged out the door.

Julie blinked back the tears that filled her eyes, as she watched the arrogant boy who had turned suddenly into a man.

What would he do?

She watched from the window.

Minutes later, she doubted her own sanity.

She watched him cross the school yard. Was this the same mature young man she had just spoken to? His slouch had returned. Even from a distance, his attitude reeked "trouble."

He had put himself into the middle of the crowd, and was busily heckling Joe, the older brother. The students laughed.

Julie was mortified, quickly pulling up her skirts for a dash across the school yard.

She was too late.

Joe had plowed into Jeb, and the two had hit the dust, wrangling with each other as fists and feet flew. Bill stood on the side, body tense, and ready to fight.

Julie arrived at the scene, grasping for a solution, before anyone got hurt.

Trust him? She was going to throttle him.

Instinctively, she picked up the water bucket that sat beside the stall. The boys were rolling around wildly in the grass, as the students howled and cheered. Coming closer, she thought she actually heard the boys talking to each other as they fought.

But she didn't have time to wonder about it. She raised the bucket over the tangle of legs and arms, and dumped the cold water on them.

"Yeowlll!" they screamed, instantly pulling apart. The crowd went dead silent.

She looked down at the two young men, sprawled now in the mud. Jeb looked up at her and winked, then pulled himself off the ground, dusting dirt and muck from his clothes. He reached down a hand and pulled Joe to his feet, grinning.

"Hey, this guy is ok!" he exclaimed in his low voice, full of attitude. And full of respect. "Great fighter. You gotta teach me some of those moves, ok?"

Joe grinned back. "Anytime." He too, was dusting dirt from his clothes. They shook hands.

"Nice to meet ya," Jeb said seriously. "Except now we have to stay after school tomorrow for fighting on the playground."

He looked over at Julie.

"That right, Miss Bright?"

She opened her mouth and then closed it again.

"Yes, that's very right, gentlemen. You may take your hooligan behavior somewhere else besides the school ground. And I will see you both after school. Now Jeb, it is time for you to ring the bell."

The students piled back into the school yard, the tension from the morning gone, but a new kind of excitement in its place.

Julie sighed, refilled the bucket for Devil, and headed back to the schoolhouse.

She was not alone. She stared in horror.

Leaning against the porch rail was a 6'6" man in a big hat. Sheriff Jack White had seen the whole thing.

"Having a good day, Miss Bright?" he said sarcastically through his grin.

"The best," she said defiantly, swishing her mud splattered skirts around him, up the steps and into the classroom.

He watched the back of her sway up the steps, and had all he could do to keep from reaching out to pull her into his arms.

She was a troublemaker, stubborn to the point of being pigheaded, about to turn his town upside down. And he was madly in love with her.

Shaking his head, he mounted his horse, and headed back to town for the wave of outrage that he was sure was going to come when the town of Grey Eagle heard about the happenings at the schoolhouse. He would handle it, because she was right. And because she made every one of his 6'6" turn into butter when he thought of her.

The town reacted just as he thought it would. While the kids seemed to accept the two Blackfoot students in the schoolhouse after Jeb's stamp of approval, their parents did not.

On the very first night, a group had gathered at the hotel for a meeting. After demanding his presence so that they could complain, they had demanded the removal of Julie Bright as schoolteacher.

He had stood his ground.

"It ain't fittin'," one rancher ranted, "We expect our younguns to be safe in school."

"Why, they're savages," exclaimed Peter Newby from the bank. "It's ridiculous to teach them to read and write."

Jack smirked at that one. In his eavesdropping outside the schoolhouse, he knew how much they already knew.

"They know all their letters and numbers. They can already write many words. They learn as good as you or me. Maybe better, in some instances."

There was a hush over the crowd.

"I don't care about any high falutin' ideas, Sheriff. I'm not going to have my kin exposed to that."

Jack White stood tall, his heart heavy. "I'm sorry to hear that, Peter. But I stand by my decision. This here is Montana, and we worked hard to be part of the United States of America. And that means that people are free to do what they choose. And in my opinion, that includes the Blackfoot. But also you. You do as you please."

So the town was divided. The very next day, half the benches in Julie's schoolhouse were empty. It made her sad, but even more determined.

Half were here and ready to learn, she reminded herself. She taught.

By the end of the week, a handful had returned, encouraged by the fact that the atmosphere at the schoolhouse had been reported as calm. Julie greeted each family as they arrived back, and said no word about the issue that had first divided them. Joe and Bill watched with dark, worried eyes, but they steadily and seriously did their work each day.

Would life in Grey Eagle every return to normal?

Sheriff Jack White sat in his office, feet up on the desk, listening to yet another rancher's complaint about the fact that there were Indian children in the schoolhouse. It had been that way for weeks. When each family would come to town to do errands and pick up supplies, they all seemed to have a visit to the sheriff on the list.

"It ain't right," the tall man with stooped shoulders complained in a low tone. "It's trouble just waiting to happen. We ought to send that schoolteacher back east."

Jack grunted. He had heard it all before. And his answer was the same. He thanked the man for voicing his concerns. But he stood behind the schoolteacher's decision to educate all the children in the area. He was keeping an eye on the situation. But he was not sending Julie Bright back where she came from.

As if he could. As if he could put her on a stagecoach and send her out of his life, out of his mind, out of his dreams. Because, though he truly did support her decision to teach Joe Horse Lover's kids, she was driving him crazy.

He traveled out to the schoolhouse every day, on the pretext of keeping an eye on what was going on. Truth was, he already knew what was going on. It was fine. There were several families who refused to send their young ones to school, and that was their own problem, in his opinion. And there were a few ornery ones attending, who took care not to socialize, and would make trouble if they could. But they couldn't.

Because Julie Bright had stood tall (despite her being no bigger than a mite)and had the schoolhouse humming along like a bee in a flower patch.

He would stand outside the schoolhouse door, and listen to her stories, to her reading lessons, and to her laugh. He would marvel at the feelings that romped around inside of him as he stood there, and wondered how she managed to turn his insides to mush. Julie Bright had gotten under his skin, and she didn't care at all.

She paid him no mind. It wasn't as if she didn't see him. She came to town almost every day after school, had a cup of tea at the hotel and visited Jane, waiting until the shout from the stagecoach driver announced his arrival. She was obviously waiting for mail, and was disturbed when it didn't arrive.

Awaiting news from back home, he was sure. When he ran into her in town, he'd offer her a ride back to the schoolhouse, and he got the same polite dismissal. The pain of that sometimes hurt like the sting of a rattler.

She simply wasn't interested. And he wasn't really surprised. She had no need to tie herself down to a small town sheriff with nothing to his name. The thought stung.

When the next Sunday night rolled around, the attendance at the women's meeting was sparse, and some were only in attendance to question her actions.

"I know you're not from around here, Miss Bright," said Mrs. Davis, "but this is just the way it is out here in the west. This is just the way things are done. We don't mix."

Julie sighed, having heard the issue before. Another time, another place. But still the same theme, prejudice.

She remembered her father's biting tones. "Young lady, you have been brought up to be better than them. They are here to serve you." That was about the Irish immigrants that worked in the kitchen.

"They are not your kind!" That had been his complaint about the children who had taught her baseball in the park.

But to Julie, people were people. Here in Montana, where folks had settled to build a new life, perhaps they could learn to live a new way.

"I teach children. All children. That is what I am here to do."

She thought of the two sets of dark eyes that looked trustingly at her each morning, still not feeling like they belonged in the schoolhouse, though they wanted so much to learn.

"They deserve a chance."

"A chance?" Mrs. Davis shrilled. "Did they give Lilly Mills a chance when they overran her stagecoach fifteen years ago? She has been a cripple since that accident, living up there on top of the stable, sad as can be. Do we forgive the Blackfoot for that?"

"These boys did not overrun that stagecoach, Mrs. Davis. I am not here to judge the actions and reactions of the people who had land quarrels here many years ago. I detest violence in any form. What I know now is that those days are over, and Montana is a state. These boys and their families have done nothing wrong. They deserve a chance. I intend to give them one."

Jack watched her from the shadows at the back of the church as she faced the crowd, his heart swelling with pride as he watched her take her stand. She hadn't turned them all, but she had turned a few. Did she always have to take the high road? Did she always have to stand up for what was right even when it caused such a God awful fuss?

With a sigh, he turned and looked down at the little blond-haired woman who sat in her wheelchair beside him, and who he had just unloaded from the wagon.

"Thanks, Sheriff Jack," she whispered, reaching out and squeezing his large hand. "I can take it from here, if you just get me in the door."

Tired blue eyes looked up at him with a sweet smile.

"You sure you're up to this, Miss Lilly?" he said.

She nodded, her face showing determination. "That young woman is right and she needs some help, and I'm set on helping her."

With a grin, he easily hoisted her wheelchair up the last steps, and she wheeled into the room. "Well, I wouldn't place bets on anybody standing up to the two of you!" He said under his breath.

"I've got something to say!" Lilly said in her soft voice, easily heard as the whole room went silent as she wheeled her chair to the front of the small crowd.

"I will never forget the men who attacked that stage-coach fifteen years ago, but they have absolutely nothing to do with these children and their families. I say judge every man, woman and child on their own merits. I want no revenge or bad feelings on my accout. These children want to learn. So I say, let them learn in peace! I applaud you, Julie Bright!"

The silence echoed in the room, and then there was the sound of her single clap, which exploded into applause that all but shook the rafters of the church.

He smiled as he slipped out the door, knowing that just like that, with the quiet determination that some-times magically makes right prevail over wrong, Julie Bright and Lilly Mills had won their battle.

He didn't want to stick around for conversation, not wanting Julie to know how worried he had been, or how he had kept an eye on her. He also thought that one of these days, she was going to find out what he really was, a dumb cowpoke who could not even read or write.

Yes, she'd always make a fuss when she thought there was a wrong that needed righting. And she hated illiteracy. That was one of the things that he loved about her, even if the thought of it made him feel like dirt.

Pushing away thoughts about Julie Bright that would make it hard for him to get his work done, he left her drinking tea with the ladies at the meeting, and headed back for his office, to wait until it was time to get Miss Lilly safely back home.

Chapter Seventeen

It's a peculiar thing how the world can settle right down after a storm. That's what happened in Grey eagle. After Lilly's quiet but strong endorsement of Julie's determination to teach every child in town, the gossip and bitterness dwindled almost overnight to a few cackling voices, and the schoolhouse once again became a place of peace and learning.

It made Jack White shake his head at times, but it seemed, once again, that the pint-sized schoolteacher from the east had won her latest battle without a nick.

People just seemed to take a liking to her, no matter if her beliefs and ideas tended to put ruffles in their old feathers for a spell. Himself included.

A few weeks later, he stood outside the Sunday night meeting on an early fall evening, picking at a horseshoe on his horse, Murphy, like he didn't have a care in the world, watching the ladies cheerfully take their leave as they did every Sunday evening, piling into wagons and buggies to return to their families. The town of Grey Eagle was learning to read. That made him feel proud. Even he was learning his letters, with the help of Jeb and his deputy Marcus. He wished for all he was worth that he had the courage to find a way to officially get some learning, to speed up the process. But his pride was not going to allow that. But he was learning, slowly but surely.

The thing that bothered him most these days in town was the presence of a certain young strapping gentleman, that cowboy, Hank, from the Circle B Ranch, who seemed to have a bold determination to win the hand of the hard-working schoolteacher, Julie Bright.

How the man ever got a day's work done was beyond the sheriff's understanding. He seemed to be spiffed up and present in town lately at the most inconvenient moments, just as he was at this very moment.

Leaning against his powerful chestnut stallion, black hat tipped back casually on his head, boots shining even in the limited light from the church porch, Mr. Cowboy stood waiting for the schoolteacher to emerge from the church.

As soon as she was in sight, he crossed the road in a quick clip, and met her before she reached the bottom step. Putting one boot up beside her, looking like the perfect suitor, he took his hand from behind his black shirted back, bowed his head, and presented her with a bouquet of flowers.

Jack White all but felt his stomach lurch. He squeezed his horse's foot, and was almost rewarded with a swift kick in the face, which he would have more or less deserved.

"Sorry, boy," he grumbled, patting and reassuring the horse. No need to take his frustrations out on his loyal critter, that was for sure.

He dropped the hoof and stood up, watching. Julie's head raised, and her eyes seemed to meet his from across the roadway, but in a flash, they turned away and she focused her attention on the man before her.

Jack watched the interchange as if in slow motion. Flowers, gestures, smiles, nods. He couldn't hear the words, but his fired up mind could sure imagine them. He watched her leave the porch with the cowboy, walking beside her as she headed down the long street toward the schoolhouse in the distance, with his giant horse following slowly behind them. In the moonlight, with his shiny boots and pretty flowers, he was walking Julie Bright home.

Jealousy surged in him. Why did this woman make him react this way? And why was he powerless to do anything about it? The thought of anyone else bringing her flowers, of holding her in his arms in a dance, gave him the feeling of a tea kettle ready to explode.

Man, did he hate that guy.

"Been wanting a chance to talk to you, Miss Bright," Hank Smith said in his deep voice. "Nice night for a walk."

He watched Julie pull her shawl closer against the nip of the crisp fall on the walk home. Hank strode beside her in the darkness, the gentle crunch of their footsteps, along with the hooves of his horse behind him the only sound in the quiet night as they left the lights of the town behind them.

"Julie," she said quickly, uncomfortable with the formality. "Call me Julie."

He smirked in the darkness, looking out over her head, out onto the empty night prairie. Julie it would be. And maybe his first plan would work after all. His pulse quickened. She was a pretty little thing, as well as a rich little thing. Because he was sure that her real identity was Julietta Brightingham. A man could do much worse than be saddled with the likes of her as a wife. At least until the will was settled, and he was settled for life. He looked down on the top of her head, visions playing in his mind. Yes. She would be most useful. And most enjoyable.

"Nice town," he said conversationally. No need to rush his plan.

"The best." She smiled up at him, and he saw the unease in her eyes. She didn't yet trust him. Imagine that. He'd better start his pitch.

"I'm going on thirty soon, Miss Julie. I'm thinking it's time for a man to settle down. To pick a place to settle for good. To pick a woman to raise up a family with."

"Thirty's a good age," she said gently. "But I'm sorry, I'm just not looking to be courted right now. I'm only twenty-four myself. For another week. And then I turn twenty-five. But I'm not sure of what path my life is going to take yet. Not sure at all."

"Your birthday's coming up? Well, I will have to get you a present to celebrate. Twenty-five is a special birthday." He was not going to take no for an answer.

"Not so special. It's just a day. No presents necessary. Thanks for walking me home," she said pleasantly, but firmly dismissing him.

Was it possible that she didn't even know? He ran his

hand over his face, thinking hard. Was it possible that she didn't know the significance of this "unimportant" birthday? That by her father's will, her estate that had been left in trust by her father would be dissolved, and that she would be in control of her fortune, and no longer in her uncle's control. Wasn't that what she was waiting for?

He had heard the story from her arrogant uncle. He had heard how she had run from home and left her life behind her to avoid being forced into an unwelcome marriage while the trust was in effect. He had been hired, in fact, to find her, before she reached the ripe old age of twenty-five, and he had done just that.

Her uncle had no illusions that he could change her mind. Her uncle had no plans to bring her back to follow his rules and make himself a rich man. No, he had been hired both for his ingenious ability to locate missing persons anywhere, and for his total lack of moral conscience. He was to find her, and he was to kill her. And all before her twenty-fifth birthday.

With proof of his beloved niece's death before her estate was turned over to her, dear Uncle Edward would inherit it lock, stock and barrel. And that was a lot of barrels.

The price he had been willing to pay for this completed mission was a high one, and had motivated him to leave the comforts of New York City life behind, and learn and live the disgusting life of a cowboy for a short while to achieve his goals.

But then he had laid eyes on the spritely little Julie Bright. And he had formed his own plan. If he was to marry her, her whole fortune would be his fortune.

Which was a much bigger payoff than the fee that her desperate uncle had offered.

Chances are, he would still have to kill her. But if he had a choice, he would marry her first. To make that plan work, he had to get her to succumb to his masculine charms. He would get both the adorable Julie, and her adorable estate, until he was tired of her. But time was running out.

So if she put up too much more resistance, he would simply revert to plan two, and kill her sooner and collect his fee. Either way, he couldn't lose.

Bill and Joe Young Son had lingered at the schoolhouse to review a lesson at day's end, and as Julie walked them to the door, they heard Devil's snort and hooves pounding on the hard dirt outside.

The sun was hot and high, despite the fact that it was fall. Julie scanned the horizon, appreciating the big blue sky. And then she saw the smoke. It rose from the end of town closest to the schoolhouse, black and billowing. She squinted her eyes against the sun, her careful look confirming her fears. The livery was on fire.

Panic rose inside of her, thinking of the dry hay and straw inside Harvey's blacksmith shop, and the resting horses. Her heart hammered at the next thought: Harvey's sister, Lilly, bound to her wheelchair, lived in the rooms above the stalls with her brother. Was she there? How had the fire started?

There was no time to think. The boys had seen the smoke only an instant after hers, and with a shrill whistle, Devil's head perked up and he stopped by their side, nostrils flaring, head held expectantly.

"Come on!" yelled Joe, as he flung himself through the air and onto Devil's twitching back. A long brown arm hung down for his brother, who wrapped his hands around the taut wrist, and flung himself high onto the horse, landing gracefully behind his older brother. In no more than an instant, the arm appeared again.

"Now, Miss Bright, get up here and let's go!"

No time for propriety! Julie gathered her skirts, held them high and tucked them in her waist band. Then reaching up, and taking a deep breath, she leapt with all her might, and landed behind the boys with a thud.

Devil turned his head and gave her one of his wild-eyed looks, and she had the sneaking hunch for a split second that the horse was laughing at her. But then he reared up on his hind legs, listened to Joe chanting in his ear. He spun around, and streaked toward town and the now billowing smoke in the distance. If he found flying along the prairie any extra effort with three riders perched high on his back, he gave no indication of it.

The pounding hooves brought them close to the smoky livery in record time.

Devil thundered to a stop when they arrived alongside the livery, where a wall of heat greeted them ominously, flames popping through the roof in the back of the structure, making crackling sounds in the hot air.

There was no one in sight. Julie's eyes pierced through the smoke, seeking out the windows of the rooms upstairs. Lilly was there.

In the far corner window, they could see her golden hair, pale face, and eyes large and terrified. Lilly was alive.

Her arms were stretched on each side of the window

frame, pulling herself as far forward as she could manage, stuck powerlessly in her wheelchair. She was gasping for air.

"Help!" she croaked.

"Help!" Julie screamed with all her might for anyone who might hear. "Fire!"

Mouth dry, eyes burning, Julie frantically looked around. How could they save her? They needed help! Her eyes darted around, no ladder or help in sight.

In the distance, she could hear the ringing of the new fire bell, and knew that the cart with water barrels would be lumbering its way through town, and knew that the alert had been sounded. But she looked back to the little face in the window, to the flames that were dancing on the roof. They would not be in time to save that sweet, gentle lady trapped in the window, already framed by smoke.

"Quick," yelled Joe, his voice already harsh from the smoke. "Calm Devil. He will listen to no one like you."

She slid down off the horse, her feet hitting the dusty ground as she darted to the front of the horse.

"Quiet boy, quiet," she coaxed the excited animal.

"Close. Bring him close. I will climb up and get the yellow-haired lady. Keep him still. Cover his eyes if you have to."

His voice was soft but determined, calm, but authoritative. She could see in that instant the man he would become. She followed the directions, gently moving the horse sideways, closer and closer to the building wall right beneath the window.

She ripped the clasp of her skirt, and slid out of it, taking the material gently and tying it around Devil's now tossing head.

"Quiet boy, good boy," she crooned, as the smoke stung her throat and eyes, and the heat made her feel like she was going to melt. The horse's muscles quivered, but he held his stand.

With gentle step, and awe inspiring balance, Joe stood up on the horse's back, barefoot now, his brown toes kneading the stallion's back as he took his stance. He wasn't tall enough to reach the window.

"Up," he grunted at his brother, who wasted not a second. He flung himself through the air, onto his brother's back, then scrambled to crouch on his shoulders, where he balanced his body, like an agile circus performer, then stood and took himself to his full height.

Like a human ladder, boy upon boy upon horse, Bill's black head was within reach of Lilly's window. She was crying now.

He reached his arms for her, locking them around her small back, but with the distance, and his small size, he did not have the strength in that precarious position to lift her weight from the wheelchair.

"Closer," he called, and she gently nudged the trusting horse. He stepped.

Bill leapt. He left his brother's shoulder, threw himself into the window frame, and hopped into the flaming inferno.

Julie's heart was hammering hard inside her chest, and her face was wet with both sweat and running tears. What was this child doing? Helpless, stuck on the ground, she prayed. The fire bells sounded closer, and the sound of yelling could be heard as the townspeople began to arrive to help, gasping at the spectacle.

Bill appeared in the window again, this time with Lilly in his arms. Her face was streaked with soot, and her clothes were spotted with burn marks. He gripped her under her armpits, carefully dangling her legs out of the window to his brother below, leaning as far out the window has he could. He couldn't reach. There was still a several foot gap between her feet and his brother's outstretched arms. To drop her with her sickly physical condition would be fatal. They needed help.

"I'm coming up," she yelled, dropping the reins, hiking up her petticoats, and preparing to leap back up on the horse.

There was a rumbling behind her. "I've got it, Julie. Hold the horse."

It was Jack. Thundering up on his Murphy, his giant horse, he pulled up beside Devil, and stood, one foot on the saddle, one on Devil.

With a move born more of trust than common sense, Joe jumped up on Jack's back, seating himself on the tall man's shoulders. With the extra height, he could reach Lilly's dangling legs. Gently, he brought her down into his arms, then to Jack's and then to Julie's on the ground. Bill came next, leaping with a loud whoop, he landed on his brother, then scrambled down to the ground.

The crowd that was rapidly building let out a cheer of relief. At that same moment, a giant cracking sound was heard as the beam that held the roof gave way, and the building collapsed behind them, plummeting to the ground with a crash, flames rising high.

Lying safely on the ground, Lilly wrapped her arms around Julie, crying softly.

"It's all right, Lilly," she calmed, secretly terrified about what had happened to the kindly blacksmith Harvey, not knowing whether he had perished in the flames.

The water wagon arrived, and a bucket brigade was in full force, when Harvey galloped up in a panic on his roan colored horse, a frantic look on his face. "Where's Lilly?" he yelled jumping from his horse and running toward the flames.

"Whoa," said Jack, stopping the man with a big hand in his chest. "She's okay. Right over there."

The story of the rescue was filtering through the crowd; the brave boys and their daredevil heroics, the life threatening fire that had begun by a stray ash from the blacksmith fireplace, the joy that both Lilly and her brother had escaped unharmed. Gentle hands lifted Lilly into a wagon to take her to the doctor's office.

Jack looked over at Julie. After all of the fear and excitement, Julie didn't even seem to notice that she was sitting on the hard packed ground covered only by her ash covered petticoat. He smiled. She wasn't going to like that when she thought about it.

Quietly, he went over to one of the town matrons who has wearing a large wraparound apron over her skirt and blouse. With a hearty laugh, the woman took off the apron and handed it to him.

Julie was sitting totally still, not even moving a muscle. He lowered himself to the ground beside her.

"That was mighty brave of you and the boys. That was quite a rescue."

"They're amazing boys. They did much more than me, really."

"Well, in a way. But if it wasn't for you, they wouldn't have been in that schoolhouse and able to help. They wouldn't have known Devil, and been comfortable enough to dare to help. They wouldn't have had the courage to rescue a settler."

"Perhaps." She was thoughtful.

"You know, it was an attack by a Blackfoot rebel tribe that made the stage crash that put her in that chair. Seems only fitting that it was Blackfoot that saved her life."

"They are good boys."

"You knew it. Now everybody knows it. Good for this town. Good for Montana. Folks have to accept folks for what they are today."

She turned toward him then, something leaping in her heart. He touched her so with his words.

But before she could react in any grateful way, he went on.

"Like folks have to accept what they are today, even if that means they are half naked sitting on the ground in front of the whole town." He paused.

She looked down, and noticed her state of undress. The color began to mount in her cheeks.

"Oh," she cried in despair, as he reached around and brought the ample apron from behind his back. "This'll about do it to get you home, young lady. Not that anyone minds seeing your most attractive petticoats there."

She grabbed at the apron, grateful beyond words, but not willing to show it. It wrapped around her and covered her completely.

Standing, she faced him, face flushed. "You are not a gentleman, Jack White!" she said, turning on her heel.

And maybe she was right. He was having very ungentlemanly thoughts right about now concerning one adorable if a little sooty schoolteacher.

"Hold on," he laughed gently. "Don't get a bee in your bonnet. And I'm giving you a ride home. The boys are taking Devil and heading back to their family. They have had enough action for one day."

He was right. And her legs were wobbly, truth be told. So she swallowed her pride, and followed him to his horse. He gave her a lift, and she landed solidly in his saddle. He climbed on behind her, and slowly, they ambled toward the schoolhouse, as the sun began to dip below the horizon.

She leaned back into him, breathing deeply, enjoying the feeling of his chest against her back. He felt strong, and secure, smelling still of the smoke from the fire. His left arm was firm around her middle, holding her close. She imagined she could feel his heartbeat, though the sensation was probably more from the beat of the horse's hooves on the hard ground.

In front of her, the schoolhouse loomed far too quickly.

"If you're not in a hurry to get home, how about taking a ride?" His voice was low in her ear.

She turned her head to answer him, and her cheek touched his. Feelings jolted through her, making her head spin, her stomach take flight. She swallowed hard and found her nerve.

"Yes." She forced air out of her lungs to say the word.

Then she leaned back into him again, closed her eyes,

and enjoyed the ride. For as long as it lasted, she would relish this magic moment feeling so attached to this man.

The horse thundered across the plain, leaving the town and schoolhouse behind. He slowed as they traveled the rocky path that led into the foothills. She opened her eyes and smiled, recognizing the area that she and Devil had roamed.

When he took the turn up the narrow path that led to the hidden pond, she inhaled sharply, turning again to look at him.

"The pond?" she asked quietly. "Are we going to the pond?"

"Nothing like it after the hot smoky day we've had."

He caught her questioning look.

"I promise," he said with a grin. "I will swim in my clothes. And you may do as you please."

She laughed then, her spirits rising, and feeling like an errant child who had just been sprung for a day in the park.

They climbed down from the horse, and clamored together over the last rocks to the edge of the water. Jack pulled off his boots, put his hat on top of them, let out a shout and cannonballed into the water. He came up gasping and laughing.

"It's very warm," he said through chattering teeth.

"And you, sir, are a bald faced liar, I imagine."

Jack disappeared under the water.

She had unlaced her boots and pulled off her stockings, standing on the edge of the water. She looked down at the heavy apron that she had donned when she had lost her skirt. Jumping in with such a bulky garment would take her right to the bottom of the pond.

Jack was swimming away from her in broad strokes, not even looking at her. With a shrug, she pulled the apron over her head, standing in her chemise and blouse. She had already appeared in public in this half dressed state, and she simply wasn't going to miss out on this delicious-looking swim.

In a flash, she leapt into the water, feeling its cold fingers grab at her and take her breath away as she went under. She reveled in it, splashing and kicking her feet with delight as her body got accustomed to the coolness.

Suddenly he was there beside her, his face now cleaned of the ashes and soot from the fire, his hair slicked back and shining in the sunlight. He was looking right at her. But he wasn't smiling. His eyes were wide with shock and surprise.

The cold water had taken his breath away for a moment, but he had recuperated quickly. The shock of seeing Julie fling off her apron out of the corner of his eye, before leaping into the water in such a carefree way had taken his breath away momentarily, too. But nothing had prepared him for the shock that he got next.

She had gone under, swimming and splashing like a child at play, and she had come up again—as an angel. As his angel.

Her long hair, now flowing free from its pins, was not its usual brown color, it was pale blond, laying in wet strands down the sides of her face, down her back, and in her white blouse and white chemise, he knew he had seen her before in this very spot. His heart was hammering in his chest. He swallowed hard. And stared.

Julie looked back. She didn't understand his expression at first, but when she looked down and saw the blondness on her shoulder, she remembered. She had forgotten about her hair.

"I dye my hair," she stammered. "It washes out. Sorry for the shock."

It was time to tell Jack the truth. About her past. About who she was, and who she had become.

"I have a lot to tell you."

"Are you running from the law?"

Always the lawman. She smiled.

"No. Not the law."

"Then you may tell me all about it later." He reached out his arms, gathering her close to him, her wet tresses flowing around them. He kissed the top of her head softly, then, gently pulled up her chin. Slowing, he lowered his mouth to hers.

It was a tender kiss at first, but then his mouth demanded more. He lifted her up as he stood in the water, holding her high against him. She gasped at the feel of him, of his mouth claiming hers, her arms encircled his neck, fingers entwining in the hair that lay wet against his neck. Her entire body tingled, every inch alive.

Slowly, hesitantly, he released her, letting her slide down his body until her feet touched the pond floor again.

He groaned.

"This is dangerous," he said huskily. "For an angel, you sure bring out the devil in a man."

Not trusting her shaky emotions, she decided to keep things slight.

"Is that so?" She pulled her arm back and sent a wave of cold water splashing over him. "Think you can beat me to the rock on the other side?"

And then, without missing a beat, she dove under the water and swam with all her might. Kicking and pulling at the water eased some of her anxiety, and her challenge ended the tension between them, at least momentarily. He caught up to her, laughing and breathing hard, and they played like children a few more minutes, before climbing the rocky ledge to come out of the water to dry off.

They had eased the tension of the kiss, but not the searing memory, and as they mounted the horse to head home, as Jack looked at the now blond head of the angel in front of him, his mind was full of questions and wonder. And he was hoping beyond hope that the answers to those questions were going to be something he could live with.

Chapter Eighteen

They climbed up the wooden steps, and Julie opened the schoolhouse door, moving the lantern inside.

She gasped.

The place was a mess.

The orderly piles of books she had left, ready for the new day, had been overturned. Her crates, boxes, and shelves had been emptied on the floor.

Crossing quickly to her living quarters, she found her possessions in the same disarray.

With wild eyes, turned to Jack, searching his face.

"He found me." The words came out softly, like the knell of death.

He saw the fear in her face. She might not be afraid of the entire population of Grey Eagle and their reaction to her decision about the Blackfoot, but at this moment, she was filled with fear. From her past? Was this the result of an angry settler, or was their something terrifying in Julie Bright's past? To his lawman's eye, it looked as though the place had been thoroughly seached. For what? What was going on?

He reached out and took her shaking body in his arms. She nestled gently into his warmth, letting the anguish seep over her, until the tears fell.

When she stopped crying, he sat her down at her kitchen table. It was time for some tough talk. One way or another, he needed to know what Julie was running from.

Western towns were amazing places, springing up practically overnight with the discovery of a good mine, the proximity of the railroad, or the relocation of choice ranch stock. People arrived almost overnight to fill those towns. There was one thing Jack had learned. Like himself, the new settlers in the west had often left sorrow and failure and problems behind. No one with a productive, successful, happy life picked up their belongings and moved across the unwelcoming and dangerous plains. No, many of the inhabitants of Grey Eagle had left a set a problems behind, in their quest to start anew. And most wanted those past problems to stay a secret. He respected them for that. He hesitated to pry. But now, with this, and seeing the look in Julie's face, he had to know.

He turned her toward him now, her face golden in the wavering lantern light, her eyes wide.

"What is it, Julie? What did you leave behind, and who is it that you think has found you? And what were they looking for here?"

"Oh," she stammered, panicked inside. She had kept her fears and her secrets to herself for such a long time. It had been so long, that she actually had days when she could pretend that her past didn't exist. But it did.

This havoc was not caused by townsfolk angry at the inclusion of Blackfoot children in the school.

This was the result of her past catching up to her. This was the result of her awful uncle and his awful plan and his greedy need to control her estate. But why? Why had he searched her out? Why hadn't he just let her go?

The thought began in the back of her brain, and exploded like a firecracker. Her mother's jewels. He wasn't satisfied with taking over her father's inheritance. He had sent someone to find her mother's jewels.

"Oh," her voice said again, only this time it wasn't a little sigh, it was a call to action.

She leapt to her feet, taking the lantern in her hand, bounded out the door and around the schoolhouse to the barn.

Had the searcher discovered the jewels? With a knot the side of a baseball in her stomach, she strode toward the stall, freezing in her tracks as a fierce snort, and the sound of a pounding hoof filled the air.

It was Devil. He was standing proud in the small stall, shaking his magnificent head as he heard her approach.

"It's me, Devil," she cooed, and instantly the horse mellowed and stepped forward.

Jack had followed her swinging skirts out the door, determined to follow her, especially as she had taken the only light in the place. He stood behind her now, not saying a word, watching as her presence stilled the wild horse.

The horse stepped forward. In the scattered lamplight, Jack realized that the horse had not been gated into the stall, had not even been tied. He watched in wonder.

"Good boy, what a good boy," she cooed, as the horse approached her and nuzzled her neck. Her small hands ran through his mane, and down his flanks. "I think you saved the day."

She stepped past the horse then, who offered no resistance, and moved to the back of the stall. With a strong heave, she pulled aside the wooden water trough, dropped to her knees, and began digging in the dirt beneath.

With a long sigh, she pulled out a rectangular leather pouch, and clutched it to her breast. The jewels were safe. The searcher had not found them. Whether this was by chance, or because Devil had magically decided to protect her, she did not know. But she was filled with gratitude.

"Good horse," she said, rising to her feet and crossing to stroke the horse. The majestic animal raised his head and snorted, then spun his muscular body around, and took off across the plain, hoofs thundering in the black night long after he was lost from sight.

Her knees were wobbly as she took a step toward Jack, who had stood silently watching the whole event. It was time for truth. And this was the man to hear it.

"If you want to hear the story, I will tell it. Can you stay?"

The truth was, not even wild horses, not even the wild Devil could have pulled him away. He wanted to know everything about Julie Bright, good or bad. There was nothing, nothing about this little woman that would surprise him, because she had stolen his heart. That was scarier to him than looking down the barrel of a loaded shotgun, or facing any natural disaster so far in his life. But it was a fact. He loved her.

He nodded, for some reason not trusting his voice.

She had lowered herself to the ground, outside of the stall, jewel pouch in hand, and he sat down beside her. The lantern on the ground in front of them wavered gently in the night, casting its orange glow.

"My real name is Julietta Brightingham, and when I came here to follow my dream of being a teacher, I left quite a little chaos behind."

She told him then, about her father's death, her inheritance under her uncle's control, her absolute refusal to accept marriage to her uncle's greedy cohort.

"And so I left. When Mrs. Mayberry offered me this job, it was like a gift from heaven, and I grabbed at it, and ran. I left it all behind, Jack White, and want it to stay there. Except for the fact that I took my mother's jewels, which were legally and morally mine."

She clutched the leather pouch to her breast, eyes wide.

"And I guess he sent someone to find me and retrieve them. But he didn't find them."

"You mean to say you buried valuable jewels in the stall?"

She nodded, face red. "It may have been an unbelievably stupid plan, but it worked." She was blinking back tears.

Jack's mind was buzzing with the things he heard, and bit by bit, as his mind chewed over each fact, a lot of things began making sense.

He had wondered about her fierce determination to be independent and face a challenge, from her dedication to Devil, to her insistence on roaming the dangerous plains without thought of safety. She had come to the schoolhouse at Grey Eagle with no experience, but with a dream, and had avoided any conversation about her past.

People came to Grey Eagle with their secrets and their pain. Some were avoiding the law in another part of this vast country, wanting a fresh start. He had learned to judge a man by what he did today more than by rumors of his past. Some came to start new because of loss. A generation back, families had been torn apart by the Civil War. More recently, folks had come on the search for open spaces, more land, more ability to make a good life for their kin away from the bustle of cities.

Cowboys arrived as ranches grew, looking for an honest day's work. Some people had come to escape memories of lost loved ones, preferring the adventure and danger of a new life to the constant reminders of their past. But Julie Bright had never seemed to fit any of those categories.

Nowhere in his past could he remember anybody confessing that they were running away from their money. Or from the indignity of a forced marriage. He looked at her, sitting in the dirt beside the stall, clutching her leather pouch, eyes brimmed with tears, and shook his head. This little lady was, as his stomach had told him from the first time he had seen her, one of a kind. And frustrating. And stubborn.

"OK, teacher lady," he said gently, squatting beside her and pulling her to her feet. "We're going inside, and we're going to make a plan."

"And I've got to get ready for tomorrow. Somehow, I've got to get ready for the children."

When he stood, his face was above the lantern light, and he was mighty glad. Because he couldn't help grinning at her determined little voice.

She walked with him, arm linked in his, glad for his giant strength, and with each step she took toward the schoolhouse, she felt her own strength and resolve return.

"More light," she said, rummaging around in a cupboard until she found an extra lantern. "I'm going to chase away these shadows and get this place cleaned up."

The light glowed and brightened the room, cheerful on the one hand, but clearly showing the results of the vandalism.

She was already hard at work, stacking, counting, shelving books.

He looked around at the mess around them, glad to see that except for a few broken slates, her supplies and belongings had merely been overturned and thrust out of the searcher's way. Still, it was more than she could do on her own, and he wasn't done talking yet. Not by a long shot.

"I'll start on the heavier furniture in the other room, and you can get organized about what goes where," he said.

She stopped mid step and turned to him.

"You don't have to stay. I can do this. But I'm glad you were here when I had to face it."

She shivered, then poked her chin up high in that stubborn little way she had when she wanted to prove herself. "I can do this."

He turned away so she would miss his grin again. No sense getting hit with a book.

"No problem, Miss Julie," he said with the utmost sincerity. "While I'm sure you could, I've got the knee-nippers of Grey Eagle to think about. Those little ones are going to arrive tomorrow to attend school, and I can't have this place looking like a major tornado went through. Or have a schoolteacher who looks like she was up all night. Two is faster than one."

He stepped across the room, righted her overturned desk with one quick heave, then headed for the door to her living quarters, like he didn't have a concern in the world.

"Oh," she said softly to his back, while her heart soared with relief and gladness that he was there.

Was that all it took to handle a woman? Jack put the bureau back against the wall in Julie's room, and slid the drawers back into place. He reattached a broken drawer pull with his pocketknife. Her clothing was scattered on the floor, but he dared not touch it. He stared at the scattered feminine slips of material and swallowed hard. How to handle a woman? No, he didn't have all the answers yet, he thought, as his body reacted to the thought of her.

The mattress had been overturned, and one post of the bed frame was loose, so he reassembled it best he could, and put the mattress back in place. Would it hold?

Without much thought, he turned around, and plopped himself onto the bed, waiting to hear the wood crack if it was going to give way.

What he heard instead was a giggle.

Julie stood in the doorway, hands on hips.

"Tired already, are you?"

He scrambled to his feet.

"I was testing the bed," he stammered.

She blushed to the roots of her hair.

"I see."

Eyes locked.

"To make sure it would hold."

"I see."

They stared at each other, until Julie looked away.

"Well, obviously it will hold." She bustled over and picked up the strewn bed sheets and quilt, and began making the bed. Automatically he stood on the other side, grabbing the sheets and tucking them in on his side. It was such a normal, everyday thing to do. And yet it wasn't. Thoughts were swimming around in his head, and his mouth felt dry.

When even the pillows were in place, he willed himself to breathe again.

She started picking up clothes. He couldn't deal with the clothes.

He cleared his throat, hoping the nervousness didn't show. "I'll do books," he grumbled, and moved as fast as his 6'6" frame would let him, back into the school-room.

They stacked, they sorted, they reshelved, and then they swept. It took almost all night. The sun was beginning to creep up over the horizon by the time that the schoolhouse was back in order. She sighed happily.

"Thank you, Sheriff. I feel like I have my life back."

He nodded, knowing what she meant about the school-house, but wondering, deep down inside, whether some part of her wanted that old life back. She had walked away from wealth and a life of comfort for this little rugged schoolhouse, in this little one horse town.

He looked at the pouch of jewels that sat on her now organized desk. Would the would-be thief come back again for them? They hadn't talked much as they had worked, but his sheriff's mind had been far from inactive as they had stacked and sorted.

"I want you to trust me with the jewels, Julie," he said firmly but softly. "I have a safe in the sheriff's office, and that will keep them safe. And keep you safe."

She swallowed, and nodded.

"And I want to have someone patrol out here, to be sure that there aren't any more episodes like this. The jewel thing, that all sounds like a real good reason for all this, but we can't be sure. If I had my way, I'd have you come stay in town . . ."

Violently she shook her head, and he went on with a grin, "But I know I don't have a snowball's chance of getting you to agree."

Her body relaxed.

"I want you to keep this somewhere safe. In case you need it." He reached behind his back, and pulled a pistol from his belt. "It's loaded."

She stared at the ugly and dangerous thing. "I could never use that, Jack."

"In case you need it. You really don't know what was behind this break in, Julie. And you are alone here at night, and alone with the children in the day."

She thought about the children, and nodded slowly, taking the weapon and putting it safely away on a shelf, behind her heavy books.

"But if anything else like this happens, Julie Bright, no matter what the cause, I'll do everything in my power to keep you safe and get you out of this schoolhouse, including firing you and sending you back east on the first stage that arrives. That understood?"

She wanted to sass him, but she knew he was right. She nodded, meeting his eyes.

"Thank you for understanding,"she said in a little voice. "And thanks for your help."

Morning light was spreading on the plains around them.

He put his hat on his head, and they walked to the porch. In a last gesture, he put out his arm, and pulled her close, wrapping her in a gentle embrace.

"Keep alert, Julie Bright. I am worried about you." He pressed his face into her hair, closing his eyes and breathing in the smell of her.

"Thank you, Jack. It will be all right. You will see." She pulled away and pressed the pouch of jewels into his hands. The brave and determined look was coming back into her face.

He tucked the jewels into his shirt.

He knew he could keep the jewels safe. He wished he had as much faith that he could keep Julie out of harm's way.

"Well, too bad, you'll just have to put up with it," said Jane a few days later. "We're your friends, we want to celebrate, and you can just go along with it. A twenty-fifth birthday is nothing to sneeze at, so you are going to have a party."

"All right," she conceded, knowing full well that she would not win this argument with her stubborn friend.

"Good," said Jane, rubbing her hands together. "Be here tomorrow at one in the afternoon, and make sure you act surprised."

Julie laughed. "Thanks for the warning. I'll practice acting thrilled."

Jane laughed and squeezed her arm. "I'm glad you're my friend, Julie Bright." Then she grew somber. "Are you sure you have to go back?"

Julie had shared her past with Jane, as she had with Jack, and with each telling, she found she had a stronger sense of self, and more determination to right her past. She was not going to run and hide anymore.

"I'll be on the Monday stage, Jane. It's time for me to face the life that I left behind, to stand up for myself."

There were tears in Jane's eyes.

"Grey Eagle will not be the same without you."

"And I will not be the same without Grey Eagle. But this must be done. I'm just grateful that Mrs. Newby has agreed to take over the schoolroom temporarily. Until a new teacher can arrive."

"Will I ever see you again?" Jane wrung her hands, and Julie's heart felt heavy.

"I don't know what I will find when I return home, or how long things will take. I will write when I know. But I know my heart will be here in Grey Eagle."

Jane nodded and didn't push. "We will celebrate your birthday in a big way before you go."

She watched Julie with misty eyes cross the street to make arrangements for her passage out of town on the Monday stagecoach.

As Julie got the details about the Monday stage, Jack walked into the office behind her, and listened to her inquire about a ticket to take her back east.

Not Julie Bright, the ornery bespeckled schoolteacher he had come to love, but Julietta Brightingham. Heiress and socialite.

He was trying to think of her in that light, trying to remember that she had a whole different life somewhere else, a whole different complicated history that did not include Grey Eagle and its inhabitants.

The one main inhabitant that he was concerned with was himself, of course. Because no matter what he tried to remember about Julie Bright, what he remembered most of all was the feel of her in his arms up in the secret pond, the glow of her smile, and her soft white blond hair (which he saw was neatly tucked up into her bonnet so only those who paid strict attention would notice that the wisps that peaked out were now blond and fair).

The sight of her standing at that ticket counter hit him like a board to the side of his head. He knew that sooner or later, she would have to return home to confront her uncle and face her old life. But he had been hoping beyond hope, that there would be time. He had been hoping that life in Grey Eagle could go on just as it was for a little bit longer, that he'd have time to deal with this tornado of emotion that threatened to set him spinning at any time.

But here she was. She would be gone. And the question looming now was when.

He came up behind her.

"Julie." She didn't jump.

She turned slowly, and he saw the sadness in her eyes.

"I'll be on the Monday stage. I shall go and face things while I know I have the courage to do it."

He nodded slowly. He would never ask her to stay. He would never risk the pain of her rejection, and understood that she had to go. But it was like a rattler lashing out, tearing up his insides.

"When your things are packed, I'll help you get your bags to town."

She nodded. It seemed like only yesterday when she had arrived on that first stage, book loaded bags weighing her down. So much of life had evolved.

"You need a ride to your surprise party tomorrow?" he asked.

She nodded. "Is there anyone in town that will be surprised at this party? Seems a little silly to keep calling it a surprise party!" she grinned.

"Makes the ladies in town happy to be surprising someone, I reckon."

"Well, since I am truly surprised that they want to do such a nice thing, I will simply be surprised on the spot."

"Good girl. No more trouble at the schoolhouse?"

"None at all. Since you've got my jewels locked up safe, I'm sure I'm of no interest to anyone."

"And the gun. You've got the gun."

She smiled, and his heart melted. "You know I'm not going to use that gun."

"You got a problem, you just shoot it off into the air. I'll hear it. Travel safely, Schoolteacher."

"And speaking of school teaching, I did speak to Mrs. Newby and she is planning to tutor you every Wednesday night at the schoolhouse. Between Marcus and Jeb and Mrs. Newby, you'll be reading Shakespeare yourself in no time at all."

He grinned sheepishly. "I see you're on to me. I'll catch up to the seven-year-old Morton twins any day now."

"See that you do," she said primly, but her mouth was trying to hide a grin. She tossed her head, and headed out of town.

*   *   *

Sheriff Jack White's mood did not improve with the dawning of the new day, nor did it show signs of brightness as Saturday morning wore on.

In fact, he was such a grump that both Marcus and Jeb, who had taken to hanging around the sheriff's office, were living dangerously by making jokes about his black humor behind his back.

"Enough, you two!" he bellowed at noon time, lifting his head from the copy of the *New York Times* newspaper that had arrived on the morning stage. It was his weekly challenge, as he slowly and belatedly learned to read, and he was determined to fight the battle of sounding out vowels and consonants, no matter how unsettled his mind was. But it was taking him even longer than ever to decipher even a paragraph.

Marcus ambled over, daring to near the growling lion in his den. He looked over his shoulder at the newspaper.

He let out a long low whistle. "Whew, sheriff. At the risk of getting something thrown at me, I think you are reading the wrong article."

He pointed to a column at the top of the opposite page. Jack's eyes followed. And frowned. At the top of the article, was a picture of a certain Miss Julietta Brightingham, and an inch high headline: MISSING HEIRESS OF THE BRIGHTINGHAM SHIPPING FORTUNE. While it didn't look like the Julie that they had come to know, even with her newly displayed blond hair, he recognized her. In the formal pose, with no glasses on her nose, wearing an elegant dress, hair piled high on her head,

and neck adorned with jewels, there was still no mistaking that it was Julie. Julietta. In her New York world. He felt a stab in his heart at the thought.

"Read it," he grumbled, not willing to attempt tackling the whole article with his barely basic skills.

Society, as well as the world of business, is ticking down the days until March 24th, which will mark the twenty-fifth birthday of missing heiress Julietta Brightinghan, only daughter of the deceased shipping magnate James Brightingham.

Shortly after his demise, Miss Brightingham disappeared, leaving no trace, to the chagrin of her uncle, Edward Brightingham, who, as sole trustee to the Brightingham fortune, has been diligently searching for her.

"The search has been exhaustive," the sober faced trustee stated at a recent press conference. "At this point, it is sadly assumed that Miss Julietta met with some unfortunate accident and is no longer alive. For the good of Brightingham Shipping and its employess, it is now necessary to pursue legal remedies to have my niece declared officially dead."

These comments were recorded two weeks ago, as the twenty-fifth birthday of the missing heiress looms on the horizon. According to James Brightingham's last will and testament, the entire holdings have been kept in a trust, with Edward Brightingham as trustee, which has allowed the company to operate while the search for the heiress was underway. On her twenty-fifth birthday, as the trust is legally dissolved, as

stated in her father's will, the estate would have reverted to Miss Brightingham in her own right.

If there was proof of her death before the trust was dissolved, or with the legal declaration of her death, the estate will revert to Julietta's uncle, as her only living relative.

"We had hoped that we would have found the dear girl by this time, or have received proof of my niece's demise, if that is the sad case. But we have the assurance that the courts will move quickly on this matter, so that the employees and structure of Brightingham Shipping will not suffer in the interim," stated Edward Brightingham.

Jack growled, picked up the paper, and crumpled it into a ball.

"I guess this is why she's heading home," said Marcus thoughtfully. "If she doesn't claim her fortune, she'll lose the chance. You can't blame her for that, Jack."

Jack ran his hand through his hair, and hated the fact that his hand was shaking.

"I don't blame her for any of it, and that's the truth."

His throat felt tight. "It was too much to handle, and she ran away. And now she's going back. That's the end of it."

No matter that his heart felt like it had been pierced by an arrowhead. He pushed away the pain and stomped over to his desk.

"The end of it for us here in Grey Eagle," Marcus said absent-mindedly, staring at the ceiling. "But the beginning of a new stage in New York, for sure. I mean, can

you imagine how shocked they are going to be when Julie just waltzes in again?"

Jack narrowed his eyes.

"What do you mean?"

"Well, they say how hard they looked. I guess they are sure she is dead, and yet, here she is, fine and dandy the whole time. And the uncle thinks he is going to inherit her fortune. But he's not. Hey, it's like some kind of drama out of Shakespeare, you know?"

Jacks thoughts started turning. There was a lot to what Marcus was saying. A little uncomfortable feeling started nagging him, like a burr under a horse blanket. How exactly ecstatic was the uncle going to be to see her when it meant that his inheritance was gone? How hard did he really look for his missing niece, with the idea of turning a fortune over to her when he found her? What if the uncle had been searching for her, not, as Julie had feared, to bring her back, but to make sure she did *not* come back?

He sure didn't like the path his thoughts were taking, but he let the thoughts flow because truth to tell, if she died before her twenty-fifth birthday, and it was proven, it would have been easy and automatic for him. He'd inherit without a single question asked.

Was he somehow responsible for the things that had happened to Julie? He didn't like the thought. Today was her birthday party. Tuesday was her birthday. Monday, the day before her birthday, she would leave on the stage. And he, he decided suddenly, would be going at least part way with her, to get her safely to the train in Helena. He absolutely hated the fact that she was going to return to New York and her heritage there. But if that was what she needed to do, he was going to make darn sure that she got there safe and sound. There would be no attacks on Julie Bright while there was a breath left in his body.

Chapter Nineteen

The hotel was packed with well wishers for Julie's un-surprise party. A fiddler stood on a temporarily erected dais in the corner of the dining room, where tables had been moved into position along the wall to make room for dancing.

The roar of greeting that arose when she entered had her heart pounding, and her throat tight. How she had come to love this town in the past year!

The punch was flowing, feet were stomping, and presents overflowed a table by the door. A handmade quilt from the town's ladies graced the top of the pile.

The mood was bittersweet. After the miraculous rescue of Lilly from the fire, the wariness of the native children in the schoolhouse had lessened to the point that it was almost unnoticeable, and the sense of well being in the town had returned. And now their young school-teacher was leaving. As the word had spread through the ranches and streets of town, that Julie Bright was getting back on the stage and returning to New York City, people had objected.

"Make her stay!"

"How can she leave us now?"

Julie had asked herself that same question, hating in her heart to leave the new world she had found. Yet, she knew she must. She had to face her past and bring it to closure. She had to face her cruel uncle, and make sure that he never had the power to inflict such harm again. She, who had so willingly stood up for others, now had to have the courage to stand up for herself.

Glancing at the doorway, she saw that Jack had arrived at the party. He, she knew with a heavy heart, was the one person who had *not* asked her to stay. He was the one person who didn't seem to care one way or another about who was teaching in his schoolhouse, as long as Grey Eagle had a teacher. She blinked away unwelcome tears.

They came from two different worlds. Since he had learned of her not-so-humble beginnings, his whole demeanor had changed. He didn't seem to think that all people could be accepted for who and what they were. He had accepted the Blackfoot boys. But he could not accept Julietta Brightingham, heiress. He did not seem to believe that she belonged in Grey Eagle.

Julietta straightened her hair with a tired hand. She had been up late packing, and making sure the schoolhouse was in good order for its new teacher. Perhaps Sheriff Jack White was correct. Perhaps people from different worlds were too different to mix. When Jane looked across the room at her with an expectant smile,

Julie pushed the melancholy thoughts away. She would appreciate her dear friend Jane, and the efforts she had put into the birthday party.

As the fiddle music filled the air, she turned to face the person who had tapped her on the shoulder. Hank, the cowboy from the Circle B Ranch, stood there, offering her his hand.

"Let's dance, birthday lady. Not good to waste a lively tune like this one." His smile was charming though it did not reach his eyes.

Julie did not notice.

"Certainly," she said with all the politeness she could muster. "Let's dance."

He smiled as he made his way through the crowd to the dance floor, leading her smoothly to an open spot. "Let's dance like there's no tomorrow."

Jack watched the tall cowboy work his charms on Julie Bright. Julietta Brightingham. The name stuck in his throat. Didn't that cowboy see that he didn't belong with her one little whit? Didn't anyone see the ludicrousness of the whole situation? His heart did a jump in his chest as he watched the man's big hand caress her back on the dance floor. He was holding her too close.

She was his, blast it, he wanted to scream. But he didn't. He had no right. He was just a dumb ignorant cowboy, and Julietta Brightingham deserved much better. She may not know it or believe it, but she did. And his one and only job in the world would be to make sure that she lived long enough to find that out. He had spent the better part of the day making plans with his deputy Marcus to maintain order for the next few days.

The independent little schoolmarm was going to have a fit when she found out he was accompanying the stage all the way to the train line, to make sure she was safely on her way. But she couldn't stop him. She was also going to have a fit when he told her about the article that he and Marcus had deciphered, his theory about her uncle's nefarious plans. He was learning to read, and that fact might save Julie Bright's life. Who would have thought it?

He hadn't wanted to upset her before her party, and there was not much to be gained by her knowing, as long as he assured her that she was safe. He'd see her home when the party was over, and he'd spend the night on the porch, without telling her, to keep her from harm.

He sighed, watching her flit across the floor. A new song was playing, and the dark cowboy still held her in his arms. Jack shook his head in disgust.

She was safe enough amidst a party in the Grey Eagle Hotel. He didn't have to stay and watch as his heart was ripped from his chest. He'd come back when it was done. He turned on his boot heel, bounded out the door of the hotel, and across the street to his office.

He got half way there, before his temper got the best of him. Was he going to walk away and let some two bit cowboy with snake eyes and a fancy horse take away the one woman who had set his head to spinning? Just what kind of a man was he, anyway? He made a sound that was mighty close to a growl, turned around, and marched back into the party.

"Excuse me," he said to the cowboy through thin lips,

as he tapped him on the shoulder, barely in control. "I have business with Miss Bright. I'll take over this dance."

Hank frowned angrily, but had no choice but to let go of Julie. She slipped into Jack's arms.

"Sheriff!" she said softly, not even able to hide her delight. His stomach tightened, and his collar felt tight. "You're finally dancing with me!"

The brown eyes twinkled up at him, and instantly, all felt right in the world.

"Yep, I guess I finally am."

"I'm very, very glad. I've been waiting for you."

His heart soared.

The music played, one song ended and another began, this one slow and melodious. They continued dancing. She was pressed close to him, he could feel the warmth of her body, the way she just fit against him, despite her small size.

The world around them seemed to melt away as they swayed gently to the music. They were totally unaware that the crowd had parted, slowly, smiling, encircling them, watching the magic of the dance.

He nuzzled the top of her hair, mesmerized by the softness, the gentle smell of violets. She lifted her head to him then, and without of thought of what he was doing, or who was watching, he bent and touched his lips to hers. She sighed happily.

When the applause began, they were startled back to reality with a jolt. Pulling apart, and looking around, the inhabitants of Grey Eagle were surrounding them, smiling and laughing.

"It's about time!" Harvey yelled, as the crowd chuckled.

Jack and Julie looked sheepishly at each other and then joined in the laughter.

She was quiet all the way home, and aside from clearing his throat a time or two, and not knowing exactly what to say, so was he. The night was clear and pretty, stars twinking in the sky above. He eyed the schoolhouse as they approached it. Were his eyes and ears playing tricks on him? In the quiet of the night, he could swear he heard the sound of a horse pounding away from the schoolhouse, thought he saw a flash of motion on the almost pitch black horizon. Was he just looking for trouble? Most probably. He saw her to the door, opening the schoolhouse and turning on a lantern before leaving her, ignoring her protests. He was glad to see that nothing was disturbed. He felt his lawman's nerves on edge, vigilant, sensing danger, even though there was no evidence in sight.

"Good night, Jack," she said softly, "It was the best party of my life."

"Good night, Julietta," he said, taking off his hat, and taking her in his arms. She sighed as his mouth came down upon hers, not so soft as the last time. She met him, on tiptoe, feeling the demand of his lips, the passion in his heart. His arms held her tightly, possessively, and she kissed him right back.

"I wish you didn't have to go," he said as the kiss ended.

"I must. Good night, Jack." She touched his face softly.

He heard the door latch as she went in, and then he quietly took the saddle from his horse, using it as a pillow, as he had many times out on the range, and lowered his 6'6" frame to the porch to keep watch until dawn.

Out on the prairie, a loan rider watched him settle for the night on the porch from a distance. He cursed under his breath. Who would have thought that the oversized and ignorant sheriff would take her home and act so gallantly and protectively? He slapped the reins to his horse, and took off into the night. He would make a new plan.

The stagecoach was scheduled to come through Grey Eagle at 10 A.M. Jack was up at first light, returning to town to get his horse packed and ready for the trip. He intended to ride right along next to the stagecoach as it crossed the open prairie, until it reached the train station at Helena, a major stop on the rail line. His office settled, he was just about ready to lock up and cross the street to the hotel for breakfast when a buckboard wagon pulled up in front, and a harried rancher rushed to his door.

"We've had thieves, Sheriff," the man cried. "My prize bull is gone from the barn. You gotta come out to our place and see what you make of it."

Jack glanced at the clock. Bill Wheeler was understandably distraught, and the Wheeler spread was right on the outskirts of town, and he still had an hour to kill before the stage arrived. It was his job to check out their losses, gather some information, and bring it back to Marcus to follow up on in his absence. This was his town, and he was responsible to make sure all of its inhabitants were safe.

"Marcus," he called into his office. "Go to the schoolhouse and fetch Julie Bright for the stage. I've got to ride out to the Wheelers, but I'll be right back."

He stuck his hat on his head.

"Let's go, Murphy," he said, resignedly, and threw a leg over his horse.

Julie arrived at the hotel at the same time that the stagecoach arrived. Her bags were not heavy on this trip, as she had left her books behind for the schoolhouse. Marcus loaded her things easily, tipping his hat good-bye as she climbed aboard. She was the only passenger on this leg of the trip. The sheriff wasn't back yet, but he knew he'd be true to his word and catch up to the slow moving stage in no time, or send a message for someone else to accompany her.

No sign of the sheriff, Julie noticed with an aching sadness. He had not even cared enough to come and say good-bye. The stage began to move, then stopped. The door of the coach opened to admit one more passenger. Julie looked up in surprise. It was Hank from the Circle B Ranch.

"Why Miss Bright!" he exclaimed in delight. "You are traveling today?"

Julie's stomach lurched, but she pushed the feeling away. Leaving this town was taking its toll. Her feelings were all jumbled up.

"Yes," she said civilly. What was it about this man that made her feel so defensive? "And you Mr. Smith?"

"I'm heading back east myself. I'm not made for this life, so it seems. Going back to civilization." He settled into the seat across from her.

The stagecoach lurched forward again.

"A boyfriend back home?"

Not quite, she thought. A mean and miserly uncle that she was going to learn how to deal with.

"Family business." She kept her answers short, and was surprised at her lack of neighborliness. But she simply didn't feel like discussing things.

When the attempts at pleasant conversation didn't succeed, the cowboy finally leaned his head back on the seat, pulled his hat over his eyes, and went to sleep.

The stagecoach rumbled out of town.

At the Wheeler ranch, Sheriff Jack White had taken down all the pertinent information, had assured the ranchers that the loss was a shame, and had vowed to do all he could to catch the culprit who had stolen the prize bull. Not that he thought he'd have any success at that feat. Cattle poaching was a high crime in these parts, at least when the thieves could be apprehended, but that was a rare event. Brands were altered, deals were made, and life went on. It was a sad but true situation in these parts of Montana.

When he was parting from the unhappy ranchers, ready to mount his horse, and congratulating himself that he would be back in town for the stagecoach departure with time to spare, the trouble began.

The corral fence, evidently not secured when they had left the barn, had been pushed open by a large brown cow, her udders full and uncomfortable. In the morning excitement, the milking hadn't been finished. Bad enough that she had escaped the fencing, but two stout pigs grunted at the open gate and followed her to freedom.

"Get them, get them," a frantic Mrs. Wheeler screeched from the farm house door, shaking a towel in her one hand, and hiking up her skirts with another as she charged after the errant animals.

With a deep sigh, Jack had dismounted his horse, grabbed his lasso, and helped the overwrought ranchers to reclaim their livestock. It took only a few minutes to get them safely back into the corral, but a few minutes more before he had calmed the Wheelers, remounted his horse and headed back to town, grumbling under his breath all the way.

He knew he had a problem when he hit the end of Main Street, and did not see the back of the stagecoach parked at the hotel door.

"Stage been through yet?" he hollered to Marcus, who had just arrived and was opening the office door.

"Left town a few minutes ago, Sheriff," he called over his shoulder. "Was surprised you weren't here to chaperone, like you said you would. But I figured you had arranged for the cowboy to keep an eye on her in your place."

"The cowboy?" Jack lifted the hat from his head, and mopped his brow with his shirt sleeve. Suddenly, he was sweating, despite the early hour of the day. His muscles were tense. "What cowboy?"

"The tall dark-haired young one who's been buzzing around her. The new cowpoke from out on the Circle B." Marcus looked at the sheriff curiously, noticing the sudden awareness in his eyes. "Oh, gawd," drawled the young man as he surveyed his angry boss. "This ain't a good thing?"

"Get your horse and follow me," barked the sheriff. "And bring a gun. They can't be far along in that old stagecoach."

He flicked the reins, and his horse spun around, hooves hitting the dry dirt of the street and thundering out of town.

The road that the stagecoach would follow was a worn path over the prairie for a short while, a common road-way out of town. But after a short distance, the signs of the road were no longer evident. At a point, wagons and horses coming and going from Grey Eagle would cut out over the prairie to whatever direction was the closest to their home, as the crow flies. Aside from a rocky ridge with scrub trees in the far distance, the vista spread out bare and uninhabited. With the prairie winds moving dirt around, and the lack of traffic to renew the trail, the stage would simply aim itself into the eastern sky, and head for its destination in the next distant town, about three hours away.

The stagecoach wasn't the fastest of vehicles, with its high boxed cabin, and its wheels made for durability as well as comfort for the patrons within. The prairie was rocky and dry at this time of year, and a smooth ride was much more likely when the horses were taken care of, and the state of the roadway was taken into consideration.

So Jack was both surprised and apprehensive when he could see no sign of the stagecoach in the distance as his horse pounded up the ground across the prairie. On this clear day, visibility was a few miles, plus or minus some distance. As he thundered across the dusty prairie, he was well aware that there should have been a noticible cloud of dust marking the progress of the stagecoach. And there was none.

Jack felt the apprehension building. The stage could not have been too far ahead. The driver had only a short

head start. Where was the stage? Where was Julie Bright?

He touched his heels to the horse's side to increase the speed, heading due east into the newly risen sun. Shading his eyes from the bright light, he thought he saw something on the trail ahead. He slowed. As he approached the spot he had kept in his sight, the dread that had begun like a hot coal in his belly roared to an inferno. Ahead of him, on the path, something or someone was lying. Still and silent, the shape of a body came into his sight.

He galloped to it, flinging himself off the high horse before it even slowed. He hit the ground in a run, reaching the figure on the ground and gently turning it over.

He knew it was not her before he even saw the face. The victim was too large, too male. The face was familiar to him. The victim was the gray-haired stage driver, Pete. He was out cold, hands tied behind him.

With a banging heart, he turned the man over and tried to revive him. He fetched the canteen that hung from his saddle, and poured it on the man's brow. Slowly, Pete moved a little, his eyes began to flutter, and then to open. He looked up into the sheriff's face with desperate sadness.

"It was the young poke," his rough voice rasped. "He bought himself a ticket, and as soon as we was out of town, he had me pull over, like there was an emergency, and then he conked me. I went down like a stone."

He raised a dusty hand and brushed it over his face.

"I'm sorry, Sheriff. The stagecoach. It's gone . . ."

"What about the girl? What about Julie Bright?"

His eyes swept the horizon, looking for a glimpse of

the missing vehicle. All was still on the horizon in front of him.

"She was in the coach when he knocked me out. I heard her screaming and making a racket. He must have tied her up before he stopped the stage. Oh, I could kick myself." The man's voice was getting more raspy, and he laid back down on the hard packed earth.

He wanted to shake the old man for letting Julie fall into danger, but he knew it would do no good. If it was anyone's fault, it was his own. He knew he should have been accompanying that stage until she got to civilization. It was his fault. The thought echoed like thunder in his brain.

"Go, Jack," whispered the old man. "Go find her."

Jack looked at the injured man, lying prone on the ground in the middle of nowhere. He needed help. Behind him, he heard the sound of an approaching horse, and turned to find Marcus bearing down on him at full speed.

"Take this fellow back to the doc," he growled, relieved at seeing the deputy. "And get a search party up. The stage is missing."

Marcus was out of the saddle in a split second. He lifted the wiry stagecoach driver up onto his horse, before climbing back up behind him. "I've got this guy, Jack. You go get him. He can't have gone far in that contraption, Jack. It's too slow."

Jack nodded, eyes scanning the horizon. Off to the north, a copse of trees survived on the plain. The area around them was dotted with large boulders. "I'll check it out, I'll find her," he said, pulling his hat down over his eyes.

"Jack," called Marcus, "You'll find her. Here. Take this with you."

He whipped the extra gun out of his holster, and tossed it lightly through the air. Jack caught it easily.

"Thanks."

Giving Murphy a kick that showed he wanted speed, they spun and took off across the prairie. The tall horse rose to the occasion, and thundered toward the trees.

His heart hammered to the beat of the hooves. He scanned the horizon. He would find her. His eyes narrowed. Since the stagecoach had so quickly disappeared, it could not have gone far. The rock filled copse of trees was the only option.

It didn't take long to reach the spot. It didn't take long to find the stagecoach. He approached it with a feeling of dread, not knowing what he would find inside. What had happened to Julie? But it was empty, and abandoned secretly behind a large boulder, its horses calmly chewing grass. On the ground, he could see signs of horse prints. He'd had a horse waiting here. One horse.

It had been a well timed plan. The horse waiting, the abduction taking place at a particular spot, near the trees. Had he known that the sheriff had planned to ride alongside the stage? Had the theft at the Wheeler ranch been part of the plan to distract him and make the way clear? And how long would he keep Julie alive?

Jack shook his head in disgust. Some sheriff he was, getting outsmarted by a two bit cowpoke. As much as he wanted to throttle himself for his stupidity, he pushed the thought aside. He had a job to do.

He scoured the ground, looking for signs of the horse's direction. Hank Smith could have taken off in any direction, and would want to avoid the direct and obvious road, knowing that he would be pursued. On a fast horse, he could have covered some miles in no time. Jack got close to the ground, looking for signs of disturbance, and he finally found what he needed. Heading south east, he found two rocks that had been hit by a horse's metal shoe, the fresh scrape marks like a beacon showing the horse's recent passing. He marked the spot quickly with rocks, showing the direction he was going. When Marcus arrived with his posse, they would waste no time following.

He breathed a sigh of hope. He would catch him. He would save her. If it was the last thing he ever did. He put his heels to Murphy's strong flank. The chase was on.

Chapter Twenty

Julie Bright had experienced a myriad of emotions since stepping onto the stage for the first lap in her long trip back to New York. She felt determination. She felt strong and able to face her uncle and to confront him about his motives and his actions. She had left New York as a scared but willful child, and she was returning as an adult. Somewhere in the Montana air, between teaching big eyed children the value of reading, and freely flying over the prairie on Devil's proud back, she had grown up. She didn't know what she would find when she returned to New York, but she knew that whatever it was, she was ready to handle it.

But with each turn of the stagecoach wheels, she felt a wave of sadness. Grey Eagle was disappearing behind her, becoming like a little dot on the horizon, disappearing like an illusion in her mind. But it hadn't been an illusion. It had been real. It had been the most real time of her life, a time filled with wonder, and excitement, and challenge, and love.

She sighed, thinking of the big tall sheriff, his enormous hat shading his eyes, his arrogant cowboy's stance and bossy ways hiding the insecurities that she had come to love as much as his assets. Each turn of the coach wheel was taking her away from him, too, and out of his world of Grey Eagle. She felt like her heart was being squeezed from the pain. Because no matter what she felt for him, she couldn't make him reciprocate the feelings.

She could feel that he was attracted to her, and in his own shy way, he had made that known. But there had been a wall between them, something that stood in the way that was more formidable that the majestic Rockies that rose to the west.

If he had asked her to stay? What would she have done? It was a mute point because he had not asked her that. In fact, he had been more in favor in her leaving. He had made that clear. He had been in favor of her leaving since that first day she had stepped off the stagecoach in Grey Eagle, and it seemed his feelings hadn't changed by the day she had stepped back onto that coach. A blanket of sadness cloaked her. She looked at the sleeping cowboy on the bench across from her, grateful for his slumber, his hat tilted forward over his eyes. She was not in the mood for polite conversation.

Her feelings were showing in her tear filled eyes, and she blinked to clear them. No sense crying over unrequited love. In all the literature she had read, she knew that she was certainly not the first woman to feel this way. The aching would go away. The feelings would pass. They had to. But she couldn't stop the unwilling tears, so she closed her eyes, put her head back on the seat, and prayed for the respite of sleep as the stage rhythmically rolled over the prairie and into the eastern rising sun.

He watched her from under the brim of his hat. Such a pretty little woman. And so rich. The thought galled him. How much better it would have been to have won her heart, and then her fortune. But she was a strong minded little thing, and not easily impressed. And time was short.

His plan was good, and her dozing eyes would make his job easier. He watched out the window of the stage-coach for the view that would initiate action.

The small row of trees came into view on the far left. It was time. Making no sudden moves, he pulled the thin rope out of his pocket. She was a little thing, but spry and strong. He would have to overcome her first. Slowly he raised himself from the seat, crossing to her left. In one fluid motion, he turned her with his left hand, thrusting his arm under her throat. With his right hand, he pressed on the pulse point in the side of her neck.

Instantly, she came to life, her feet flailing, her hands reaching up to grab at his forearm. She let out a scream, as he pressed harder. She struggled valiantly, but couldn't hold out against his strength. Finally incapacitated by his pressure on her neck, she slumped listlessly in his arms.

"You calling, Miss Bright?" hollered the coach driver, having heard a muffled voice.

Hank cursed angrily. He hadn't thought she'd be so

noisy. Quickly, he took the rope and tied her hands securely behind her back. As an afterthought, he pulled his kerchief out of his pocket and tied it around her mouth. She would not be out long, and he had a feeling that this little she cat was going to make quite a racket when she came to. And he still had the coach driver to deal with.

"Miss Bright?" the driver called again when she didn't answer.

The coach began slowing.

He laid Julie's prone body on the seat. And got himself ready.

The coach stopped, and within seconds, the door opened.

"I heered you, Miss Bright. Are you all right?"

Hank was partly out of his seat, hovering over her. "Help me, driver, she seems to have had a spell and has taken a faint."

The driver climbed in. "Not like her," he began, puzzlement on his face. He didn't get to finish his sentence. In the closed compartment, he didn't stand a chance. A gun butt came down hard on his head, and he dropped like a sack of potatoes.

He pushed the old man out of the coach and onto the ground. He bound his hands the same as he had Julie's. It wouldn't keep him long, but it would keep him. If he had time, he would have killed the man and gotten rid of the body, and so of any chance of later being identified. But he didn't have the time. It would be enough to have the body of Julie Bright disappear from the world. He would have to limit himself to that. He climbed up to the top of the stagecoach and picked up the reins. "Let's go," he barked and the team took off. Roughly, he steered them off the rough stage path and headed for the trees. His plan was working like a charm so far, and he had miles to go before he would feel like he had escaped the sheriff, and on his way to collecting a mighty large reward.

He thought of the unconscious body of the little schoolteacher in the stagecoach under him. What a waste, such a tidy little morsel. He was not going to enjoy killing her, that was for sure. But perhaps she would see her way to succumb to his charms before he had to do that. Willingly or not. He laughed viciously at the thought. And that, he would enjoy.

He brought the coach to a steady stop in the trees, behind the largest boulder. It wouldn't be hidden long, he knew. But it would give him time. Precious time. His horse stood waiting. He heaved the listless body of the schoolteacher across the saddle, and leapt up onto his horse. Without a backward glance, he headed off into the south east, off the beaten path, making a straight line toward Helena, two days trip away. He had ever intention of avoiding any pokey little cow town in this part of Montana, where the sheriff was sure to look. When he was done with this cute little package, he would dispose of her in a place that no one would ever look, and easily make his way back east to his life and his reward. His mouth watered at the thought. He kicked his horse hard, and let the dust fly.

It was the worse dream she had ever had. Her body felt like a punching bag, aching, jostled, and unconnected.

Wake up, she willed herself. *Escape the dream.*

With great determination, Julie attempted to open her eyes. The light registered on her brain, taking away the darkness. But it did not take away any of the pain. She was still aching and hurting. In fact, she felt worse. Instead of the foggy discomfort, she felt each searing jolt. Where was she, and what had happened to her?

Her wrists stung, anchored securely behind her back. Her shoulders ached. As her eyes focused, she could see the rocky prairie rushing by. She was lying face down over a horse, and he was moving fast. Her stomach felt each step of his gallop, as she bounced with his gait. She had worn the pouch that contained her mother's jewels around her waist, beneath her skirt, and each bounce made them dig into her stomach. She could feel the horse's muscles flexing beneath her cheek, smell his pungent sweat, feel the wetness on his cheek. This horse had been running for a long time.

Her head ached with blinding intensity, and her feet were numb from her uncomfortable position. She repressed the moan that fought to escape her lips. She had to think. She had to clear her memory, her senses, and make sense of what was going on.

With barely any motion, she moved her head from its position facing the front of the horse to the back, which gave her a different field of vision. She saw a black clad leg, and a scuffed brown tooled boot. Her memory registered. She had seen those boots before. On the sleeping cowboy in the stagecoach across from her. Her memory snapped into place. Him suddenly moving, his hand on her shoulder, her neck. And then darkness.

Rage boiled within her. What was going on here? What had happened to the stagecoach, the driver? How much time had passed? What was she going to do?

Think, Julie, think, she admonished herself.

Aside from the muscle soreness from bouncing on the saddle, she could tell that her stomach was empty and she was hungry. That meant that hours had passed since her breakfast at the beginning of the morning. She moved her head again, trying to get the position of the sun. It was mid way in the sky, slightly behind the horse. Was it rising or setting? What direction were they moving? She had no idea yet. She closed her eyes, and tried to organize her thoughts.

She longed to move her limbs, the stretch, to change position. But she dared not. Instinctively, she felt that being still was her best survival technique until she had a plan. Until she had figured out what was going on. She willed herself to deny the pain.

An hour passed, and she could feel the horse's fatigue under her. Sooner or later, he was going to have to rest the horse. She glimpsed at the sun in the sky. It was lower than before. It was afternoon, and so the sun was setting in the west. This meant they were moving in a south east direction, and that they had been riding for miles.

A feeling of hopelessness seeped through her, bringing every strain, every ache in her body to its full intensity. Would she die out here, miles from her old life, miles from her new life? And would anyone care? Back in New York, where the world believed her missing already, would anyone look for her? In Grey Eagle, where the inhabitants had all said good-bye to her and wished her well, they would have returned to their normal lives, assuming she had gone on to hers.

The loneliness echoed deep inside of her. A blanket of

fear brought her spirits to a darker and darker place with each hoof beat on the ground beneath her. Was she going to die here?

Julie had heard it said that your life passes before your eyes before death. What images were reverberating in her panicked, terrorized mind? She closed her eyes. She saw her schoolroom, she saw Devil's dark proud eyes as he tossed his head.

But most of all, and most clearly of all, she saw a tall and strong cowboy in a big hat, and with deep troubled eyes staring into hers. She saw Sheriff Jack White. That was her life. *He* was her life. And she was galloping away from him, across the prairie to a certain death, without ever having told him so, without even realizing the depth of her own feelings.

Her mind grappled with the fact, wrapped itself around the thought. She had undone business in New York, but suddenly that paled in comparison. She had undone business in Grey Eagle, and it was about facing feelings, and meeting that man head on. And she was going to stay alive, no matter what it took, in order to do that.

The darkness that had trapped her in hopelessness receded just a little bit. She was still alive, and there had to be a reason for that. She was strong, even if she was at a severe disadvantage. But she would have a chance to change the odds. And when that chance appeared, she would take it, no matter what the cost. She began breathing deeply forcing the oxygen into her exhausted body, tensing her ankles, slowly flexing her feet and her fingers to bring back the circulation and feeling. When she got a chance, she would be ready.

Jack's face was lodged in her mind, and she kept the vision crisp and clear. She would not die.

The sweat dripped down Jack's face, as well as down the back of his shirt, as the sun beat down on him. Murphy's gait didn't change as he sat low in the saddle, eyes constantly scanning the horizon. He had been riding for hours. Occasionally taunted by a distant cloud of dust far ahead, which may or may not have been stirred up by an escaping horse, or spurred on by the sight of a newly dislodged rock, or indentation in the hard prairie soil, Jack pushed himself forward with nothing but his heart and his keen eye to lead him.

Would he ever find Julie Bright? As the minutes ticked on into hours, and the miles added up, the odds of his success diminished to about nothing. And still he kept on. Using the logic that had built him a life, despite his lack of schooling, he knew that Hank Smith had to be heading to a town that was on the train line. He might be aiming for the anonymity of a large stop like Helena, or he could stop at one of the small spur stops on the way. But he'd need a train stop, because he'd been heading back east to New York to get whatever reward or pay had been offered for his diabolical services. And he'd be in a hurry to escape the wrath he knew would be following him.

And when Hank Smith got on that train, Jack knew that Julie Bright would not be with him. No, if he had figured the situation right, and he had every reason to believe that he had, Julie Bright's death would be his ticket to get his payoff. And Jack would use up every breath in his body to prevent that death from happening.

If time had not been an issue, he would have high tailed it to a town with a telegraph office, and would have send a message to every train stop along the way. It would be easy to prevent the monster from achieving his final goal. But that was not the goal Jack was worried about. He wanted Julie, his Julie, safe and sound.

He wiped the sweat from his eyes on his sleeve, and prayed hard to the God that he had not even believed truly existed. He kept moving forward, following his instincts, and trying to keep his pounding heart from exploding right out of his chest.

It was nearly dusk when Julie felt the horse slow its gait. She raised her head, and saw they were approaching a raised rocky area, dotted with scrub pines, and some dense underbrush. From her limited field of vision, she could see no sign of habitation. They were far from any civilization. As much as she had hated the jostling, humiliating ride trussed up and slung over the horse all day, she had been safe. But now? If they stopped? She had no clear understanding of what Hank Smith was up to, and what her part was in it, but she clearly knew that she was in great danger.

She had hoped all day that a miracle would occur, and that Jack White would find her missing and rescue her. But she knew what a silly dream that was. No, if she was going to be saved, she was going to have to safe herself.

The horse came to a stop in the middle of a group of pine trees. Hank climbed off the hot and tired horse with a groan. He reached for her body, and she kept herself limp. He took her like a sack of potatoes and placed her on the ground. Her face lay against the firm Montana prairie, she smelled the rich scent of it, and felt the warmth that had been absorbed by the long day sun.

"Where am I? What has happened?" she said softly, gathering her courage to face whatever it was that was going to happen. It was time to admit to being awake. It was time to find out whatever she could about what was going on.

"Ah, the schoolteacher awakens," drawled Hank, as he loosened the girth on the horse. He lifted two saddlebags from the mount, and threw them to the ground.

With her hands together in front of her, and her ankles securely tied together, she struggled to sit up. "Hank?" she said shaking her head, trying to get her bearings. Dizziness enveloped her as she changed position.

Hank stared at her for a minute, then spoke. "You are a cute little piece. It's a shame you didn't react to my charms, teacher lady. Though I'm sure it's better this way."

"What's better? What way?"

"Don't play coy with me, Julietta Brightingham. I knew who you were before I even knew where you were. I'm working for your uncle."

"Uncle Edward? He sent you to retrieve me? This is how he wants you to bring me back?" It didn't make sense to her.

And then, horribly, it did.

"Bring you back? Not on your life. He doesn't want you back. He wants you dead. He needs you dead. By the end of today. Before your official birthday tomorrow."

The thought stung her. For all she knew about her uncle, she did not want to believe this.

"But why? Why?" Her remorse was real.

"For the money, of course. For the inheritance. If you

die before your twenty-fifth birthday, he becomes the heir, not the trustee of the estate."

She was speechless for several seconds. And then her anger snapped.

"And you will be rewarded? You have planned this whole thing with my lily livered uncle? To be rewarded?" Her throat was dry, as so many things began to make sense.

"Grandly. Though not as grandly as I would have if you had succumbed to marrying me."

"Even if I had been tempted, which I surely was not."

He glared at her. "You're mighty feisty for someone in your position. If I had wanted you, you would have been mine."

"But my uncle would never have approved that." Her mind was working fast.

"Like that would have mattered. After tomorrow, he's got nothing to say about it, as long as you're still alive. It all reverts to you. The trust is dissolved."

"So I'd be rich, in my own right." She shook her head in disgust. "And he would kill to prevent it."

He sneered, showing white teeth, his usually handsome visage lit with evil. "If you were still alive tomorrow. Which you won't be. As soon as I'm done with you."

A chill went down her spine. Could she bribe him? Appeal to his better side? Escape? The list of options was short and unlikely. Julie Bright felt the wave of loneliness and hopelessness seep into her bones, making her feel every ache and pain in her stressed out body. Her wrists burned where the ropes cut into her skin. She had a stiff neck, a headache, and every muscle and joint felt like it had been stretched and beaten.

The future looked bleak, but she was still alive. For some strange reason, he had not killed her yet. She would hang onto that thought, and keep praying for a way out.

He left her trussed up like an errant calf while he gather sticks and dead brush to start a fire. From a saddlebag, he brought out some food, and she could smell it cooking over the small fire. Her stomach growled with hunger. There was a small stream nearby, and he filled his canteen with water. The very sound of the water made her dry lips pucker. He kept looking back at her, as if trying to make a decision.

"I have to . . . I have to relieve myself," she said finally, unable to ignore her needs any longer. He stared at her for a minute, as if evaluating her.

"I'll let you do that. And I'll let you fix yourself up. You look a mess."

As if that mattered when you were facing impending doom.

But she didn't argue. He untied the ropes that bound her hands.

"I'm keeping your feet tied," he snarled. "To keep you from running. And if you try . . . you'll pay."

One look at his dark eyes and she believed him. It was going to take more than outrunning to escape this man.

It felt like heaven to have her arms unbound. She gently swung them side by side, trying to get the circulation flowing evenly, wiggling her fingers, bending her sore and reddened wrists. She could only walk with tiny steps, with her ankles bound together, but she didn't argue. He left her alone behind the largest of boulders, where she took care of her personal needs, and then led her to the rocky edge of the running stream. She sat gratefully on the bank by the edge of the gently flowing water, first dangling her fingertips into its cool depths, then her sore wrists. The water felt refreshing and looked clear and inviting. On her knees, she bent and washed her face in the stream, finding both her body and her spirits revive. Greedily, she drank from the stream.

She wasn't stupid. She knew that this man who wanted her dead had other nefarious plans for her before completing his deed. There was only one reason, she figured, that a ruthless man like him had kept her alive so far. He had every intention of having his way with her. It was, despite being a horrible contemplation, going to be her one and only chance of saving her life.

She gulped some more water as she heard him coming up behind her. She would be ready.

"Okay, Heiress," he smirked. "Time to get to know each other." He gripped her upper arm with steely fingers and pulled her to her feet. With a lecherous look on his face, he stared at her.

She didn't flinch.

He picked her up, feet still bound together, and carried her back to the now roaring campfire. She kept her body relaxed. Her eyes darted around the clearing, taking in all they could. The horse was tethered at one end of the clearing. He had gathered a large pile of sticks for firewood, and had them perched beside the campfire.

In the fading light of the day, the fire glowed, sending its billowing smoke up into the Montana sky. Something was cooking on the campfire, she couldn't identify what kind of animal he had caught and had perched on a spit. Despite the fact that her stomach ached with hunger, the smell of the cooking animal made her feel nauseous.

He put her down on her feet beside the campfire, next to his bedroll that he had unfurled. As fear curled inside of her, she looked up at the big Montana sky, which was turning rapidly grey as the pink sun set on the western horizon. Suddenly she knew what she was going to do.

Would this be her last sight, her last vision on this earth? Because one thing was for sure, she would die before she let this man do as he had planned.

And what had her life been like, up to this point anyway? It had been struggle for freedom. A struggle to become the person she had wanted to be. She had traveled long and far to find that freedom for herself, and she had. Perhaps this was the last fight. She was not going to let this evil man win in the fight for her freedom, no matter what the cost. Even to her death, she would struggle to stand up for Julietta Brightingham to be and think and live as she pleased. Or die in the process. And she knew she had but one chance. He was bigger. He was stronger. But he did not have more to lose.

He moved quickly then, as she knew he would. And she was ready. He bent over to untie the ropes that bound her legs. With an animal like groan, one hand slid beneath her skirts and ran its way up her leg.

Next to the fire, she leaned quickly, and plucked the straightest, thickest branch that he had laid on top of the growing fire. It was about three feet in length, and as round as a man's wrist. It was smoking in the middle. It would do.

As soon as her feet were free, she parted them, which took Hank by surprise. Taking advantage of the split second his reaction gave her, she took the stick solidly in both hands, turned at the waist as far as she could go, and swung the stick with all the might that her years of secret baseball practice had given her.

On his knees untying her legs, his head was right at waist level. High and on the outside. Like her favorite pitch.

Crack!

As the stick connected with the side of his skull, the force spun his head around. He didn't make a sound as he hit the ground like a sack of grain. *Abner Doubleday would have been proud of that swing!*

She wasted not a second, not even checking to see if he was dead or alive. She securely tied his feet and his wrists with the same cords he had used on her, efficiently making sure that he could not get loose if he woke up.

He was alive. After a few minutes, she could hear his shallow breathing, and was grateful. As much as she wanted her freedom, killing a man for it was not something that she had ever wanted to do.

Freed from her bonds, she stretched her legs and moved around the campfire. She was miles from nowhere, but she was free. Darkness had descended on the prairie, and she knew that she was going nowhere until the light of dawn. She rummaged through Hank's saddlebags, and found some stored food that appealed to her much more than the roasting animal on the fire. She added all the gathered firewood to the fire, chasing away shadows. She settled herself on Hank's unrolled bedroll, sitting in the firelight, ravenously filling her empty stomach. She sat hugging her knees, thinking, with the fire burning brightly, and an attempted killer tied up and gagged only a few feet away.

Jack White was wild with frustration. He had mentally mapped routes from the site where Julie Bright had disappeared to every small stagecoach stop he knew, and had found no sign of them. He was exhausted, every muscle in his body aching, not even from hard work, but from tension. He was starving. And he could not give up.

As Murphy's hooves pounded the ground beneath him, he fought the visions in his mind of the fate of the woman he knew he loved. Was she alive? Had she been harmed? The feeling of powerlessness built up in his like the force of a steam engine, rage fueling rage, and he knew that if he ever got his hands on the arrogant criminal, he knew that the power unleashed would be both dangerous and absolute. And also, that it would feel good.

The hours of searching passed, and with each moment, the fear grew. Where was Julie and what was happening to her? Jack kept on, scouring the ground, eye to the sky, watching for signs of life. Or of death. He watched the occasional buzzard dip in the air, waiting with dread to see if others joined his dance, a sure sign that a dead creature of some type had been found. To his overwhelming relief, no buzzards circled in sight.

The day dwindled into night. The night slid its dark tentacles through the prairie sky, blocking out his ability to see. But still he kept on. He hit two towns in the blackness of night, waking the sheriff and asking about people traveling through. No sign of the cowboy, or the woman, no train had been through to head east. Until morning. The train would hit mid morning.

With ongoing determination, despite his depleted state, he kept moving methodically across the prairie. Hours passed as he covered mile after mile, eyes on guard, ears alert for any sight or sound. Finally, almost looking like a mirage, he saw an orange speck of light in the distance, the glow of a campfire shining like a beacon in the dark night. With heart quickening, and hooves pounding, he tore toward the site. Would he find her? Or was he too late? His adrenaline flowed. He would do whatever he had to do to rescue her from the devil who had taken her captive.

He wished he had more weapons. He wished he had deputies. He was ready to fight. He was ready to do anything to release her and safe her life.

But he should have know better. He found her. When he found her she was sitting calmly and cross legged, on some old blanket, right next to a dwindling fire. He found her sitting with a misshapen tin mug in her hand, quietly drinking tea as if she were the Queen of England. He found her conversing peacefully with the large, evil minded cowboy, who was laying on his side, bound up like a steer heading for market, and pleading with her to let him loose to mend his ways.

He had thought he was going to rescue Julie Bright, aka Julietta Brightingham? That would be the day.

He didn't know whether to laugh or cry with relief, and to his horrified realization, he found he was doing both. Julie stood, dusted off her filthy skirt, and crossed to him, a twinkle in her eye.

"You found me!" she said in delight. "I'm so glad. I had no idea whatsoever as to how I was going to lift him up on the horse to get him to justice."

Jack swept her up into his arms. His heart was hammering in his chest.

"I don't know how you managed this, but I'm sure you would have figured the rest out." She was such a little thing. Such a precious little thing. Such a daring and crazy little thing.

He turned and glared at the bound up cowboy. "You could have just conked him for good, left him, and let the buzzards have him." Jack was thinking of doing just that.

Hank was silent and sullen and looked at him with apprehensive eyes.

"Never," she exclaimed. "He will be an invaluable witness to what devious plans my beloved uncle had made. I want this man alive and well. And he may well mend his ways yet."

She was such a stubborn little thing. Such an aggravating little thing.

"There is not one positive trait in this man, Julie," he countered. "Tell me one good thing about him, and I'll respect my badge and bring him in alive."

She scrunched up her face and thought. And then smiled.

"He's a most excellent dancer."

Jack stared at her in disbelief. And then he laughed. Because she was right. Not that he was a good dancer. That was the most idiotic thing that she could have said. But it served its purpose. His desire for immediate revenge was depleted, like taking the top off a whistling teapot. Jack would let him live and bring him to justice. Because that was the creed that he lived by. And Julie knew that. His heart swelled with love for her.

They sat quietly around the fire in the cool night air, sipping tea, and the sharing the remainder of her stash of food. After Hank had eaten, he fell into an uneasy sleep.

Julie leaned against Jack's broad chest, and he could feel her small body relax as the hours ticked away. He could smell the sweetness of her hair as her head rested beneath his chin, he could feel the slow rhythm of her breathing, and he knew the instant she fell asleep.

Gently, lovingly, he kissed the top of her head, and then slowly guided her onto the bedroll beneath them, putting her on her side. He laid down on his side behind her, pulling her back to his body, enveloping her with his warmth. Automatically, she curled up into him, like it was the most natural thing in the world.

His body reacted with a start, but hard as it was, he pushed the thoughts away. He would be satisfied with keeping her warm and safe on this night. She had been through a harrowing day, and so had he. He didn't sleep, couldn't sleep, between the feelings of having her pressed close to him, and his wariness of the would be killer, even though restrained, only feet away. But he had the greatest sense of peace he had ever felt in his life, as he lay there on the prairie floor.

He thought of the fears he had felt for her safety, the horrors he had imagined, and he pulled her closer. She sighed, and relaxed against him in her sleep.

In her sleep. When she was awake it would be another story. But he cherished the moments as they ticked by, almost feeling a sense of loss when the pink glow of the morning sun began splashing its rays on the horizon. She would be awake soon, and these moments would pass. But not his feelings. Not his love. The brutal day he had spent praying that she was safe and sound had changed him. It had made his feelings clear. He was wildly in love with this woman. And he wanted her in his life. Somehow or other, he would make her agree. He didn't want to lose her again.

Chapter Twenty-one

News spread like wildfire in Grady, Montana, after the legendary Sheriff Jack White of Grey Eagle arrived in town shortly after daybreak on his big chestnut stallion, with the pretty little missing schoolteacher perched in the saddle in front on him. Behind him, he led a smaller dark horse carrying a sullen looking prisoner.

By the time they had lumbered down the length of the small town to the local sheriff's office and town jail, half the town had shown up to see the show. They had heard of the stolen stagecoach and the missing teacher lady. Marcus, the sheriff's deputy, and his posse, had been through the day before, looking for information, and alerting the towns along the train and stage routes so that Hank Smith had no easy escape. There had been a lot of fear for the lady in question, but there she was, sitting pretty as you please, safe and secure with the sheriff.

The residents waved as they passed.

"Good job, Sheriff Jack!"

"We knew you'd get him!"

Jack threw back his head and laughed, remembering that day not so long ago when the stage had brought Julie Bright to town, after she had clobbered the stage robber. She was strong and she was resourceful, and she didn't need anyone to fight her battles. And he didn't need to take credit for that strength.

The crowd followed them down the street, gathering like an audience outside the jail door. The local sheriff came out and took Hank Smith into custody, giving Jack a big smile and a slap on the back.

"Most obliged, Sheriff Jack. You did good work here bringing this one to custody. We'll ship him off to the capital where he'll get his just due. When you have a chance, let me ask you some questions for the records."

Jack cleared his throat. "This was good work all right, but it's not my success. Let me introduce you to Miss Julie Bright, also known as Miss Julietta Brightingham, who was the one responsible for bringing Smith to justice. I just arrived in time to help to get him up on the horse. The rest was on account of her."

He reached up and lifted Julie off the horse and their eyes met. He felt a charge go down the length of his spine. He wanted to wrap his arms around her. He wanted to hold her, and keep her, and never let her go. She belonged here. He felt it in the marrow of his bones.

"Well, you're quite a little lady, let me tell you that," said the baldheaded sheriff. "You're the stuff that this new land is made of. And we're proud of having you here."

"And I've been proud of being here, Sheriff," she said quietly. "However, I really do need to return home. I have heard that you have a train heading east coming through later today."

And with her few short words, Jack felt something in his heart die. What had he expected, after all? That the events of terror that she had been through would change her perspective? That learning the whole story of her uncle's schemes, and the right to her inheritance would be ignored, and she would decide to stay in Grey Eagle?

Even despite his dreams, he knew Julie better than that. She had run once, scared and overwhelmed by her life. But she had grown up. It would not happen again. He would have to accept it.

"The stage should leave about noon, Miss Bright," the kindly sheriff offered. "Perhaps we can offer you a room at the hotel to refresh yourself."

"That would be wonderful. And a trip to the mercantile would be appreciated. I need a few things."

And so it was arranged. The records about the event were filled out. The necessary supplies were selected and delivered to Julie's room. She bathed, and collected herself, and reappeared in a short while, dressed in a new, store bought dress, with a sunny bonnet perched atop her carefully arranged blond hair.

Sitting across from the neatly dressed young woman, Jack White felt weak in the knees. It took all the effort he had to sit there. It was harder than corralling angry cattle that needed branding. It was harder than standing up to bank robbers, heading off a lynching, or pounding the prairie all night looking for her, and wondering if she was dead or alive.

She was more than alive. She was like life itself to him. And she was leaving. The tick of the clock echoed like thunder in his brain. She would soon be getting on a train, each mile traveled east taking her farther from him, and back into her old life. The life she belonged to.

And there was nothing he could do about it. There was nothing he *should* do about it. Because if that was the life that was going to make her happy, then that was the life that he wanted for her. The thought twisted like a knife in his gut. He would accept it. He had no choice.

He would not beg her to stay. He would not try to explain how she had brought color to his life. How she had made his days richer, even when there was still no doubt in his mind that she was the most aggravating female person he had every encountered. He would not try to explain that he had absolutely no idea how he was going to recover from the loss of her in his life. He'd had lots of tragedy and loss in his life. He'd gotten by. And he'd get by again. He hoped.

So he sat there like a lump of stone, and watched her while she made polite talk and ate her breakfast, and tried for the life of him to think of other things.

A messenger arrived to say that the train was ready, and he walked her out the door, feeling suddenly numb, which was more welcome than the pain.

She looked straight into his eyes again, as if trying to read him, and gave him a gentle smile.

"I have to go, you know. There is no way that I can not go, Jack."

He nodded, dumbly. If he had tried to speak, he would have humiliated himself, because his throat was so tight, not a single word could escape.

"It will be all right. You will see. Thank you for searching for me yesterday."

He cleared his throat. He swallowed hard. Every inch of his body longed to hold onto her, to beg her not to go. Did she know that he would have searched to the end of the earth for her? But the truth was, she hadn't needed him, didn't need him.

"You did right fine on your own, Julie Bright. You didn't have a need for me at all."

Julie smiled, reached for his hand, and squeezed it. "There are different kinds of need, Sheriff White. Just you remember that."

And then she was gone. She stepped up into the train, the door was shut, and the train started forward on the tracks.

He stood, frozen to the ground, watching the train pull out of town, watched it until all he could see was the little puff of dust it left in its trail. He watched until the horizon was empty and barren again, with absolutely no sight of Julie Bright. She was gone.

One lesson that Jack White had learned in his life was that life just kept going on, no matter how hard his heart had been hurt. When his parents had died, when his life had seen better days, he had come to see that if he just kept putting one foot in front of the other, and doing the next right thing, he could get through the day.

So with his heart aching, like someone had tried to tear it out of his chest, he got up each day, and did the best job he knew how in Grey Eagle. This town was his life, and he would not let the town down.

The bold determination got him through the rest of the fall, and through the long cold winter. The snows piled high, as they always did in this part of Montana, and for the most part, people did what they usually do in winter, struggle to keep the livestock alive and fed, and struggled to keep their spirits up while being cooped up on the colder, darker months of the year.

On several occasions, he made the trek up into the hills to visit the Blackfoot family, seeing that they had the supplies that they needed for the winter, seeing that the family was safe and well, especially when Joe Horse Lover was gone on a hunt. The Blackfoot were an accepted part of Grey Eagle life now.

This particular winter, there was one other significant difference. The people of Grey Eagle were reading. When he made his occasional rounds to the inhabitants, both in and out of town, he often found an open book on the table, like *Romeo and Juliet,* that was being read out loud by the family by lantern light on the long winter nights. His town, like himself, was learning to read. The thought made him downright happy. Julie Bright may have been gone, but she had left her mark, and not just upon his heart.

Her bags had been lighter on the way home, because she had given away every one of those back breaking books she had carried when she arrived in Grey Eagle. She had left behind an important part of herself, and those books were being swapped and traded like wild fire. So he, too, had become part of the swap, and he and Marcus would while away the often quiet winter days reading Shakespeare, and reading about Abner Doubleday.

If he was a bit sullen and grouchy compared to usual, no one dared complain to him about it. It seemed like an unwritten rule that Julie Bright's name wasn't brought up in his presence. In a way, that was a relief. But in another way, he was starved for information about her, waking every single day with the thought of her on his mind, how she had fared stepping back into her sophisticated life, how it felt to be Julietta Brightingham of New York City.

He hadn't heard a word from her or about her in all these long months, and it felt at times like there was a hole in his heart. Not that he'd expected to. But did she ever think back to that short time in Grey Eagle? Did she know the effect she had on this town (let alone on himself, though he was not going to admit that out loud to a soul)?

He loved this town. It was his life. But sometimes, in the late hours of the night, he'd wake up, and stare out the darkened window. He'd wonder what would happen if he, Jack White, sheriff of Grey Eagle, Montana, dared to climb onto that eastbound train and follow that schoolteacher heiress right back to New York City, fancy world and all.

What if he begged her to come back to Grey Eagle? And what if she was happier there? What if she asked him to stay there? Would he volunteer to give up the world he knew for a world with her? Such ridiculous questions were best left in the darkness of the lonely night, because the truth is, she had left without ever asking him such a thing. But it was a thought that played in his mind in those solitary moments, a kind of wishing that kept him going.

It was the morning after a night like that when Jane Adams strolled into his office on a sunny, though briskly cold morning in early March. She wasn't working at the hotel any longer, because she had been hired to work out at the schoolhouse, since learning to read. She was helping Mrs. Newby with the children, since the numbers were increasing with several new families coming to town. He'd heard rumors that she was being courted by Fred Worth, the foreman of the Dry Gulch Ranch, and if the glow in her face was an indication of anything beyond the chill of the day, she was smitten. The ladies of the town had her married and building a family already, and he was deciding, with one look at her, that they were probably right.

"Sheriff Jack," she exclaimed with her pretty smile. "I've gotten a letter from Julie."

His heart skipped a beat, and several emotions collided. He was excited to hear. He was jealous that it had been Jane that she wrote to. He was fearing the news. Was she getting married? In love? He was dying for the news.

"How is she?" he said simply. Jane stared back at him with wise eyes, sensing the importance of his question.

"She is fine. Healthy. Excited. She sends her regards."

"Anything new in her life? She's adjusted?"

"Making great progress. She says there's a lot to do. She says she's excited about planning to get married."

He felt the blood in his veins turn to ice. He felt like time had stopped. He was stunned into silence. He had known it would happen. But he had not been prepared for the pain.

Julie Bright. Getting married. To someone else. It felt like the energy in his body was draining, flowing away. He snapped himself to attention, trying to focus on the young woman before him. She was staring at him quizzically.

"Are you all right, Sheriff? You look . . . strange."

That was a mild description. He was down and out. He felt like he had been kicked in the head by somebody's prize mule. Kicked in the head until his head spun around sideways.

One foot in front of the other, he reminded himself.

"I hope he's a good man."

"She says he's wonderful, though pig headed and opinionated. The kind who thinks he knows everything." She was grinning. "Sounds like a good match for Julie, don't you agree?"

He had to smile, even though his heart was in tatters. "Sounds a bit *like* Julie, if you get my drift."

Jane laughed out loud. "Well, it was wonderful to finally hear from her. So I thought I'd stop by and share the news. I'm in town to arrange a lease on the Thomson house, since it's going to be standing empty. Mrs. Thomson is packing to go to California to live with her daughter, now that her husband's passed."

Jack nodded, knowing about the move. It also clarified what the ladies in the hotel had been saying. Jane Adams was taking a husband. Now that would make for some good excitement in Grey Eagle.

"I've heard that you've been keeping company with Fred, Jane," he said as she was leaving his office. "He's a good man. And a lucky one."

She blushed to the roots of her hair. "Well, thanks. And he certainly is wonderful."

She smiled and left him alone with his thoughts.

Christine Bush

The town would grow. Life would go on. People would live and love, babies would be born, and folks would die. That was the cycle of life. And he would be there to help them do all those things, keep them safe, and keep working on make the town a better place.

He had plans now to build a hospital. He wanted to bring a doctor to Grey Eagle, to give the people a better chance of staying healthy, of getting fixed up when things went wrong and they got hurt. He'd put his heart and his energy there.

Because he sure needed to do something with his heart. Because although it was right there in his chest, beating away, it was filled with so much pain he could hardly stand it. People like Jane and Fred could fall in love, and share their lives. But not Jack White. Because he had fallen in love with the one woman that was on this earth for him, and she was not going to share her life with him. She was back in New York city, and planning to marry someone else.

Sometime he wished that mule could kick him just a little harder in the head, and put him out of his misery because putting one foot in front of the other was getting harder step by step.

Most folks thought that spring was the most exciting time in Montana. When the weather cleared up, and before the heat of summer scorched the prairie, a lot of exciting things were bound to happen. New families arrived, glad to be able to travel without the confines of the harsh winter. Shipments of goods and materials began to filter into town. Farmers readied themselves for the planting they had scheduled, and for the arrival of baby calves and colts that signified the growth of their herds.

The smell of sawdust was in the air again, as building began on the new hospital building at the end of town. It would be two proud stories tall, with a doctor's office and living room, and a large ward and several smaller private rooms upstairs for patients. It would be the first official hospital in this part of the state.

New homes were being constructed, and everywhere there was a feeling of prosperity and growth. The residents of Grey Eagle were excited and optimistic about life.

Except for Jack White.

Each day that passed, his heart felt heavier. Some matrons had tried to set him up with the eligible young ladies in the area. He had dutifully met a few, pushed himself through a few social dinners, but the result was the same. They were lovely, friendly ladies, and would make someone a fine mate. But not for him. His heart had been given away, and there was no way he even wanted it back.

It was a bright Friday morning at the end of April, exactly two years to the day that Julie Bright had first rolled into Grey Eagle. Jack had left his office for a quick jaunt across the street to the hotel for a cup of coffee, pulling his hat on his head to keep the rising sun out of his eyes.

Squinting against the brightness, he thought he saw the silhouette of morning stage rolling into town. Looking again, and using his hand as a sun shield, he noticed that there was more than the usual amount of dust in the air, stirred up by the stagecoach wheels. He studied it best he could in the distant and bright sunlight. It wasn't moving more quickly than usual. Instead, it seemed to be moving a bit slower.

He stood for a minute, and as the coach neared, the reason became clearer. There was a large wagon moving along behind the stagecoach, pulled by two small grey horses. What kind of shipment was this? The wagon was stacked high with crates and boxes.

He stepped into the street to greet the driver, raising a hand as he recognized Pete on the bench, reins in hand.

"Good day to you, Sheriff Jack," he called cheerfully from the top of the stage. "It was a much more peaceful trip this time, with not one bandit to outrun on the trail. Which is a good thing. For the load in this wagon weighs a proper ton, if I do say so, and we couldn't have outrun even a pregnant mare if we had tried."

"What's in the load, Pete?" hollered Jack as he walked closer to the stagecoach. "Didn't know we were expecting one. Glad you didn't have trouble on the trip."

"I am in agreement. For this time, the little one is sporting a gun. Said she wasn't going to have any mangy character steal her things. Didn't want to have to knock another one out with a rock, I imagine. Not that she couldn't do it. I sure wouldn't get in her way!"

And with that, the stagecoach came to its final stop, the door opened, and Julie Bright climbed out and stood right in front of him.

Chapter Twenty-two

When Julie Bright had started her eastward voyage back to confront her uncle and to reclaim her place in life, she had only a murky plan of what her future would bring. She had left Montana with a heaviness in her heart, her mother's jewels belted tightly around her waist under her skirt, and a strong determination that she would return.

Indeed, that was the only way that she could keep her five-foot-two frame seated in the train seat as she had peered out the little window and watched the giant man who was Sheriff Jack White shrink to a dot on the horizon, and then disappear.

It was only the anger, the feeling of righteousness, the intense belief that evil should not be able to flourish in the world that drove her on. And so she had returned to New York. When she had left New York, she had left in a quiet hush, as the ordinary looking little schoolteacher who was leaving behind her old life to start anew. When

she returned, she had returned as Miss Julietta Brightingham, Heiress Restored. In St. Louis, a news reporter
had interviewed her, and had gotten credit for scooping
the news world with the fantastic story. Her weapon had
been the truth, and the truth had done its vital work. By
the time she had arrived back to reclaim the family home
that had been taken over by her Uncle Edward, justice
had been set into motion. Her uncle had been arrested.
Auditors and investigators were reviewing the account
books for improprieties.

She had been greeted at the door by her loving staff
who had stayed on, praying for her safety and eventual
return. She had received greetings from the society matrons, had attended to household business and fended off
more newsreporters than she had ever known existed.
She had met with the Board of Directors of her father's
company, which was now hers. She listened, she read,
she discussed, and she thought.

She dined at the finest of restaurants with societal well
wishers who desired to catch her up on the who's who of
New York life. She answered the many questions about
her sojourn to a world that they could barely imagine,
trying to explain to them that her experiences had added
so much to the depth of her life, and that she had not
been in fearful exile, as they liked to imagine.

And as each day progressed, she became more and
more aware of her feelings, and of the ways that she had
grown. She had left New York an intelligent, but very
scared young woman. She had not known how to handle
the life that was expected of her, she had not known how
to stand up for what she needed or wanted. Her sheltered

life had not prepared her for that. But the time in Grey Eagle had. One year can certainly change your life.

Slowly, the plan that had begun barely a seed in her mind began to grow. Helping that little seed to germinate had taken several hard months of work. Today, at the age of twenty-six, she knew that she *could* step into her New York responsibilities and manage her father's company very adequately. She could do it. She could succeed. But she was going to make another choice.

Today, she knew clearly that she belonged in Grey Eagle, Montana, and not in the boardroom of Brightingham Shipping. She was not going to run away from her responsibilities and opportunities, she was going to make them work for her.

In a methodical manner, she met with the important business associates, attorneys, and managers. She liquidated some assets, consolidated some departments, and carefully interviewed until she could select a trustworthy general manager and administrator for Brightingham Shipping. With her uncle and his cohorts facing a prison term for their financial improprieties, the company was once again stable and strong.

She made the decision to retain her house and household, as she would need to travel at least once a year back to New York, and her loyal family staff would not have their lives disrupted. As soon as the New York details were settled, she turned her eyes toward the future.

She was going back to Grey Eagle, and to the town and life that had become her home. She was going back to Sheriff Jack White, whether he wanted her or not. Somewhere along the bouncy trail home, she came to grips with the feelings in her heart. As she had written to Jane, she was going to marry the man. Whether he knew it or not.

And Jane was helping her with still another secret. She was not going back empty handed to Grey Eagle. She had a new direction in her life. The new school-teacher had settled into the schoolhouse and by Jane's accounts, the transition had been just fine. Julie had no intention of interrupting that. But she had decided that there had been another great need in town, a need that had been suggested by Jeb Johnson, when talking about the importance of books. They needed a library. And she was just the woman to provide it.

She had instructed Jane to lease the Thomson house, when she found out it was being vacated. She would install the library in the downstairs room, and have living space for herself on the second floor. She had scoured libraries, catalogues, and booksellers all over the city for weeks. If Sheriff Jack White had grimaced about the two small but weighty bags of books she had brought to Grey Eagle when she had first arrived, he was going to choke on this load!

By the time the books had been packed, the pile in the living room had grown to eighty-four cases. When they had been packed to go west on the train, they took over half a box car to move. When she had arrived for the stage ride, she had hired a shipment wagon to accompany them across the prairie with the books in tow. Determined to protect the valuable cargo that bounced along behind them, she had gotten a pistol that she kept in her lap as they headed west.

She had plenty of time to think on the several week

trip back to Montana. The library would be called the Jeb Johnson Library, in honor of her bell ringing student who had given her the idea. That would be a good and positive start in life! Not many a young man can attest to having a library named after him.

And the sheriff? Would he be surprised to see her? What would he say? She rehearsed her opening speech to the man, practicing statements and explanations for hours at a time.

And then suddenly, they were in Grey Eagle, and she breathed in a fresh smell of it as they neared the town. Soon, the stage was slowing in front of the hotel, it was time to alight from the stage. As the door opened, she stepped down onto the familiar packed surface, gun in hand, turned around, and ran smack into a broad, hard chest. A tall chest.

She lifted her head, and looked up into the eyes of Sheriff Jack White. She was speechless, despite her best intentions. And he did not look happy. Some things never changed.

What was she doing here?
The sheriff was having all he could do to keep from exploding at her. The very idea of her getting married had sent him into a dither, and he had worked hard to try to forget and to accept it. The very idea of her living so far away in New York made him feel lonely and lost. He had worked hard to get himself back up to a workable mood. And now here she was. Climbing off the stage as pretty and fresh as a gardenia, smiling and happy. While his world had just been turned upside down . . . again.

And his heart was breaking. In his dreams of seeing

her again, he had not realized how great the pain would be. It cut him like a knife. She would visit, and she would leave again. And that would hurt even more.

But by God, was it good to lay eyes on her. He couldn't help being glad to see her.

She had something up her sleeve, he knew, just watching her face. He saw the pistol in her hand, and the large store of crates piled high on the accompanying wagon.

"Smuggling, Miss Bright?" he said quietly with a smirk. "Or had you taken to bank robbing, and that is your stash?"

"Neither, my dear sheriff. I am just glad to say that I reached here safe and sound."

"And the wagon? The crates? I'm assuming they are yours."

"The crates?" she said. "Yes, they are. They are books for the library."

"Library?" He shook his head in question. "I don't believe we have a library, Miss Bright," had said formally.

"We do now. Jane arranged it. I'll be living in the upper rooms."

His heart stopped. "Living?"

"Well, yes, Sheriff Jack. I'm home to stay."

Home to stay? His emotions exploded like fireworks, until the memory of Jane's words echoed back at him.

"But your marriage. I had heard you were getting married."

Could she hear his heartbeat from the distance?

"I am. As soon as it can be arranged."

It would be worse than missing her. Would he have to watch her, day by day, knowing that she belonged to another man? Frustration and anger warred inside of him, mingled with something that felt distinctly like terror.

"Does he know what he is getting himself into?" he asked, trying to conjure up every aggravating thing she had ever done to him, trying to restore his equilibrium.

"Not exactly. But soon he will."

"And where is he? Is he here in Grey Eagle?"

He looked around, but no one else had been on the stagecoach, and he saw no strangers in his town.

"He is already here. In fact, one might say that he *is* the spirit of Grey Eagle."

He looked at her blankly, his mind suddenly spinning with hope, trying to process what she was saying with that little smile on her face, and her blond curls poking out of her bonnet. For a moment, he couldn't speak.

She squinted at him, not sure that he had gotten what she was trying to say. She wasn't going to give up. She wanted this man, and she meant to make him understand that.

She lifted the gun. "Do I have to shoot you, Sheriff Jack, to make the point? I will if I have to. It's *you* I'm going to marry."

He pushed his hat back on his head, put his hands on his hips, let the joy and relief surge through his body. He stared down at her, looking ridiculous with that silly little eastern style pistol in her hand.

"It's a major offense to aim a firearm at a lawman, little lady. You have any idea what the punishment is for such behavior?"

"I have a feeling you're just aching to tell me."

"I am. It's a life sentence. No parole. No changing minds."

"I'll take it."

"That's settled then."

He reached out and took the pistol from her shaking hand, and dropped it into his shirt pocket.

"Good thing you didn't come across any bandits on this trip. That little weapon wouldn't stop a prairie dog." He stepped toward her and pulled her into his arms.

"Wasn't aiming for any prairie dogs." She stepped into his embrace, knowing that she was coming home, feeling right. "I've settled things in New York. I had to go back, you know. To face it. To make plans. And I'll have to go back occasionally. To make sure things are in order."

"You'll tell me all about it later. A library? You brought this town a library?" He put his face down, and nuzzled the top of her hair, loving the smell of her, the touch of her.

"I did. And I'm here to run it."

"That looks like a mighty big load of books. Good thing I can read."

"Good thing." she agreed, turning her face up to his.

He took his cue, lowered his lips to hers, and their life began.